The Attitude Girl

by

Mila Bernadkin

Five Star Publications, Inc.
Chandler, AZ

Linda F. Radke, President
Five Star Publications, Inc.
P.O. Box 6698
Chandler, AZ 85246-6698

Library of Congress Cataloging-in-Publication Data

Bernadkin, Mila.
    The attitude girl / by Mila Bernadkin.
        p. cm.
    Summary: Victoria Benson and her friends go through their last year of high school, weathering crises about love, dating, health, finances, and family.
    ISBN-13: 978-1-58985-155-9
    ISBN-10: 1-58985-155-2
    [1. Coming of age—Fiction. 2. Dating (Social customs)—Fiction.
3. Friendship—Fiction. 4. High schools—Fiction. 5. Schools—Fiction.]
I. Title.
    PZ7.B4546At 2009
    [Fic]—dc22

                                                          2009010193

Printed in the United States of America

Editing by Gary Anderson
Cover design by Kris Taft Miller
Project Manager Sue DeFabis

"A positive attitude may not solve all your problems, but it will annoy enough people to make it worth the effort."

—Herm Albright

Acknowledgments

I want to express my heartfelt gratitude to my publisher Linda F. Radke for accepting me as a Five Star author and for giving me this chance, and more; to Sue DeFabis, project manager, and the entire team at Five Star Publications for their hard work and their commitment to this project.

I would like to sincerely thank Arizona Authors Association and all the contest judges for choosing this novel and awarding it first prize.

Thanks to Patricia Netzley at the Institute of Children's Literature for believing in me and for encouraging me to make my first steps on the rocky road of writing.

My special thanks, respect and admiration go to Marcia Lusted, an outstanding teacher and an exceptional person, for having faith in me and for showing me what it means to be a writer.

And finally, many thanks to my family, especially to my sister, for their patience and understanding, for their love and support.

Author's note: This novel is not a story about me or my family; this book is work of fiction.

PART I

Analyze This, Analyze That

"It requires a very unusual mind to undertake the analysis of the obvious."

—Alfred North Whitehead

I, Myself, and Me

"I happen to feel that the degree of a person's intelligence is directly reflected by the number of conflicting attitudes she can bring to bear on the same topic."

—Lisa Alther

"What do you mean, you're unemployed?" I ask Mom after she hits me with the news—no, drops the bombshell on me would be the better way to put it.

"Exactly what I said. It means I don't have a job anymore."

"What do you mean?" I repeat the question.

She just says it so matter-of-factly, I can't believe it! *Like unemployment happens to her every day.*

School sucks. I come home for a little TLC from my primary caregiver, and that's what I get from her? Unemployment?!

"They let some people go to save money, and I was one of those people."

Mom doesn't seem too upset, but she's not her usual cheerful self, either.

"But you've done so much for that company. How could they do that to you?" I almost feel like crying. "Thanksgiving is in a few days, and then Christmas—"

"Well, it's called an executive decision. I agree, it's not the best time to lose a job, but it's nothing personal. It's just business."

She seems unbelievably calm.

"Mom, how can you be this calm? You should hate those executives. I do."

"Victoria, it's going to be extremely hard for you in life with that attitude of yours."

Here we go again. My attitude.

* * *

I, Victoria Benson, a seventeen-year-old high school senior, have an attitude problem. Actually, I don't have a problem with my attitude, but other people apparently do.

If you look up the word *attitude* in Webster's dictionary, it says: "approach to something, position toward something, way of thinking, opinion, point of view, state of mind, etc."

To me, it's not that straightforward, and it's not as simple as that. Before I form an opinion about something, I have to analyze it. I analyze *everything*. Everything should make sense to me, and if it doesn't, I'm not afraid to say it. I always stand by what I believe in.

I remember my very tough but cool fifth grade teacher wrote in our yearbook, under my picture: "To my favorite Attitude Girl."

Do you know why she called me that? Because I always had an opinion about her "special" methods of punishment (like writing the same word a thousand times for talking too much in class) and was never afraid to speak my mind (and boy, did I have a mind of my own!), but she loved me anyway.

If you ask me what my number-one pet peeve is, I'll say it's when people tell me that I should *always* have a positive attitude. I *do* have a problem with *that*. I mean, aren't you supposed to have at least one good reason to have a positive attitude? Well, I'm a happy and a cheerful person, but if I'm having a bad day, why should I have a positive attitude? Just because it's the right way of thinking or a good position to have? I don't think so.

Personally, I think that an attitude is more of a feeling than a state of mind. If I feel good, if everything goes my way, then I'll have a positive attitude, but if I feel lousy, if nothing turns out they way I want it to, then let me be negative. Please don't tell me that a positive attitude always helps. It doesn't, and that's a proven fact.

Case in point: homeless people. Why should *they* have a positive attitude? Just because "the sun'll come out tomorrow?" Yeah, right! Would it get them a warm house, nourishing food on the table, or nice clothes on their backs? I think *not*.

Or take my mom, for example. Mom believes that the problem itself is *not* the problem. The problem is *your attitude* about the problem. She's the biggest optimist that has ever lived. My mother had given years of hard work to that bank and always did it with a big smile. So what? They got rid of her anyway, didn't they? And her super-positive attitude didn't help, did it?

Has it ever occurred to anyone that there's nothing wrong with my attitude? Hello, people! Wake up and change *your* attitude.

*   *   *

"Mom?"

"Mm?"

"Listen, what are we going to do about the money now?"

It's so painful!

"Is that all you can think about?" Mom snaps. "Money? My god, Victoria! What's wrong with you? It's normal to worry about the money, but aren't you forgetting something else?"

She's pissed off, I can see that. *I wonder why.*

"What do you mean?" *God, that must be the most popular question on my Q & A list.* "Of course, I think about the money. Money is money. I totally love money. So what?"

How can she not understand that? I'm irritated now. *What am I forgetting?*

"It's okay to love money, Victoria, but money isn't everything. Money is not the only thing that matters in the world. Do you really think that money is our only problem? And what about my feelings?"

I can see that she's a little agitated. *So that's what she means.*

"You're right, Mom. Money isn't everything, but it makes *everything possible.* I also totally agree with you that money doesn't matter—its *amount* does—and of course, money is not the problem—the *lack of it* is. Have you ever thought why everybody's so fascinated with the *Lifestyles of the Rich and Famous*? Nobody's interested in or cares about the lifestyles of the poor and forgotten."

I articulate expressively, waving my hands, trying to make a point. *Is Mom getting it? What does she mean 'her feelings'?*

"Well, Ms. Clueless, first of all, we're not completely broke. Not yet, at least." Mom shrugs, shaking her head. "Secondly, I'll look for another job, but not right away. I need a break. God knows, I deserve it, and I haven't decided yet what I want to do."

She sounds confident. I'm not. *What is she thinking? Life sucks!*

"What do you mean?"

Am I stuck or something? Why do I sound like a scratched CD?

"Enough of that, Victoria. You sound like a broken record, asking the same question over and over again," Mom says firmly and definitely, as if she had read my mind. "It's not the way to recycle. You need to refurbish your vocabulary."

I think she means it. She doesn't look like she's kidding.

"But if you're not going back to work right away, how will we live?"

I'm desperate! I hear a siren in my head. *Shopping! Shopping!* I was planning to go shopping with the girls for some new clothes. *Car! Car!* Mom promised. Now both seem so unlikely.

"Mom, who brainwashed you? Maybe it's stress talking."

I hope that's the reason.

"Stress? In my life? With my work?" Mom asks in astonishment, her eyebrows raised, her big, almond-shaped, dark-brown eyes wide open. (I have her eyes.) "Nooo! Are you kidding me? Stress is a *part* of me. If it's not there, I feel like my best buddy is missing. Now that I don't have such a stressful job, I'll miss it terribly."

Is she kidding now? Is that supposed to be a joke or is it irony I hear in her voice? Is she being sarcastic?

"Mom, please don't do anything irrational. You're scaring me."

I really mean it.

"Rebel without a clue. It's so typical of you."

Mom's voice is filled with indignation. She's all stirred up.

"You're right. Stress is bad for me. That's why I need some R & R. I'll be collecting unemployment benefits for six months and will be looking into my options. It's none of your concern, but if I want your advice, I'll ask for it—and you'd better think about changing your attitude, Victoria. You shouldn't be so self-centered. Not everything's about you, you know. The universe doesn't revolve around you."

She brushes back her short, thick, wavy hair with her hand, as she usually does when she's nervous or irritated. (I also have her hair. The texture, I mean. Everything else is different. Mom's is short, dark-brown, with a touch of copper; mine's long—it goes down to my shoulder blades— and is a cross between dark-ash and light-brown, more like my father's. I also have his nose and his "swollen" lips, and unlike Mom, I'm very tall, just like Dad.)

She stops for a moment to clear her throat and then, a little softer, continues, "Hey, don't worry. I know it's my responsibility to take care of the two of us. That's what people have savings for. I don't have much, but we'll survive. We'll be fine. I promise."

I believe her. I've always believed my mother because she's never let me down, and for the moment, I feel a little more positive. God knows, my mother and I have our differences and we fight (we're at each other's throats quite often), and by no means would I call us poster children for the perfect mother-daughter relationship, but we've always been very close and love each other like crazy. Mom has always been there for me, just like her parents have been always there for both of us.

Meet the parents

"Children begin by loving their parents; as they grow older, they judge them; sometimes they forgive them."

—Oscar Wilde

Losing a job isn't the worst thing that could happen to Mom. The worst thing is telling Grandma about it. My grandmother is the classic Drama Queen. She creates drama out of nothing. Literally. I mean, give her nothing and she'll give you the most intense drama in three acts.

So later that night, Mom makes THE CALL.

"Calm down, Mother, please," Mom says after she gently breaks the news to Grandma.

"I know Daddy has a bad heart, Mother," she continues, "so don't tell him, then. Okay, tell him. Don't lie. Don't keep secrets. What do you want from me? Give Daddy my love. Victoria's fine. We both will see you Thursday. Good night, Mother."

Mom hangs up and sighs loudly.

For the next few days, Mom and I prepare for Thanksgiving. On Thursday, my grandparents come bearing gifts. After the ceremony of hugs and kisses is complete, my grandma hands me two very familiar bags from Tollan's—the name I love and cherish. (My best friend Liza Tollan's father owns the chain of expensive upscale Tollan's department stores.

Tollan's is one of my favorite places in the entire world. Liza and I spend so much time there, that we call it our "home away from home".)

"This winter will be dreadful, dear, so we brought some things to help you deal with it," Grandma announces proudly.

"Thanks, Grandma. Thanks, Grandpa," I say as I open the bags.

Inside each bag is a different color and pattern cashmere set, containing a beautiful sweater, a scarf, a hat, and gloves. One is green and represents spring to me (not to mention money) and another is classic black. The sets are so soft and beautiful that I'm speechless.

"They must've cost a fortune!" Mom exclaims.

"Well, do you like them?" Grandma asks me, ignoring my mother's comment.

"Are you kidding me? They're gorgeous! And they're my favorite colors. You remember that I have a green jacket and a black coat. Now I can match, alternate, and coordinate," I say fast, totally happy and excited.

"Not only that. I thought the colors would go incredibly well with your beautiful eyes and your gorgeous hair," Grandma declares, pleased with herself for thinking of everything.

"Way to go, Grandma! Thank you so much, both of you!" I hug my grandparents again and then notice two huge grocery bags on the floor next to my Grandpa.

"What's that? I ask.

"That's what I'd like to know," Mom says, looking and sounding suspicious.

"Don't just stand there, David. Give Libby the groceries. They have to be refrigerated," Grandma instructs Grandpa, ignoring Mom's question yet again.

Mom and I get it: they brought enough groceries for practically a month! My panicky grandmother probably thinks that since Mom's unemployed, we're totally poor now and should go on public assistance and receive food stamps. (Look who's talking! Didn't I ask Mom how we would live now?)

"Here, Libby," Grandpa finally says, handing my mother the bags of groceries.

"Mom, what did you do this for?" Mom asks quietly and looks at me, her eyes begging for support.

I remain silent.

"Libby," Grandma replies, "if you don't understand why, then we did it for the child. Please don't start now. It's Thanksgiving. Let's be thankful we can do that. Okay?"

"Victoria, don't you want to say something?" Mom asks me.

What does she want?

"I'm very thankful," I say, squeezing the bags with my new cashmere sets as hard as I can.

Nobody is taking them away from me. Let them try!

Mom knows she's just lost. She looks completely perplexed and defeated. She slowly picks up the groceries and takes them to the kitchen. We all walk into the dining room. The table Mom and I set looks beautiful.

The dinner is delicious, as usual, but Grandma overdoes it when she tells Mom what a wonderful cook she is, taking credit for making all of this possible.

"Do you remember, Libby, how I talked you into learning how to cook?"

"Yes, Mother, I do, and I'm so glad I listened to you," Mom answers, turning away from her mother and rolling her eyes. (She'd say anything just to please Grandma.)

"I only wish you listened to me when I asked you not to marry that loser. Everything would be different if you had," Grandma says with her mother-knows-best attitude.

Oh-Oh. She just had to stick in the knife and twist it.

"Stop it, Rose!" Grandpa cries out with an I'm-all-fed-up-with-you expression on his face.

We all look at him, surprised. It's so not like him to interrupt my grandmother, or anyone, for that matter. My grandfather is the nicest, sweetest person I know. He's adorable. I have such a unique relationship with him. We can talk about everything, or we can just sit and not talk at all and still understand each other. It's hard to explain. He's *sooo* special, my grandpa.

"That loser," of course, is my father, and I hate to admit it, but my grandmother's right (it doesn't happen often, but in this case, I have to agree with her). My father *is* a loser because only a loser could do what he did. I haven't seen him in ten years and I'll probably never see him ever again. There's not much I can remember about my father, but I feel like I know everything about my parents, thanks to my mother, who has told me their story many times.

*   *   *

My parents, Elizabeth Fine and Richard Benson, met in college, where they both majored in finance. Dad was on his third year and Mom was a freshman. My father noticed the feisty, vibrant, intelligent young woman, so different from others, right away and fell head-over-heels in love with her. Richie and Libby, as everybody called my parents, were perfect together—a golden couple with a bright future ahead of them.

After my father graduated, he was hired as an intern in a large investment firm in downtown New York, and Mom continued living in a dorm. They could only see each other on weekends. When Mom had just one year of college left, they decided to get married so they could spend those two nights a week as husband and wife.

The Fines weren't very happy. They didn't have anything against Dad. Of course, they wanted their only child, their beloved Libby, to marry a nice Jewish boy, but it wasn't that. They were afraid that if Mom got married, she'd get pregnant right away, drop out of college, and never graduate. It was their greatest nightmare. No education and no degree wasn't good enough for their daughter. *It would be the end of the world,* they thought.

The Bensons, however, were more graphic.

"No son of ours is going to marry a Jewish woman," Mrs. Benson said.

"And if you do," Mr. Benson added, "we'll cut you out of our wills and our lives."

Mom didn't want to stand between my father and his parents, but Dad said that they were miserable human beings and they weren't that rich anyway, so he wouldn't lose anything. So with two friends as witnesses, they went to City Hall and became Mr. and Mrs. Benson. Mom never told her parents she got married, and Dad stopped talking to his parents altogether. They never called.

Everything went well at first. Mom and Dad loved each other, and then one winter night my father, the future investment broker, unconsciously made a nine-month investment in Mom's oven, not expecting any gain or growth, but he got both. It happened, and he panicked! He didn't know what to do with that. And Mom? Well, she's been saving up for my education ever since the stick turned blue.

"Richard, call your parents," said Mom. "Their first grandchild might change the way they feel. It might change everything."

Dad called. His mother picked up, heard the news, and then hung up on him. (Speaking of bad attitudes!)

I've never met my paternal grandparents, but if I ever have, I wonder, would they complain about my attitude—and if they did, would I say, "Look who's talking?"

Anyway, in all those years my father lived with us, he neither saw nor heard from his parents. (I wonder if it's hereditary, since I haven't heard from my father after he left us.)

"Libby, are you telling me you got married six months ago and you didn't tell your parents?" Grandma asked when Mom told her about the marriage. She was shocked and hurt. "We've talked on the phone so often, you came for a visit several times, and you didn't even bother to tell us you were married? You lied to us!"

"No, Mom, I didn't lie. I just kept it a secret. When I told you I was going to get married, you didn't approve, so I decided not to tell you," Mom defended herself. "If you had approved, you and Daddy would have been there, right beside me, when I got married."

"Since you didn't listen to us and married him anyway, I would have preferred that you told us so we *could* have witnessed that event," Grandma insisted. "So why are you telling me this now?"

"Mom, that's not why I called. I'm telling you this now because I have great news: you and Daddy are going to be grandparents."

"What? When? David! Come here! We're having a grandchild!"

She called Grandpa to the phone and then Mom patiently waited until she told him why his daughter called. When Mom told her how she and her new husband lived, my grandmother, the general, decided that there was no way her only daughter and a father of her future grandchild would live like that. So the next weekend Mom and Dad were expected at the Fines' house in upstate New York to discuss their options. Nobody dared to say 'no' to Grandma, so when my grandparents offered to put a down payment on a house just a few blocks away from theirs as a belated wedding present (so they could help with the baby when it arrived), my parents accepted. And I think that no matter how much my grandmother insulted my father since then, he never talked back to her because he always remembered that his own mother hung up on him.

Finally, Mom graduated, and then I was born. My parents had a new house and a new baby. In a few months Mom was hired by a local bank as a financial analyst. She dropped me at my grandparents' house before work and picked me up on her way home.

My father was commuting to Manhattan, but soon the golden boy (and others) realized he wasn't as golden, and his future wasn't as bright as everybody had believed. He made a few bad investments for his clients and lost his first job, then another. He opened his own investment firm with a partner, but it didn't go well and he lost a lot of money. Then he went to work for somebody else. He started changing jobs again. His professional life was a mess.

Unfortunately, Dad's personal life was also a complete disaster. Every time Mom tried to talk to him, he pushed her away. The more she wanted him to open up, the more he kept to himself, his face gloomy all the time. His depression started to hurt their marriage.

"Richard, talk to me please. Tell me what's bothering you," Mom said to Dad. "You've become a different person. I don't recognize you anymore."

"Just leave me alone!" he snapped. "Can't I just be left alone for a while?"

He didn't want to talk to her. They talked less and less, until they had nothing left to say to each other.

As for my dad and I, it became obvious that he never wanted me—he only wanted Mom. If I'd been a boy, maybe we could've bonded, but we were two complete strangers. We didn't know what to do and how to behave around each other.

By the time I turned seven, my father had left. Though I remember just pieces and bits of my parents' last conversation, I remember their faces and voices on that day very well.

"Forgive me, Libby," Dad said. "It isn't the life I wanted. I didn't sign up for it. I didn't ask for it. I'm not ready for it. Don't you see I'm suffocating? I need to get out fast, before I lose my mind. I don't know who I am. I have to find that out."

"I didn't hope for a life like this, either," said Mom. "I also don't know who you are anymore. I married a different man, but he's gone. You do what you have to. Do what you think is best for you. Don't worry about us. We'll survive without you."

I'll never forget how my Dad looked at me before he left and how he patted my head. His eyes were so sad, and his hand was icy cold.

He left to find himself. I never even knew he was lost. I wondered sometimes if he existed at all, if I ever had a father—except that I'll always see his eyes and feel his hand.

*   *   *

"We'll never see him again, will we?" I ask quietly. "My father, the loser, I mean."

"I don't know," Mom answers with sadness in her eyes. "Why do you ask?"

"Why do you care?" Grandma adds and shrugs.

"Mom," I say, ignoring Grandma, "when a man says he wants to find himself, does it mean he wants to be someone he's not or does it mean he wants to be someone, but can't?"

"No, it's more like he's trying very hard to be *somebody*, but doesn't know how," Mom replies, and suddenly it makes sense to me. I hope my father finds himself or that *somebody* he's looking for soon, because otherwise there's a chance that one day he just might cease to exist.

"Well, Libby, you've outdone yourself this time," Grandma says, changing the subject. "Hasn't she, David?"

"Yes, dear, everything was delicious," Grandpa confirms. "I'm so full."

"I'm glad you liked it," Mom says, "but, Daddy, you hardly ate anything—"

"You know, Libby, your father isn't a big eater," Grandma puts her two cents in. "Girls," she changes the topic again, "we'd like to give you something."

She puts five hundred dollars on the table. *Green is definitely my favorite color.*

"Oh? What's this for?" Mom just *has* to ask. "It's not Chanukah yet, and you already brought your no-reason-just-because presents."

"Yes, dear, but we didn't bring anything for *you*, and we know that Victoria is planning to go shopping with her friends next weekend. Let's not ruin her plans," Grandma insists.

Let's not, I think and continue stuffing myself up with food. (I always eat a lot when I'm nervous, upset, or depressed, and this moment definitely qualifies as all three.) Unfortunately, it's not up to me. It's up to Mom, the spoiler.

"Victoria, don't you want to say something?" she asks.

"Thanks, Grandma and Grandpa," I say with a full mouth and a long, meek look, playing innocent, my favorite game.

"I meant, thanks, but no, thanks. We can't accept it and we don't need it," Mom, the ruiner, says.

She gives me THE LOOK and her eyes say *two can play this game.*

"I *can* accept it and I *do* need it," I hurry to say, afraid Grandma will take it away.

"Take it back, please, Mother," says Mom, the destroyer. "And you, Victoria, stop making those grimaces, especially your *cranky* face."

(When I'm not pleased with something or disagree with someone, I lower my eyebrows and wrinkle my forehead and one side of my mouth. Mom calls it my *cranky* face.)

"But why?" I yell at Mom. "It's not your money."

God, this woman makes me mad!

"Libby, if you don't want it, you don't have to take it, but please let the child have it," Grandma says.

There you go, Grandma. Go ahead, tell her. Let her have it!

"Mother, please stay out of it. You don't understand. Money is the only thing that matters to Victoria. Yes, it's important to everybody, but to her, it's everything! As long as she can go shopping, she has a life. Otherwise, her life is over. Isn't it true, Victoria?"

"And what's wrong with that?" I yell again, pretty loud this time. "If you want to know, it's all *your* fault. You've always bought me expensive clothes. You've never deprived me of anything, you've never said no to me when I asked you to buy me something. I've gotten accustomed to this lifestyle, so what do you want from me now? You've created a monster, and now you live with it," I scream out in one breath.

Mom just stares at me, crushed and speechless. I'm not sure if it's because she agrees with me and feels guilty for creating a monster or because she doesn't know how to fight that monster. Anyway, both scenarios are scary.

"Victoria, stop yelling at your mother," Grandma demands. "You can't talk to her in that tone of voice. You'd better drop that attitude of yours, young lady!"

"That attitude of mine? There's nothing wrong with my attitude," I almost shout. *It's getting tiring already.* "Whose side are you on, anyway?"

I feel my eyes getting wet.

"David, say something, please," Grandma says to Grandpa.

"I think it's between Libby and Vicky," my ever-tactful Grandpa says softly. He turns to Mom and continues, smiling. "It's time to go home. Thank you so much, Libby, for a wonderful dinner. Give me a hug, darling. You, too, Vicky."

He smiles at me as well. I hug him and kiss him on the cheek. *God, I'm so loaded with food, I'm about to explode!*

As soon as my grandparents leave, I lift up my shirt, unbutton my jeans and sigh easily. Mom and I start cleaning the table in silence. The money is still there, but we ignore it.

Finally, when there's nothing left on the table but the money, I ask quietly, "What do we do with this?"

I'm afraid to look at Mom, but I do it anyway.

"I think we established it earlier," Mom says calmly. "You have two options: you can give it back or you can go shopping. It's your decision." She shrugs, tilting her head and pressing her lips together. "It's up to you."

"But it's a no-win situation. If I do the first, you know I'll hurt Grandma, and if I choose the latter, you'll hate me. So you see, I can't win either way. I don't know what to do."

"I could never hate you. I'll always love you unconditionally," Mom says tenderly, smiling at me. Her eyes are filled with tears. "Go shopping with your friends. Have fun. It's no use to argue with Grandma."

Is she for real or is this some kind of a trick?

"Do you mean it?"

Forgive me if I'm a little skeptical.

"I know you're skeptical, but I mean it."

God, she's good. She should be a psychic or something. I always feel like she's reading my mind. Or maybe my *I'm skeptical* face says it all. (My *I'm skeptical* face is practically the same as my *cranky* face, but I also add a little from-the-corner-of-my-eye glance.)

"Okay, Mom, I believe that you mean it," I reassure her.

Mom sits down and suddenly asks, "Tell me something, Victoria. Do you really mean it?" She gulps and makes that brushing-back-her-hair-with-her-hand gesture. "That it's my fault that you love money and shopping so much because I taught you to?" She gives me a long stare. "Because I'm *not* as obsessed with money as you are. I'm sorry you feel that way."

She's actually apologizing to me! Suddenly I feel ashamed of myself.

"Mom, I'm sorry I said that."

I mean it. *Should I take the money, though?*

"No, don't apologize for saying what you feel. You're right. It's my fault. I always made sure you felt like you were privileged, but I failed to teach you how to appreciate every-thing you got and never take it for granted. I think we both have a lot to think about.

Mom goes to the kitchen, and I'm left with lots of ques-tions: Am I a spoiled brat or just plain selfish? Do I just have a bad attitude about the money or am I the ultimate material girl? And whose fault is it anyway? I'm more confused than ever. I get the money for now, but do I win? Even though I come out victorious in this situation, is it a victory in a long run?

My name is *Victoria,* after all.

The Name Game

"A name is the blueprint of the thing we call character. You ask, what's in a name? I answer, just about everything you do."

—Morris Mandel

What's in a name? Well, sometimes nothing, sometimes everything.

When I was born, Mom wanted to give me a strong name, a name that could make a statement, so she named me *Victoria*. It speaks for itself. I just don't know what exactly my victory was. If you don't count two dance competitions I won when I was younger and took tap dance and ballroom or several tennis tournaments over the years, I haven't won or conquered anything. Not yet, at least. Maybe what Mom meant was her own victory over Dad. He didn't want a kid, but she had it anyway. She picked the name and he didn't object. (Translation: anything that made Mom happy was fine by Dad.)

He just called me Vic. That made me realize that a boy might not be that terrible, but a girl . . . so I was forever and ever Vic to him, well, at least for the first seven years of my life, until he left. They could as well have given me a boy's name, like my friend Alex, for example—strong, manly, and much better than Vic. Anything would be better than Vic.

What are parents thinking when they name their children? Come to think of it, take the girls in my school from the "popular-but-dumb-and-mean" club. All their names have something to do with jewelry. Check it out: Brianna Gold, Ruby Gorman, Heather Stone, Amber Livingston, Bridget Silverstein, and last, but not least, Tiffany Lawson— the leader of the pack. I call them the *Jewelry Collection*.

Let's analyze. When their parents named their daughters, did they do it because they were rich? Did they do it because they saw their little darlings as precious gems? Or perhaps they did it because with names like those, their little darlings would grow up to become rich by default?

*   *   *

It's the Monday after the Thanksgiving weekend. We're in History class. The first few hours are killing me. I can't wait till the break. I feel like I'm going to fall off the chair.

"Do you hear me?" Liza whispers. "I just said 'School sucks!' Where are you?"

"I'm in the *twilight zone*," I whisper back. "I don't hear anything. I don't see anything. I'm sooo sleepy. My head is pregnant. I have my *own* history in it."

"Your head is whaaat? Care to translate?"

Liza looks at me, astounded.

"My head is heavy and all messed up. It's full with tons of thoughts and questions, and everything is sooo mixed up. You're right, school sucks!"

Life stinks!

"Shush! Please don't talk," our substitute whatever-his-name-is teacher murmurs and presses his finger over his lips, looking straight at Liza and me.

Finally, it's lunchtime. We go to the cafeteria. As usual, it's the *haves* on the right side and the *have-nots* on the left. (Translation: those who have a life and those who don't.)

So, who do we have on the right? The *Jewelry Collection*, of course, and their eternal knights—the *Jocks*: the captain of the football team and Tiffany's boyfriend, Jordan Baker, with all the king's men (other football players) and several basketball players, including their captain and Amber's boyfriend, Nickolas Carson. (Nick is considered the hottest guy in school. I personally don't think so. *Liar!* Okay, he *is* hot. I think he just looked at me. *Or is it just my fantasy?* Wait . . . yes, he did it again. I swear it! *Stop it!*)

On the left side I see strange people. What you'd usually call *freaks and geeks*. Freaks look weird and . . . well, freaky. They're fashion misfits. They don't know how to dress and either don't wear makeup or their makeup is: a) so colorful and messed up that it would be great for the circus, or b) so dark and gothic that it would be perfect for Halloween. Some of them are dummies. They're so dumb that it's written all over their faces. Geeks (aka nerds) are very smart, usually wear glasses, look boring, *are* boring, are constantly laughed at, are victims of cruel jokes, are the best students in school, and are hated for it.

To sum it all up, we have winners and choosers on one side versus beggars and losers on the other. It's the name game, and it's all in the attitude. The nerds don't understand that they can be winners because they're so intelligent, so they just sit there on the left side, being losers. Meanwhile, the stupid right-siders treat them like losers just because they can, not realizing that *they*, the airheads, are the actual losers.

Then there's us, sitting on the back, in the middle. By *us*, I mean myself and my four best friends: Liza, Alex, Jackie, and Chloe. We're *Switzerland*. We're neutral. We don't belong to either side (by choice).

"Look at Tiffany and Jordan. Aren't they cute together?" says Chloe in a cutesy, robotic tone of voice.

"Yes, they are," Alex confirms, mimicking Chloe. "Just like Barbie and Ken."

"They make me want to puke, but yeah, they're adorable together," I say, kind of sugary-syrupy. Then I angrily add, "Those creatures just make me sick."

"Come on! They're stupid, but you have to admit it, they *do* look good," Liza laughs. "By the way, guys, are we still on for Saturday? Shopping, I mean."

"Can we do it Sunday instead?" Chloe asks. "My brother is coming over on Saturday."

"Whatever," Liza says. "Is it okay with you guys?" she asks Alex, Jackie, and me.

"I'm fine with it," Alex replies. "Saturday, Sunday . . . I don't care."

"I'm busy this weekend. Lots of stuff," says Jackie, looking at her sandwich, but we all know what the real problem is: she doesn't have the money to shop.

That wakes me up.

"I'm afraid I can't make it either," someone says.

Huh? Who said that? It sounded a lot like me. Was it really me? Did I lose my mind? Perhaps it's just temporary insanity? I do have that money from my grandparents. Well, I still have six days to reconsider. Perhaps my sanity will restore by then. A girl can hope, can't she?

"Whaaat?" Liza, Alex, and Chloe exclaim in unison.

Jackie just looks at me with an open mouth. That expression on her face is priceless.

I think for a long time about what to say. *Shit! Can I use a lifeline and get back to you?* I look at Mrs. Roberts, our teacher-monitor, talking on her cell phone, her face a little disturbed. Suddenly I see her quietly sneak off out the door. *Maybe it's a family emergency.* Soon, others start to notice

Mrs. Roberts' absence and I hear some commotion beginning to develop.

"Watch where you're going, you dork," I hear suddenly from the right side. It's pretty-blonde-but-really-dumb-and-mean Heather Stone, insulting a quiet, brilliant nerd, Norman Fixx, for accidentally touching her shoulder with a food tray he's carrying to his table.

"I'm sorry," mumbles the always-so-polite Norman, "I didn't mean it, honestly. I'm so sorry."

His apology apparently isn't enough for Heather. She's out for blood.

"Listen, Bates, you psycho!" she continues to torture the poor guy.

"His name is Norman Fixx, not Norman Bates," I yell from my seat. (Switzerland breaks the rule.) "Leave him alone. Didn't he apologize? Didn't he say he was sorry? What else do you want from him, his blood?"

"You shut up! Who asked you?" Heather shouts back, and then narrows her eyes and asks, "Who are you, his mother?"

"Norman Fix-me-up, come here. I want to talk to you," calls Ted "The Jaws" McAlly, Heather's "bodyguard." (McAlly isn't the only one "guarding" Heather's body.)

"No, Norman Put-me-down sounds much better," Heather declares and starts giggling.

Does she actually believe she's being funny? They all laugh. All except for Nick and Brianna, that is. Brianna Gold is the only one from that group I can tolerate. And Nick . . . I look at him appreciatively. He smiles at me and sends butterflies down my spine. He's so sexy, I feel a warm wave all over my body. *God, he's gorgeous! If looks could kill, I'd be a corpse right this moment.*

"Look who's talking! McDummy and McUgly."

As I say it, I look at Heather first and then at Ted, in case their brains can't figure out who is who. I just can't help myself. Now everybody's laughing, but not Nick. *Does he approve?* He doesn't smile at me anymore.

Poor Norman just stands there in the middle of it all, his face as white as the wall.

"Norman, don't just stand there. Go back to your table," I yell at him, pointing with my hands.

He obeys and slowly walks to his table.

"Yo, Benson! Who are you calling McUgly?" I hear Ted's bass. "Nobody calls me ugly. I'm THE MAN. Got it?" The Jaws-slash-McUgly angrily expresses his protest against my definition of *him*, but it doesn't bother him that I called Heather McDummy—a real gentleman. "You can talk the talk, but let's see if you can walk the walk," he says as he walks toward me, trying to provoke me even more.

I give him a finger-down-the-throat. *You piece of shit, don't push me. I'm not in the mood.*

Heather, on the other hand, doesn't notice his betrayal and defends her man as well as herself. She runs in my direction with her fists and teeth clenched. It's not a pretty picture.

"What did you just call us? You bitch! I'll show you McDummy and McUgly," she screams.

Her face is a picture of rage—all red and wrinkled, her eyes squinted and flashy.

"Bring it on, you, resident whore!" I retaliate. I'm dumping all my anger about Mom losing her job and me losing all my financial privileges on that slut. "You're sooo going to squirm after I'm done with you!"

I feel my blood boiling. I stand up. I'm ready to rumble.

"Vicky, stop it!" Alex, Liza, Jackie, and Chloe yell in unison.

They all look distressed, but I'm so pissed off now, there's no stopping me. *What if Mrs. Roberts walks in now?*

"Well, she *is* a slut and a whore. It's the truth, and everybody knows it," I insist.

Everybody does, but Heather doesn't agree with it, obviously. She's in my face now, and suddenly Switzerland breaks a second rule: Now Alex, Liza, Jackie, and even little Chloe are by my side, ready to protect one of their own. The *Jewels* are also right there, by our table. Amber, Ruby, Bridget, and Brianna just look on with horror, but Tiffany looks as mad as Heather does—same red and angry face, same clenched fists and teeth. She's ready to fight beside her best friend. It's war! The *Bold & Beautiful* versus the *Beautiful but Dumb*. The gloves are off! It's going to be the showdown of the century.

The cafeteria workers just look on and whisper to each other.

"Whatever you do, make sure you don't throw food and dishes around," says one of them.

How very touching and caring of them. Such sensitive guys—I can't hold back the tears.

It seems that a huge bomb, with all the hate inside it, is about to explode, but suddenly Jordan stops Tiffany as she's about to join Heather in a cat fight.

"Let's stop this shit before Mrs. Roberts comes back," he says to her. "Take Heather and let's go."

Tiffany and Jordan try to pull Heather away from me, but Heather's mad, mad, mad.

"I don't understand why you had to start this."

Tiffany looks infuriated as she tries to blame everything on me. *God, I hate that bitch! I hate her and Heather with a passion.*

"So you think it's me who started this?" I blow up. "You know what? You can crawl back into the hole you just crawled out from. Don't you have something else to do? Like some-body's life to ruin or someone's reputation to smear? And for the record, you stink, too."

Suddenly I feel all worn out. I don't want to fight any-more. *Thank god Mrs. Roberts isn't back yet.*

"What kind of bullshit is that? What's up with the atti-tude? Chill!" Jordan says to me.

He then grabs both Tiffany and Heather and drags them away.

"Everybody back to the table! Cut it out!" Nick loudly says to his co-siders, trying to end the spectacle, a fiasco that was about to happen. "Shame on you guys. You're all behav-ing like first graders." I think he means all of us. Then he turns to me and says quietly, "And you . . . I'm disappointed. You're so much better than that."

Omigod! Am I blushing? I'm so embarrassed right now, I want to die. *Please, someone, shoot me! Wait! Let's analyze. It's not that bad. I mean it's bad that he's disappointed in me, but it's good that he thinks I'm so much better than that.*

Nick then turns to Norman and says firmly, shaking his head, "And you, Norman, have to learn how to stand up for yourself. Be a man, for god's sake!"

As soon as we all sit back down in silence, Mrs. Roberts walks in and says, "I needed to take care of something. Sorry it took me so long. Is everything all right here?"

God, that was a close call.

"Yes, Mrs. Roberts," we all answer.

Then we notice that Brianna is still here, by our table. We all look at her, waiting.

"That was bad," Brianna says, wrinkling one side of her mouth. "Thank god Mrs. Roberts didn't walk in a minute earlier. We'd all be in trouble. Nick is right, we did behave like little kids."

"You didn't do anything," says Jackie, shrugging.

"Yes, but they're my friends, and I'm ashamed of the way they acted."

"So what do you want, a medal?" I ask angrily, unable to help myself.

"No, I just wanted to invite you guys to a party I'm having at my house Friday night. My parents are out of town, so I want to take advantage of it. Will you come?" Brianna asks, looking me straight in the eye. "It's a good way to bury the hatchet."

"Are you insane? Kiss and make up? I don't want to bond and become friends with people like all of you," I say in disbelief.

Why would she even think that I'd want anything to do with *that* crowd?

"Sorry you feel that way. Even among people like *us* you can stumble across some who are nice and smart," Brianna says calmly.

I can see that she's a little hurt, and I feel bad.

"Listen, Brianna, I'm sorry I said that. It's nothing personal," I say—and I really mean it. "I just can't stand those stupid, self-righteous bitches—Heather and Tiffany, I mean. No offense, but you know what they say, *you are who your friends are*, or *tell me who your friends are and I'll tell you who you are*, or *tell me who your friends are, and I'll tell you everything about you*. Well, something like that. Get it? Maybe you need to re-evaluate your friendships. Anyway, I apologize for being rude to you. You didn't do anything wrong. And thanks for the invite. I just don't see myself socializing with you-know-who."

"I appreciate your apology, Vicky. You don't have to hang out with people you don't want to," Brianna says, smiling. "Anyway, invitation stands. You're all welcome to come. If you change your mind, I'll give you my address and the details."

She walks away, and the girls stare at me in silence. Finally, I break it.

"You have the right to remain silent. However, I'd appreciate a little speech."

"You're *our* friend, and we're ashamed of the way *you* behaved," Alex replicates Brianna. "It was extremely neurotic." She thrives on giving lectures. She just needs to be in charge. She takes on her motherly attitude and tone of voice and continues, "And your attitude toward Brianna just now was unacceptable and uncalled for. She was incredibly fair, and it was totally nice and gracious of her to invite us to her party."

"I apologized to her, Alex, didn't I? So give it a rest."

What does she want from me?

"Yes, you did, but did you mean it?" The relentless Alex doesn't give up.

"Yes, I did. As a matter of fact, Brianna is the only one from the *Jewelry Collection* I can stand. Amber, Ruby, and Bridget aren't that terrible either, but for them, whatever Heather and Tiffany say and do, goes." I pause a moment and then add, "But admit it. You *were* about to join me in a fight, weren't you? By the way, you were welcome to jump right in a little earlier."

"You're wrong. We just didn't want you to get hurt and tried to prevent the fight," Alex replies. "What did you expect us to do? Be your personal cheering section? Or maybe your personal firing squad?"

Maybe she's right. Why should they join the fight? I don't answer. Shopping is forgotten. At least for now.

After a moment of silence, Liza suddenly asks, "Who was that girl? Who was that imposter, and what did she do with our best friend, Vicky?"

"You're such a smartass," I reply, irritated. "A little support from my best friends wouldn't hurt. Anyway, I wasn't going to turn that debacle into actual physical combat."

"Please, guys, not again," cries Chloe.

"Chloe's right. We've had enough for the day," Jackie says and then sighs heavily.

"Why are all of you against me?" I ask, annoyed. "Would you rather that smug, self-righteous bitch abuse poor Norman and nobody do anything about it?"

"Nick's right," Alex states. "Norman should learn how to stand up for himself. Eleanor Roosevelt once said, 'No one can make you feel inferior unless you agree with it.' "

Alex loooves to quote famous people. She has a quote ready for everything, Miss Know-it-all.

"Are you kidding me? Are you out of your freaking mind?" I can't believe she said that! "If wishes were horses, beggars would ride," I quote Mother Goose. "He doesn't stand a chance against them. Those monsters will eat him alive. They'll chew him up and spit him out. Next time it could be one of us, you know. Remember: bite or be bitten, eat or be eaten, kill or be killed."

"Vicky, please, don't be so melodramatic," Alex says, waving her hands.

Whaaat? Am I becoming my grandmother?

"Heather was damn wrong, but so were you, and two wrongs don't make it right."

Alex just can't settle down, can she? Does she ever?

"Well," I soften a little. "Sometimes I just can't sit and let some freaking idiot abuse the underdog. Sometimes we have to speak up for those who won't. You know, help those who can't help themselves."

I look at Norman and suddenly I see Tina Perelli, sitting next to him. Tina has black hair with a white strand covering half of her face, and wears very dark Goth makeup. Every part of her body is pierced. Her clothes are too complex to describe.

"Case in point," I say, pointing my chin in Tina's direction. "Look at Tina. Her family is filthy rich, I heard. Did you see that BMW she drives? Regardless, when she's coming, I can feel and smell a wardrobe malfunction. But she's actually an attractive girl. As a matter of fact, with a normal haircut and color and human makeup, she could even be quite pretty. Once you put her in some nice clothes, of course. I'm just not sure she knows what it means. Maybe someone needs to show her, to fill her in."

"Why would a person consciously look like that?" Liza asks, making a frown.

"Beats me," Alex replies, "but it's sooo sad."

"Maybe she likes that look," Jackie, the advocate, says seriously. "Everyone's entitled to his or her own image. Maybe it's her way of expressing herself. Have you ever thought of that?"

"Like maybe she's trying to say something with it, to make a statement?" Chloe asks.

"If it's a statement of individuality, well, it's not a very good way to make a statement," says Liza. "It's a fashion disaster and a style abuse."

"Has it ever occurred to any of you that maybe she's crying for attention?" I ask.

"What attention? Whose attention?" little Chloe wants to know.

"Maybe her rich parents are so busy with themselves that they don't pay any attention to Tina, and that's the way she rebels," I speculate further. "Maybe she wants help and the only way to get people's attention is by looking freaky."

"My rich father doesn't pay any attention to me, but I don't look scary," says Liza.

Her eyes look sad. *We'll need to address that issue later. I think she also needs a lot of help.*

"That's because you have us," Chloe says. "Poor girl. Tina, I mean. She doesn't get any attention from her parents and she definitely doesn't get any attention from anyone else."

"We don't even know if that's the case," says Jackie. "That's how the rumors start."

"I just know that she needs a lot of help," I insist, confident that it *is* the case. "I don't even think she *wants* to look Goth. I'm telling you, I don't think that's who she is."

"What do you mean?" Chloe asks, looking at me with her big blue eyes wide open.

"How do you know?" Alex and Liza ask at the same time.

"Goth people usually have attitude," I answer. "A *real* attitude, I mean. Tina is completely opposite. Look at her. She's so shy and she has a quiet demeanor, so if her look *is* a statement, it's a *help-me-I'm-in-trouble* statement."

Then I think, *Why don't we make Tina our project? We could find out what it is with her and we could take her with us when we go shopping next time. If I ever shop again . . .*

"Vicky, do me a favor," Alex interrupts my brainstorming. "Stop your psychoanalysis of Tina's character. Come out of your *psychoanalyst* mode and step back into your *writer* mode." She takes my hand and adds, "And please don't fight. Write!"

"What is that supposed to mean, Alex? Be a writer, not a fighter?" *When will she leave me alone?* "Where are you going with this?"

"It's very simple. Bullying happens everywhere every day. So instead of fighting with worthless bullies like Heather, write about it. You're the editor of our newspaper, right? Here's a great topic for your next article: 'Bullies Among Us.' "

"Hmm . . . I haven't thought of that. Maybe I *should* write about it," I say with a sigh. "Those nobodies always mock and rag on poor Norman. Well, I'll put it on my things-to-do list."

"Vicky, tell me something," Alex continues tormenting me. "Are you at least a little bit remorseful or completely guilt-free?"

"Alex, don't be a pain in the ass," Liza comes to my defense. "Cut it out already."

"Okay, okay," Alex softens a little. "I hope it doesn't happen again, though. Ever."

"I promise," I say, tucking my hair behind my ears—a sign that I'm nervous.

"By the way Vicky, you never answered what happened. What's wrong with you today?" Jackie asks. "I don't recognize you. If something's bothering you, we'd like to help."

Duh! Everything sucks. Everybody stinks. I hate my so-called life.

"I have no idea what happened," I lie, looking down. "It's sooo not me."

It's not!

"Ya think?" Liza asks sarcastically.

"I don't think. I know," I answer. What can I say? *I'm not mean; I'm just in a bad mood?* But it's true. "Something just came over me."

As soon as I say it, the girls' faces change. They all stare at me, taken aback, and say in unison, "No kidding!"

"All right, let's end this, please," I beg. "I regret I behaved that way. I won't do it again."

"Wait, I have a question," Chloe says with hesitation. "Vicky, why do you call Ted *The Jaws*, and why did you call him McUgly today? Do you really think he's ugly? I personally think he's totally sexy."

"I agree. He's stupid, but hot," Liza says and then asks, "What's up with that, Vicky?"

"Isn't it obvious?" I ask, surprised. "His jaw is square. He has an overbite and a space between his two front teeth. You'll see something like that in a dream (or should I say, in a nightmare) and you'll never wake up. He doesn't even need a mask on Halloween. Blind people might find him attractive, but you?"

Ooops! I've done it again. I'm baaad!

"What a mean thing to say," Jackie says with indignation. "Do you really hate them *that* much? It's too much even for you. Are you sure you're okay?

"I think that his jaw makes his face very manly, and that space is kind of charming," Chloe persists before I have the chance to answer Jackie—and I'm glad I don't have to.

"I think our little Chloe likes the big guy. How cute is that?" Liza says and smiles.

"I do not!" Chloe declares, blushing and twisting a strand of her curls around her finger.

"You do, too!" the four of us tease.

"Okay. What if I do? He's with Heather anyway," Chloe responds, still blushing.

"He doesn't deserve you, babe," I say, "but honestly, if it makes you feel better, I called him McUgly because it goes well with McAlly, and because he insulted Norman. He's a jerk, but he's a *hot* jerk."

We all laugh.

"By the way, about the party," Alex suddenly changes the subject.

"What about it?" Liza asks, looking at Alex.

"Sounds interesting. As a matter of fact, I'd like to go. Why not? We've never been to a house party without parents before. Well, with more than five people, I mean. I think we need to unwind."

She looks at all of us, waiting for a response. I don't believe *Alex* said that.

"I second that," Liza says. "So we need to go shopping before Friday night. Are you with me?"

She suddenly becomes giddy. I swear the girl lives to shop. She'll probably die shopping. Going back to her favorite subject makes her the happiest girl alive.

"As I recall, we *were* talking about shopping when we were so rudely interrupted," she starts.

Does she ever want to talk about anything else? But why does the mention of shopping bother me so much? Because everything's changed? I have the five hundred dollars my grandparents gave me. Why then? *What if it's the last five hundred dollars I'll ever get? Maybe because I might need it for something more important, like Christmas shopping for my family and friends, for example.*

"Two things I want to talk about: shopping and Nick," Liza goes on.

Whaaat? Why does she want to talk about Nick? God, I'm going to kick her ass! What is it, open house for let's-take-a-hit-at-Vicky day?

Dzzzzzzzz, we hear. *Saved by the bell,* I think, but I'm dead wrong. On the way to class, Liza brings it up again.

"By the way, did you see how Nick kept staring at you through the entire lunch?"

She winks at me. I shake my head and turn away.

"Of course, he kept staring at her. She behaved like a maniac," Alex puts her two cents in.

"Nooo, he stared at Vicky like there's no tomorrow," insists Liza. "God, he's gorgeous!"

"He's built like a Greek god," Chloe says. "He's to die for."

Better than McUgly?

"Yeah . . . he's dreamy," Jackie supports Liza and Chloe. "Alex, don't you think so?"

"He's okay, I guess," Alex replies coldly, not looking at us. "In case you forgot, he's taken. He's Amber's man, so why are we talking about him? What's the point?"

"Amber Shmamber. The point is that I think Nick Dreamy is hot for Vicky," Liza persists. She turns to me and says, "You haven't said a word. What do you think?"

I give her an intense look and say, "He's not hot for me, but even if he is, I should care about it because?"

When will this torture stop?

"How do *you* feel about *him?*"

Liza doesn't want to give up.

"I don't care one way or the other," I answer, turning away.

Liar! You do care, admit it!

Now it's my turn to blush. I can tell that I am. My friends look at me and smile at each other.

At last, we're in class. The inquisition is finally over. *God, it was a long lunch.*

*   *   *

After school, Liza reminds us that we need to discuss the upcoming party and shopping (fashion and shopping mean to Liza exactly what lecturing and being in charge mean to

Alex—everything), so she suggests we go to the Indulgence Café, our favorite hangout.

"At least there we won't be interrupted and we can finish our conversation," she says. "Hopefully, it's going to be just the five of us."

The Fab Five

*"Friendship is the hardest thing to explain.
Friendship is not something you learn in
school, but if you haven't learned the meaning
of friendship, you haven't learned anything."*

—Muhammad Ali

Once upon a time, there were five little girls. For as long as I can remember, the five of us have been together. We started calling ourselves the *Fab Five* long before America discovered and fell in love with those five famous, adorable gay guys that tried, with their "queer eyes," to make over the entire straight male population of the country. *We* are the original *Fabulous Five.*

Alex Malone and I have known each other practically since we were born. Alex comes from a family of doctors. Her grandfather has been our family physician forever. Her grandmother is a big shot gynecologist. She actually delivered Alex and me, exactly three weeks apart. Alex was born on August 10 (she's a Leo, which explains her need to be in charge) and I was born on September 1. Alex's parents share a dental office that members of my family visit when needed. Our mothers and grandmothers used to take Alex and me to the park on play dates together. We missed each other like crazy when we were apart.

When we turned three years old and our parents decided it was time for us to be with other kids, they brought us to a fancy daycare center. There, out of all the children we played with, one pretty, blonde, blue-eyed little girl stood out. We liked her the most. That girl was Liza Tollan. The three of us soon became inseparable.

Liza's mom died when she was just two years old, and Liza only knows her by pictures. She was raised by her rich father, who gave Liza everything, except for his attention. After losing his young wife, he started changing nannies because Liza was acting out. He didn't realize why she did it (she was crying out for him and his love), so he put her in a daycare.

Then he started changing girlfriends. The older he got, the younger they got (his current girlfriend is hardly older than Liza). Since Liza's grandparents (her father's mother and her mother's father) live in other cities, Alex and I were all she had then, and are all she's got now, plus Jackie and Chloe.

Liza and I paid a lot of attention to our looks even then. We could stand in front of the mirror for a long time, arguing about who was prettier or who had a better dress. Alex, on the other hand, was more interested on what was inside, literally. (Several "opened" dolls and un-stuffed animals might attest to that.) So it was a given that when we got older, Alex announced that she had decided to become a surgeon. (She even looks like one—very serious, with straight light-brown hair always taken back in a knot or a ponytail, and glasses over her hazel eyes, since Alex can't tolerate contact lenses.) Liza declared that she wants to be a supermodel. (Now, realizing that she's not tall enough, she wants to be a professional clothes buyer.) I, however, though sharing Liza's love for style and fashion, found myself writing down all my thoughts and recording everything that was happening with us in a journal. I knew pretty early on that my real passion was writing. (To this day I keep a handwritten journal. I thought of starting a computer journal, but then decided against it—I didn't want to lose my personal touch and sense of security. I actually love to write, and this pen-on-paper journal is really intimate; it belongs only to me. I also like the fact that it's portable, which is very convenient. I use my computer for writing newspaper articles; blogs and Facebook aren't for me. I know, everybody does it these days, but I'm not like everybody else. Besides, there are millions of people surfing the Web and so many hackers invading our cyberspace and breaking into our files, it's scary. I've heard that prospective employers look at online stuff every now and then. I'm a forward-thinking kind of girl and I don't want anybody to know anything about me that can haunt me later. Even Mom could probably more easily see something online than by reading my journal.)

The three of us met Jackie and Chloe when we started kindergarten and hit it off. Right away we just clicked. Later, we all went to a private school together, and the rest is history.

Adorable, chubby little Chloe Wilmore, with her curly ash-blonde hair, baby face, rosy cheeks with dimples, and big, round blue eyes, was our "baby." She was a little artist even then. She used to draw us pretty pictures and make beautiful statuettes out of clay. Chloe, who's totally naïve and innocent, still looks and acts like a baby, and we all mother her. She's extremely talented and hopes to become a famous artist some day.

Chloe's father is CEO of a large computer consulting firm. Her mother owns a catering business, so for Chloe, like Liza and Alex, money is *not* an object.

If there ever was a perfect child, every parent's dream child, it was definitely Jackie Millerman. Jackie looks stunning without even trying. She's tall, and every part of her body is perfect. She's so naturally beautiful, she doesn't need make-up: creamy complexion, huge dark-brown eyes with the longest black eyelashes, a "sculpted" nose, and the most luscious pink lips. Her dark-brown hair is thick, long, and silky, and though Chloe and I need to straighten our hair and Liza and Alex need to curl theirs, Jackie doesn't have to do a thing with hers. It's straight, but not *that* straight. It's wavy, but not curly. It's very fluffy and full of body. It's . . . well, you know, just perfect.

Jackie's parents are probably the only attorneys in America who hardly make any profit. Just like their perfect daughter, the Millermans like to help the needy and take more pro bono cases than cases that bring in money. So, just like my mom, they have to deprive themselves to pay their daughter's tuition.

Jackie is their pride and joy. She's one of the best students in school (the other one is Norman Fixx). She's the smartest one of us and has always helped us with our schoolwork. Of course, it's a no-brainer that Jackie wants to be a lawyer. She hates unfairness and fights for justice, just like I do. She just does it with grace. Maybe someday she'll run for office. I can see it right now: Congresswoman Jacklyn Millerman, Senator Jacklyn Millerman, or even Jacklyn Millerman, the President of the United States. (That might be a bit pushing it: an Independent *Jewish woman president.* It could probably make the shortest punch line ever in a stand-up comedy act.) Then again, Jackie most likely wouldn't make a good politician—she's very honest and too sensitive for that.

*   *   *

We're in the Indulgence Café. The setting is very modern, but at the same time extremely warm and cozy. I love everything about the place: the atmosphere, the interior, and of course, the most scrumptious desserts.

As we give our orders to the waitress, I look at my friends. I love all of them the same, yet each girl differently because they're so different.

Liza is my *playmate*. We're more alike than the others. We discuss fashion, shop, and do some crazy things together, just the two of us, when the others don't feel like it.

Alex is my *rock*. When, after analyzing everything, I still can't make a decision or am afraid to make the wrong one, Alex always can straighten me out.

Chloe is my *serenity*. She always supports me, and sometimes deep inside I feel that's exactly what I need. Chloe's reassurance often gives me peace of mind.

Jackie is my *shrink*. She listens, doesn't interrupt, doesn't judge, doesn't get annoyed, and always knows what to say, when to say, and how to say it. Her opinion is the voice of reason.

Altogether they make a perfect *soul mate*. I need all of them. I can't even imagine what my life would be without any one of them in it.

*   *   *

"Are you okay?" Liza asks me, taking her stuff off the tray the waitress just put down.

"Yeah, I'm fine," I reply, nodding. I take a bite of my éclair and wipe my lips. "Why?"

"Just wanted to make sure. I've never seen you not being excited about shopping, and you usually talk and laugh a lot. Knowing you, I'd say this condition you're in right now is a catatonic state."

"Or a coma," Alex adds, "compared to how you were acting in school earlier."

I don't say a word, just keep stirring sugar into my latté.

"Are you sure you're okay?" Chloe asks softly and touches
my hand.

"Yes, I'm positive," I answer, annoyed. "Can we please
talk about something else?"

"We worry about you," Alex says. *Here we go again.* "You
snapped today and now you're quiet. We know you said that
nothing's wrong, but we don't believe you and want to know
the reason you're behaving like somebody else."

As usual, she speaks for everybody.

"But nothing *is* wrong, really," I lie, shrugging and looking away.

"Vicky, how can you say that? We have eyes and ears."
Alex persists loudly.

"Leave her alone, Alex. If and when she wants to talk,
she'll talk," Jackie, the diplomat, intervenes. "Let's talk about
something else."

"Sure," Alex replies and makes a grimace. "Whatever."

"I can't wait till we get our SAT scores!" Jackie says,
excited.

(Scores and grades mean to Jackie exactly what fashion
and shopping mean to Liza and what lecturing and being in
charge mean to Alex—everything.)

"Of course, you can't wait," says Liza. "I bet you'll get,
like 2,500."

"Liza, 2,400 is the highest score," Jackie, the overachiever,
laughs.

"I know, but I bet you'll go over the limit and get extra
points," Liza also laughs, but then makes a serious face and
says, "I'm personally scared to see mine."

"Tell me about it," I say, making a shivering gesture. *God, what a reminder!* "I don't even want to think about it."

Like I don't have enough to think about.

"Well, I'm glad we're done with our college applications and essays," Alex says with her *teacher* face and tone of voice. "As soon as we get our SAT scores, we can send everything out—and then . . . a new beginning, a new life. NYU, here we come!" (NYU is our first school choice. I, for one, want to attend it because they have a strong journalism program.)

"Do you know what I often think about?" Liza suddenly asks with a dreamy look.

"Sure, we do. That's easy. Shopping," I answer sarcastically and sing, "It is a-a-a-lways on your mi-i-i-nd . . . It is alwa-a-a-ys on your mi-i-i-nd . . ."

"No, seriously," says Liza, not offended. "Maybe I should ask Daddy dearest to buy me a magazine? Something that has to do with fashion and style."

"Can't you buy it yourself?" Chloe wonders, innocently.

"I think she means like a company. She wants to publish a magazine. Right, Liza?" I ask.

"Yeah. You could be my editor-in-chief, Chloe would be our art director, Alex and Jackie could be our company doctor and lawyer, respectively. Wouldn't it be cool?"

"I want to be a surgeon, thank you very much," Alex says and shakes her head.

"And I'm going to be a social issues attorney, like my parents, not a corporate one," says Jackie, also turning Liza's offer down. "Sorry, Liza, but there are more important things in this world than fashion and style."

"Well, I still think it would be great to work together," Liza says.

"I knooow," Chloe cries out, "but I don't want to grow uuup!"

"Don't worry, you never will, baby," Liza tells her and pats her on the head. "Come to think of it, guys, waiting for our SAT scores is the only thing that spoils the mood. This should be the most exciting time in our lives. The next few months, I mean. We're going to shop till we drop: for the party, for Christmas, for the prom—"

"Do you ever think about anything but shopping?" I snap. "I don't *want* to go shopping, I don't *want* to go to that stupid party! I don't know what's going to happen with me tomorrow. I don't know how we're going to pay my college tuition, and I don't think I'll ever enjoy shopping again. Mom lost her job. There! Happy now?!" I finally spit it all out.

Suddenly I lose my appetite. There's a long pause. Nobody talks for a while.

"That explains it," Jackie speaks first. "I'm so sorry, Vicky."

She takes my hand and squeezes it.

"Explains what? Sorry for what?" I ask, knowing very well what she means.

"I think she means that explains your neurotic behavior and mood swings," Alex clarifies for me. "And I think she's sorry for your mom losing her job. So am I."

She starts to caress my elbow.

"Me, too," Chloe adds, sticking out her lower lip and stroking my shoulder.

Why does everybody feel it necessary to touch me?

"Sorry. When did it happen?" asks Liza as she puts her hand on my back.

"Just before Thanksgiving."

"And you're only telling us now?" Alex raises her eyebrows in disbelief. "We *are* your friends, and that's what friends are for, you know."

I feel a lecture coming on.

"Listen, it's been only a few days. It's not like there's a deadline on it. Please, let's not discuss the time frame, okay? I can't."

I feel completely drained. Still, I tell them the entire story about Mom, about the Thanksgiving dinner, about the five hundred dollars, and about our argument because of money.

"Can I ask you a question?" Alex asks, looking like it affects *her* somehow.

"Can I stop you?"

A counter question from me. *Maybe I should try and stop her.*

"How's your mom? How does she feel?"

Alex really looks concerned.

"I can only imagine," says Chloe, rolling up her eyes.

"I don't know," I shrug. "How am I supposed to know?"

"Have you ever thought of asking her?" Alex sounds irritated and looks like it. "You only thought about what will happen to *you*, right? Vicky, *she's* the victim here, not you."

"Sorry, Vicky, but I happen to agree with Alex," says Liza. "You're taking it too personally. It's not the end of the world for you, but your mom probably feels like shit, betrayed by her employers, and needs some support and understanding."

"Yeah, it's not that bad, Vicky," Jackie adds. "Your mom will find another job and everything's going to be all right."

The girl is such an optimist. That's the difference between Jackie and me. I see a squirrel as a rat with a fancier tail, while she sees a rat as a squirrel with a shabby tail. I call 'em like I see 'em. She calls 'em as she wants to see 'em.

"I wish!" I exclaim. "That's the problem. She's not going to look for another job right away. She wants to 'look into her options and figure out what she wants to do next'," I say, imitating Mom. "She thinks she deserves to rest for a while."

"And she does!" Jackie declares. "Let her do what she has to do."

"I don't believe you!" I snap again. "I just spilled my guts and served them to you on a platter. Would you like some blood with that to wash it down with?"

"What is that supposed to mean?" Alex asks, looking at me strangely.

"You only worry about Mom's feelings," I say, offended. "Where's your concern for me?" *Whose side are they on? Some friends they are.* "Don't you see? If she doesn't go back to work right away, we'll have to live on her savings, and when that's over, she'll have to dig deep into my college fund. Yes, she's saved some money, but considering how much she was spending on me every year and how much the cost of education went up, we could probably afford one year of NYU, maybe two, if I get enough financial aid."

"Of course, we worry about you, too, but we're sure your mother knows what she's doing," Alex reassures me. "You shouldn't worry about anything yet."

"I agree," Jackie says. "I know your mom and how much she does for you."

"Me, too," Chloe joins in. "She just needs your support right now."

"Your mom will figure out what to do," Liza says. "As for you, my beauty, you need a diversion. I insist that you take your five hundred dollars and buy yourself something sexy, gorgeous, and expensive, and then go to the party looking stunning and *kill* the enemy."

Don't teach me how to live. Better help me financially.

"Liza, are you having a blonde moment?" I ask, agitated. "What part of *I don't want to* don't you understand? Shopping is *your* life, but it's not mine. Maybe it used to be, but it can't be anymore. You want me to buy something expensive? How very rich and blonde of you! Read my lips, Blondie, *I don't want to go to that stupid party! Leave me alone!*"

"Vicky," Liza says in Alex's tone of voice and with a serious face, "you know how much I resent those *blonde* references, and you've just made three. Are you comparing me to Heather? I'm nothing like her! I don't consider myself the dumb blonde, and I'm offended that you think of me that way. You'd better soften your attitude a little bit."

What am I thinking? How could I say that to Liza? She's such a good friend to me, and she's so smart—and the others are only trying to help. Am I becoming a difficult bitch?

"I'm sorry. I didn't mean that. You just piss me off sometimes."

I really feel bad about what I had said to Liza. Now I stroke *her* back.

"I don't know . . . I want to keep the five hundred dollars for Christmas shopping, and I'm not sure I want to go to that party. There probably will be too many people I can't stand. I'd rather go to a place 'where everybody knows my name' instead of going to a place so crowded that people will hardly notice me."

"Trust me, they'll notice you, all right," Liza tries to change my mind.

Is it working?

"And they know your name," Chloe, who takes everything literally, says with confidence.

"You know what I mean."

Actually I'm not sure she does. *Does she?*

"Let's go! Let's go!" Chloe keeps at it for a while, happy and excited that there's a chance it might actually happen—a party with boys, and *without* grown-ups.

"It's four against one," states Alex. "It's settled then. We're going! I'll tell Brianna."

"And tomorrow we're going shopping!" Liza exclaims. "Nick will be at the party," she whispers in my ear.

Like I care!

"Come on, it'll be fun."

She's very persuasive.

"I don't know . . . I don't want to go," I murmur, but don't sound that convincing anymore.

"Okay, guys, let's have some fun!" Jackie seals the deal.

Girls Just Want to Have Fun

"Girls just want to have funds."

—Adrienne E. Cusoff

It's Tuesday morning. Liza picks me up for school. (I don't know where Mom went, but she took her car, and since I probably won't have my own car for at least another five years, somebody has to.) As soon as we walk in, we see Alex, Jackie, and Chloe waiting for us by the lockers.

"Wait till you hear what just happened," Chloe announces, all giddy as she looks at Alex.

"Whaaat?" Liza and I also look at her, impatiently.

"Oh, nothing much," Alex says proudly. "I just talked to Brianna."

"Okay, spill it already," Liza insists.

"I told Brianna that we decided to accept her invitation and will come to her party," Alex continues. "She seemed genuinely glad about it—and guess what she told me? Heather won't be there! She's not coming because of McAlly."

"Nooo!" Liza cries out.

"No way!" I exclaim.

"Yes, way!" Alex insists. "She's pissed off at Ted because he didn't stand up to you for her. Someone probably pointed that fact out to her, and they had a huge fight and stopped talking. No matter how much everybody tried to change her mind, it was no use—she's not coming."

Alex looks smug and pleased with herself.

"That's great news," I say. "I'm happy that I don't have to deal with her after yesterday. It's one thing to handle her in school, but it's a different story to deal with her at a party without parents or teachers. I don't want another fight, a real one."

"That's not all," Chloe says with a sneaky smile. "Tell them, Alex."

"Tell them what?" Alex asks, turning away. "There's nothing else to tell. Let's go."

I notice Jackie raising one eyebrow, tilting her head to the side, and giving her I-can't-believe-you kind of look, but she still doesn't say anything. *What does Jackie mean by that look? What does Alex not want to tell us? I'm dying to know.* Liza and I exchange glances.

"It's about Nick." The naïve, innocent Chloe rushes to satisfy our curiosity. "He asked us about you, Vicky. He wanted to know if everything was okay, how you were, and if you have calmed down. Wasn't that nice and thoughtful of him?"

"Yeah, it's cool," Liza answers and pinches me.

"Ahhh!" I scream. "Ouch! What the hell did you do that for?"

"I did it to wake you up, you stubborn asshole," Liza says. She really enjoys this. "I was right, he *is* hot for you. Mmwa, mmwa, mmwa," she makes kissing sounds.

"Thanks, but no, thanks," I say and smack her on the back lightly, though I'd like to *really* punch her, "and while we're at it, thanks for the *asshole*."

"Any time, bitch!"

We all laugh, but not Alex. She looks a little distressed.

"Did that slip your mind?" Jackie asks Alex, giving her an intent, piercing look.

"What are you talking about?" Alex asks, pretending she's confused.

"I'm talking about you forgetting to mention Nick to Vicky and Liza."

"Oh, yeah, I completely forgot about it," Alex answers, turning her eyes away again.

"Alex, do you have a crush on Nick?" Liza asks. "How interesting. A triangle."

"A quadrangle," Chloe corrects her. "You're forgetting Amber."

"I don't have time for this. Let's go to class," Alex huffs and walks away while we follow.

"Stop talking about Nick, asshole!" I hiss, paying Liza back, "or we won't talk at all."

"Okay, chill. I'm sorry. I won't do it again, I promise," says Liza and adds, "You're becoming very difficult to deal with. You get pissed off too easily and too often. Let's go."

On the way to class, we see Norman. He looks at me with admiration, poor little genius.

"Good morning, Vicky," he says, smiling, and adds, "good morning, everybody."

"Good morning, Norman," the five of us answer in unison and keep walking.

When I'm sure he can't hear us anymore, I say to my friends, "I can't look at him without tears. I just want to hug him, squeeze him, and cry my eyes out." I joke, but mean it. "He looks like a lost little boy and I feel the need to protect him."

"Do you feel the need to adopt him, by any chance?" Alex asks, and everybody laughs.

"I have a better idea," Liza says. "Why don't you go together on that TV show, *Beauty & the Geek?* You might even win."

"FYI: that show hasn't been on for quite some time," I chuckle.

"Too bad," Liza says, making a crying face. "What a loss!"

Now we're hysterical, and it feels kind of nice.

All day long the left-siders look at me like I'm some kind of a hero or something, especially Norman and Tina. Though I get some hateful looks from Tiffany and Heather, no words are exchanged. However, it's a different story with the *Jocks*. First, Jordan and Ted pass by and make comments.

"Hi, Vicky," Jordan says. "Have you chilled already? Man, some attitude you've got there. It's kind of a turn-on."

"So what's the problem?" I look at him with disgust. "Go to Tiffany. I'm sure she's always willing and ready."

He shrugs, waves his hand, making an I-give-up gesture, and walks away.

"Hey, Benson," *The Jaws* starts with me, "I've got to hand it to you, you've got balls! But don't call me ugly anymore. Deal?"

He reaches his hand out, but I ignore it.

"Deal," I answer and walk away.

Should I take their remarks as compliments? It seems that they started treating me with respect after yesterday. *It's sad and scary.*

Then during a break, Nick comes up to me and asks, "Are you all right, Vicky? That was some outburst yesterday. What gives?"

What right does he have to ask me those questions? Who does he think he is? Some nerve he's got! I feel blood rushing to my face. I have this burning sensation in my cheecks. I can bet that I'm blushing.

"I'm okay," I answer, looking down. "And what do you care? You should worry about your friends, like Amber, Heather, and the rest of the company."

"I worry about everybody. Well, you're obviously still in a bad mood, so I'm not going to bug you anymore. I'll leave you alone."

He walks away and I just stand there, thinking, *Are Heather and Liza right? Am I really becoming a bitch or just plain stupid? He'll never look at me or talk to me again.* The day is ruined, and it's all my fault.

*   *   *

Finally, the day is over. We're going shopping. I go with Liza in her car, and Jackie and Chloe drive with Alex. On the way to the mall, I apologize to Liza for my outburst and admit that I do like Nick. A lot.

"Well, he's gorgeous and he's obviously not stupid," I try to reason out loud. "He's a great student, unlike other jocks, and he's very articulate. I just don't understand how he can be friends with those nobodies—and how can he be with that airhead, Amber?"

"I'm not even sure he's *with* her," Liza says. "Are you?"

"I don't know. They often come in together in the morning and he always sits next to her. Why then, if they're not together?"

"I don't know. I can see that he likes you, I can almost swear to that. And you're saying you like him, too. I just don't get why you had to talk to him that way."

"Beats me," I shrug. "I have a split personality, and it was my alter ego. Or maybe it was my evil twin. No, I know: I was possessed by the devil! Anyway, let's say I had extremely extenuating circumstances."

We both laugh.

"By the way," Liza says, "You're a hero to some people. Did you see how Norman and Tina looked at you today? They worship you now, I think."

We laugh some more, as we approach the parking lot. Liza and Alex park their cars and we get out.

"Okay, ladies. Let's hit the mall!" Liza exclaims.

She's sooo happy—it's her paradise (as it was mine just before a few days ago). As we walk to the main entrance, we see a familiar dark figure coming out.

"Speak of the devil," Liza says. "It's Tina!"

She does look scary. She opens her purse, so huge it looks more like a knapsack, takes out a pack of cigarettes, pulls out a cigarette, and pushes it between her black lips. She lights it up, sucks on it, and blows the smoke out.

"Hi, Tina!" we all say.

Tina looks around, probably reassuring herself she's the only Tina there and that she really *is* the one we're talking to.

After she's gotten her answer, she says quietly, "Hi. You're here. You're talking to me."

It sounds more like a question than a statement.

"Yes, we are," I confirm, smiling.

"What are you doing here, shopping?" Liza asks.

"Yeah . . . no . . . just looking around. I came out for a smoke," she says timidly.

I was right. She's very shy and meek; not at all like gothic people.

"Do you guys, uh, smoke?"

"I do. I'm a bad girl," Liza answers. "Vicky tried a few times, but she doesn't care much for it."

"I want to, but they wouldn't let me," Chloe complains, frowning and sticking her bottom lip out like an abused child who's been denied her favorite toy. "She's watching me like a hawk," she says, pointing at Alex.

"You don't need that shit. If those two want to kill themselves, let them. But not you," mother Alex announces rigidly.

"Alex, relax," Jackie lightens the atmosphere. "Nobody's killing anybody." Then, turning to Tina, she says, "Listen, Tina, we're going in. Since you're already here, do you want to join us?"

Jackie looks at the four of us, asking with her eyes if we mind. We all silently indicate that it's okay. *I was just thinking about it yesterday.*

"Join *you*?" Tina asks, first looking surprised and then very confused. "Me? Come with you?"

She's alert and reserved, like she's thinking maybe there's a trick here somewhere and we want to play a cruel joke on her. When she sees that this is really happening, her eyes say, *I can't believe my luck. I'm not worthy of such honor.* Poor girl.

"Come on! Let's go, guys," Liza says.

(She's in a hurry, probably dreading there won't be enough time to purchase the entire mall.) Tina throws away her cigarette and we walk in.

"Listen," Tina says suddenly, turning in my direction and looking at me with admiration. "You . . . What you did yesterday in the cafeteria—it was sooo cool! And long overdue."

"Thanks, I think," I chuckle. "*They* think I behaved like a neurotic."

"You did," Alex says, turning to me and then to Tina. "Tina, don't encourage her, please. God knows what she'll do the next time. She's got some attitude!"

"Oh, shut up, Alex!" I shout. "You should talk!"

"Not agaaain!" Chloe cries. "Please, guys, let's not argue. Let's have fun."

"Listen to her," says Liza. "We're here to have fun, right? Tina, do you have something in mind that you want to buy?"

"I'm not sure," Tina answers. "What I want to buy, I mean."

"Well, do you have money or a credit card or an account in some store?" Liza asks. "If you do, we can certainly help you make some choices. Vicky and I are professional shoppers."

Speak for yourself, poor little rich girl. From now on you're on your own. So enjoy it for both of us.

"Yeah, I have a couple credit cards."

"How much can you spend?" Alex wants to know.

"Whatever."

"What do you mean? What about your parents?" I ask. "Won't they be pissed off if you spend too much?"

I wish I could say whatever. I wish I could have some funds fast.

"They don't care. As long as I don't bother them," Tina replies.

Her eyes seem very sad. I glance over at the girls, telling them with my eyes, *I told you so.* They glance back at me, as if responding, *You were right all along.*

"They work all the time. When they don't work, they go out without me. That's how I pay them back: I spend their money."

"Sorry to hear that," I say, and mean it.

Money isn't everything in Tina's case.

"I know how you feel," Liza says. "I have the same situation at home. Except that I only have a father and he gives me everything except for his love and attention. My mom died when I was two. The old pictures are all I have left of her. People might think that my 'happy childhood' was handed to me on a silver platter, but the truth is, it wasn't that happy at all. Expensive, maybe, but not happy."

Miss Fashionista looks kind of vulnerable.

"Sorry to hear that," Tina says softly. "I had no idea. Umm . . . your father . . . is he the owner of Tollan's?"

"Yeah. The rich father I don't see. He works late, and by the time he comes home, I'm in bed. He changes girlfriends every week, and every time they get younger and younger. The current one is turning twenty-one soon. I heard her talking on her cell phone to someone, saying, 'Jeffie is making such a big deal out of it.' Jeffie, of course, is my father, the great Jeffrey Tollan."

Liza looks and sounds upset.

"And how do you and your dad celebrate *your* birthday?" Tina asks. "What does he do?"

"Ha!" Liza exclaims. "He probably doesn't even remember *my* birthday. I know his secretary is the one who sends me flowers every year. As for a birthday gift, I can buy myself whatever I want, so I pay him back the same way you do. I celebrate my birthday all year long by spending his money, and I enjoy every minute of it because shopping is my life. But enough about me. Let's talk about you, Tina. You're such a pretty girl, but I think you need a change. What do you think?"

"Thanks," Tina says shyly. "Do you really think I'm pretty?"

"You bet," I say. "Never doubt it, and don't forget to remind yourself as often as possible."

The girls all agree with me.

"You said I needed a change." Tina turns to Liza and asks, "What should I change?"

"Tina, umm . . . let's change your whole image. Your current one doesn't do you justice," Liza says, trying not to offend her. "What is your natural hair color?"

"Dark brown."

"Why do you color it black? And why such dark makeup?"

"And about those . . . umm . . . decorations—" I say, pointing at her piercings, "Don't get pissed off or anything, but it's too much. Why don't you keep the one in your nose and the one in your tongue, but lose the two from the brow and the lip? It's just a suggestion, and you don't have to listen to me. If you want to keep them where they are, it's your business."

"I'm not pissed off. I don't even want them myself. Do you think I like the way I look? I hate it! I know you're right, but it's just . . . Well, I try *everything* to get their attention, but they still don't notice me. They just don't care, I guess."

She shrugs and removes the two rings I suggested as the five of us exchange glances. *So I was right. Tina is crying for attention.*

"Have you tried talking to them?" Chloe asks.

"When? They're never home."

"Okay then," says Liza. "Let's pay them back with a vengeance!"

We take the mall by storm. First, it's all about Tina. We start at Tollan's, where Liza is met like a queen. She takes Tina to the cosmetics counter and asks the girls to give her a free makeover. They fuss over Liza and Tina while we look around. One of the salesgirls even trims Tina's bangs a little and tells her what to buy to take that raven black away and make her hair look more natural.

"For a while," the salesgirl says, "until your hair grows and you can snip all the black split ends off for good and forget all about it."

In twenty minutes, Tina looks like a completely different person.

"Omigod!" Tina exclaims when she sees herself in the mirror. She can't contain her excitement. "Is it really me?"

"You'd better believe it. You look so pretty, Tina," I say, and everybody agrees. "Do you think you'll be able to do the same makeup yourself?"

"I think so. I just need to buy some stuff here."

And that she does, spending a fortune.

"Good. From now on, you look like this," Liza orders her. Then she tells the salesgirls, "Thanks, ladies. You did a great job. I appreciate it. Now, if you'll excuse us, we need to dress."

We go further into the store, where the clothes are.

Liza looks around (and she knows *how* to look) and asks Tina, "Do you have something particular in mind? I mean, what style do you like?"

"Well, I like the way you guys look. You and Vicky always look so stylish, trendy, and beautiful."

"Should we be offended?" Alex asks, looking a little like she is.

"Yeah, what about us? Are we chopped liver?" Chloe says, making her *abused child* face.

"Come on, guys. She didn't mean anything by it," Jackie defends Tina. "Everybody has their own taste. Tina likes Vicky's and Liza's style. What's wrong with that?"

"I'm sorry," Tina mumbles. "I didn't mean to offend you. You all always look good, but Vicky and Liza look like models. I just always admire their style—clothes, hair, and makeup."

"Thanks, Tina," Liza says, pleased, "but believe me, it's not easy to be us. It takes a lot of work."

And a lot of money, I think.

"Yes," I say, "being us is incredibly time-consuming."

"I know!" Liza suddenly exclaims, as if she's just had a brainstorm. "We'll take a little bit of everything: a nice dress, a sweater or two, a skirt, maybe pants, and some accessories. What size are you, Tina?"

"Two," Tina replies.

God, she's so skinny! Lucky girl.

We choose a few things for Tina: two sweaters, two shirts, two pairs of pants, a nice black mini-skirt, and a little black dress. When we find the dress, I see another one, similar, but the pattern is different, and it's just my size. It's by BCBG (okay, it's not Dolce & Gabbana, but it's still very pretty) and it's on sale for two hundred dollars.

I need that dress. I want that dress. I desperately want it! No, no, no! I can't buy it. Can I?

"Vicky," Liza interrupts my mental activity. "You'll look hot in this dress. Why don't you try it on?" She points to the dress I want, and takes it off the rack. "You wear jeans too often. You need to show your beautiful long legs as often as possible. Just try it on."

"Okay, but I'm not buying it!"

No way I'm buying it! I am sooo not buying it.

When we look at sweaters, I show the girls the ones my grandparents gave me. The price is a hundred and twenty dollars. Black and green are all sold out. *Grandma knew just what I'd want. How cool and thoughtful was that?* Jackie and Chloe try them on right there, on top of their shirts, without going into the fitting rooms. Jackie, with her dark-brown eyes and hair, looks stunning in red. Chloe loves the turquoise one—it goes perfectly well with her bright blue eyes—and decides to get it. Jackie, however, puts the red one back.

"Ladies room," Jackie suddenly whispers to me.

I get it: she wants to talk only to me.

"I have to pee," I announce, pressing my legs together and shaking.

"Me, too," Jackie plays along. She makes the same gestures and says, "Let's go."

"Can't you wait?" Alex inquires, irritated. "Hold it for a while, for crying out loud."

"Sorry, if you've got to go, you've got to go," I reply, pointing at my crossed legs and making a grimace, meaning, *Can't you see, I can't wait?*

I actually wouldn't mind peeing because I'd last peed in school, and that was a long time ago.

"We'll be right back," I tell the girls."

"You guys browse a little more while we're gone," Jackie adds.

We run to the ladies room. Once there, we get inside the stalls and pee in silence. I come out first. Jackie follows.

"Vicky," she says. "I wanted to tell you something. Don't pay any attention to Liza. She doesn't understand what it means to want something and not be able to buy it. Don't let her pressure you. Don't be all torn up about it. You're used to being in Liza's club and now you're joining mine. It's not that bad. You just have to get used to it. That black dress is nice, but if you don't want to buy it, you shouldn't. It's as simple as that. We've never been to a party with those guys. They've never seen our party clothes, so we'll wear something we already have. No big deal. It's not the end of the world, you know."

"But that's the problem!" I shout so loud that Jackie flinches. "I don't want to be in your club. I want to be in Liza's, and I do want that dress. Not for the party. I wouldn't wear it to that stupid party anyway—it's too dressy for that. I just want it. I want it so badly, I can feel it on my body. Why can't I buy it?"

"You can. Jeez, you don't have to yell like a crazy maniac. Thank god there's nobody here right now. You'd scare them to death. People would run out of here with their pants down to get away from you. I didn't think you felt that way about that dress. I couldn't imagine it was possible to feel that way about *any* dress. Go try it on then."

"I'm sorry, Jackie. I didn't mean to yell at you. I'm just in a bad mood. No offense."

"None taken. Let's go."

"Wait. I remember when Liza first mentioned shopping yesterday, you said you were busy on the weekend. You lied, didn't you? It's because of the money, isn't it?"

"Yes, and yes. I didn't want to argue with Liza, but when we decided to go today instead, I couldn't think of another reason, so I went with you guys."

"You look so gorgeous in that red sweater. Are you sure you can't buy it?"

"Positive. I wouldn't waste a hundred and twenty dollars on a sweater. But you know what? I'm not you. I can browse and even try clothes on, and see others buy things and not get upset because I can't afford to buy the same things. I'm here with you guys and I'm having fun. That's what's important to me."

She really means it. *Awww . . .*

"I wish I could feel the same way. I envy and admire you so much."

My eyes are wet.

"Awww! Come on." Jackie hugs me and says, "I love you, too, Attitude Girl."

When we come back, we see only Alex and Chloe. Liza and Tina are in the fitting room. Liza comes out first.

"Voila!" she exclaims, pointing her arms in Tina's direction.

Out comes Tina in a black dress. She has a good figure and nice legs. She looks great.

"Ooh La La!" I exclaim. "Who is this beautiful super-model? Look out, world! Here she comes." I break into song, "He-e-e-re she co-o-o-omes, Mi-i-iss Ame-e-erica-a-a-a . . ."

"Me?" Tina asks seriously. "Do you really like how I look? Do I look that good?"

"Are you kidding me?" I ask, wide-eyed. "Tina, you're happening, from head to toe! Gisele Bündchen has nothing on you."

Alex, Jackie, and Chloe agree and approve. Tina then tries on some casual clothes and several outfits for school. She looks cute in all of them and decides to buy everything that fits her.

"Vicky, go try on the dress. I'm still holding it," Liza says to me.

I look at Jackie and she nods in approval. So I take the dress and schlep to the fitting room. As soon as I put it on, I feel like I was born to wear this dress. No, like I was born *in* it.

I come out of the fitting room, and judging by the girls' faces, I can see that they agree: I do look great in this dress. I feel like running away in it.

"Wow!" Chloe exclaims.

"It becomes you," Alex states.

"You look great, Vicky," Jackie confirms.

"Well, clothes do tend to look impeccable on me," I joke.

"You've already sold me on that. It's you, only better," Liza finally declares.

"I'm taking it off," I say and go back into the fitting room, where I take the dress off, and leave it there.

I come out, but don't say anything.

"So?" Liza asks.

"I left it there," I reply. "Let's go."

"You're not buying it?" Liza asks, looking at me as if I'm committing a crime.

"No, Liza," I reply, annoyed. "I'm saving my money for something more important and meaningful."

"Wait for me next door, at Angelino's Shoes," Liza says. "I need to say hi to someone."

We go to the shoe store. Suddenly I hear that familiar siren in my head, *Buy it! Buy it!*

As soon as Liza comes out of the store, I run back in, as the girls just stand there, lost.

"I'll be right back," I yell at them. "I forgot something."

I run back to the fitting room and ask the lady about the dress I just left there.

"It's been just sold," she says.

Crushed and miserable, I walk back to where I had left the girls. They're waiting for me in the shoe store.

"What did you forget?" Jackie asks.

"Never mind," I answer.

"Ran back to get that dress, huh?" she whispers into my ear.

"Too late," I whisper back. "Just sold."

At Angelino's, they're having a sale on boots. I suddenly realize that they're something I can actually buy without hesitation because I really need new boots. I buy a pair of high black leather ones for a hundred and eighty dollars and still have three hundred and twenty left for Christmas shopping. Alex and Chloe also buy nice black boots. Liza and Tina buy two pairs each—black leather and brown suede. Jackie gets none.

After visiting several more shops, where Liza, Alex, Chloe, and Tina spend a small fortune, we decide it's time to leave the mall. By the time we get outside, it's getting dark.

As we walk to the parking lot, Tina says, "I had so much fun. Thanks, guys. You're the greatest."

"You're welcome," we all say.

"I've never had so much fun," Liza announces. "Tina, I want to see you looking like this tomorrow in school."

"I'll try," Tina promises. "Liza, you're so great with this shopping stuff."

"She really is," I confirm. "She just goes overboard sometimes. She's sooo bad!"

"Yeah," Liza says, "when I'm good, I'm sooo damn great, but when I'm bad, I'm over the top, and I go higher and higher."

*   *   *

Finally, we reach the parking lot. Tina says her thanks and goodbyes and drives away.

"Vicky," Jackie whispers to me before I get into Liza's car. "I can see that you're still upset. I'll come over tomorrow after school and we'll talk some more, just you and me."

Good, understanding Jackie. She always knows what I need.

Suddenly I realize that I didn't call Mom to let her know I'd be home late. *Shit! How could I forget?* It's useless to call now.

Something's Not Kosher

"Jesus was a Jew, yes, but only on his mother's side."

—Stanley Ralph Ross

By the time I get home from the mall, it's very dark outside. Mom's on the deck, smoking. She smokes quite rarely—only when she's nervous, upset, or angry—and always outside.

"Where were you? It's dark already, for god's sake! I was worried sick!" she yells.

"Relax! Jeez, I was at the mall with my friends. Is that a crime?"

"No, it's not a crime, but couldn't you call and inform me of that fact?"

Mom's quite pissed off. I can see it on her face and I can hear it in her voice that she's angry with me. Well, I did screw-up, didn't I? *Think of something fast.*

"Come on, Mom! I knew you weren't home because your car wasn't there when I left, so I assumed you wouldn't worry."

It sounds like a lame excuse, but it'll have to do.

"It's a lame excuse, Victoria."

She's doing it again. She's reading my mind.

"Lame reason, lame explanation—whatever you want to call it," she shrugs. "I left in the morning. How did you know I'd be out all day? How could you make any assumptions? You should've called anyway."

"Okay, chill!"

That's all I need right now. Like I didn't get enough lecturing from Alex.

"Don't you *chill* me, young lady! Please be more considerate next time."

Mom calms down a little bit, but she's still upset with me.

"So you *were* out all day, huh? Where were you, by the way?"

I'm curious.

"It doesn't matter. Don't change the subject," Mom says firmly, not looking at me.

"Mom? You don't want me to know where you were? Is that a secret?"

Now I'm intrigued.

"Um . . . well . . . I attended a seminar in Manhattan. Satisfied?"

"A seminar?" I'm surprised. I raise my eyebrows. "What kind of a seminar?"

"For people interested in interior design."

Mom still doesn't look at me.

"Are you interested in interior design? Since when?"

Any more surprises?

"Since always. Haven't you noticed? Of course, you haven't. You've never cared about my interests. You've always only cared about your own," she shrugs.

"Well, I love what you did with our house," I start, ignoring her remark, "but I didn't think you were that serious about it."

Actually, that's not completely the truth. Mom decorated our house with such pleasure and love, it was unbelievable. She took care of every little detail—fabrics, patterns, colors, and styles. She chose every piece of furniture and every accessory very carefully, perfectly combining antique and contemporary pieces. I must say, she put her heart and soul into it, and I have to admit, she does have a talent for that. People coming to our house always admire what she's done with it. I love our house. It's not nearly as huge as Liza's, or even Alex's or Chloe's, but it's so tasteful and pretty, cozy and homey that I sometimes don't want to leave it. I like to stay in my room and read, listen to music, or just watch TV. Mom and I also spend a lot of time in the kitchen, snacking and talking.

"I don't know yet how serious I am, but I'm very interested. I wouldn't mind having it as my new career," Mom says, suddenly looking excited.

"New career?" I almost yell, jumping from the chair.

I'm not taking it sitting down! I want it straight up! I swear, this woman scares me more and more.

"What about your old career in finance? You know, the only career you've had for years, the one that brought us income and a good life?"

Wake up, Mom, and smell the money. Be a responsible adult.

"And the one I've always hated," Mom says.

Whaaat? She looks and sounds like she really means it.

"I've always fantasized of giving it up. Just walking away and never turning back. In some crazy way, being fired was the best thing that could have happened."

"Do you care to elaborate on that?"

What else don't I know? How many more surprises can I expect? Do I know my mother at all?

"I would've never just walked away myself because I needed to make a living. I just needed a little push. Losing my job was somehow a blessing in disguise, that little push."

"Wow! I never would've thought you felt that way. But why did you major in finance in college, then?"

I sit down again. Maybe it's easier to grasp sitting down.

"In those days, everybody took either finance or computer programming. So did I, but it's never been me. I've always wanted to do something creative." *Of course, she wants to do something creative. She's a Gemini. It's a given. But how come I never even suspected?* "By the way, do you remember Nora Brickman? She used to work at the bank with me seven or eight years ago."

"Wait! Is she the one who came here with her kid one day? He wore glasses and didn't want anything to do with me?"

Why is she telling me about that Nora woman?

"Yes, that's her. I met her in Manhattan today and we spent the day together. Nora lives there now. We had lunch, went to her place, and then she came home with me. She left an hour ago. She loved the house and what I've done with it." She pauses for a second and then continues, "Nora thinks I should do it professionally."

Whaaat? Is she crazy?

"Mom," I say without hiding my resentment. "What are you talking about? Do it professionally? It's like being an actor. Before they become famous, they wait tables. Is that what you want for yourself? Do you remember that infamous phrase, *Don't quit your day job?* Well, I think they say it for a reason."

I'm very concerned. For her and for myself. *It's not like she's got clients with money.*

"You're not worried about me. You're worried about yourself," Mom retorts. "You're concerned with the fact that there'd be no money unless I have some rich clients."

She does read my mind. Definitely.

Mom stops for a moment, coughs to clear her throat, and goes on, "Well, that's true. Any new business takes time to establish itself. That's why I want to take some classes while I collect unemployment benefits. Then I need a few clients and to do a good job for them so they can recommend me to other potential clients."

"But, Mom, you need to know someone who can recommend you to those first few clients. You need a mentor. You need connections. It's not simple. You're not acting responsibly," I say, alarmed.

What is she thinking? She's supposed to be the adult here, not me.

"Victoria, I'm not starting a new business yet. I don't have the money for it. It's just that Nora wants to take me to meet her friend tomorrow. That woman wants to redecorate her house. Nora will introduce me to her and give me a reference. Perhaps the woman will come see our house and want to hire me to do hers. I have nothing to lose, do I?"

"*That* you can do," I say.

"Thank you for giving me your permission," says Mom sarcastically.

"Just don't invest all our savings, Mom. Don't do anything drastic!" I almost scream.

"Is that a demand or just a rigid request?" Mom raises her eyebrows, tilting her head. She sounds annoyed. "Don't tell me what to do, please. I haven't lost my mind yet—and your attitude toward my feelings is very touching," Mom says, sarcastic again.

What does she expect? Am I supposed to support her in making a stupid decision, a dumb choice?

"Do you want to have a good laugh?" Mom asks suddenly, changing the subject.

It would be nice for a change.

"Laughing is good," I answer. "Laughing is healthy."

"You've heard about those parties for single people they organize so they can meet, right? They usually take place in clubs or restaurants."

"Like matchmaking?" I ask, curious.

Where is she going with this?

"Well, Nora has been attending those parties since she got a divorce and she wants me to go with her the next time she goes. It's for Jewish singles, and it's in the Tavern on the Green in Central Park. She wants to set me up with someone she met at one of those parties. Isn't it crazy?" Mom laughs.

I personally think it's a great idea.

"Why don't you go, Mom? When did you last have a date?"

"I don't remember, but that's not the point. I've never been on a blind date, and I don't intend to start now. A blind date is like a box of chocolates. You never know what you're going to get."

Very funny. It seems Mom has already decided against going. I need to try to change her mind. She needs to go out, meet one or two professional men. Maybe then she'll start missing her career and realize that her R & R time has to be over and it's time to stop fooling around, get serious, and make some money again. *Or maybe marry a rich guy?*

"But it's different, Mom. It's not really a blind date. You won't be one on one. There will be a bunch of people with the same goal. Nobody's forcing you to do anything. Just go look around."

I'm anxious, but she doesn't seem to care.

"That's even worse," Mom says and takes a pack of cigarettes out of her pocket. "Do you see this?" she points at the *warning* sign. "It says, 'Smoking causes lung cancer,' et cetera. On a box of pills, you'll see *side effects*, but when you look at a man, you don't see a warning saying, 'Alert: Armed and Dangerous' or 'Beware: Serial Killer.' You don't see a sign saying, 'Knight in Shining Armor. Will Always Protect You. Hold on to Him' or 'Intellectual. Marriage Material. This One's a Keeper.' It's more like there are several doors, and there's a man behind each door, and you have to solve the problem: open the door that has the right man behind it. Do you get my point?"

I do get her point. I now understand exactly what she means. *Actually, she makes a lot of sense.*

"I haven't even thought of it like that."

And what about Nick? Don't I act reserved around him? No, Mom really makes a lot of sense.

"Mom, can I ask you something? There is this guy in school. Well, he's unbelievably handsome, smart, and polite, but he always hangs out with the wrong crowd, with people I hate. How do I know if he's like them or not?"

Am I actually talking to my mother about Nick? Am I out of my mind?

"So you've been bitten by a love bug, huh?" Mom laughs. "I'm intrigued."

"Mom, be serious! Forget it. I can't believe I asked you a question like that."

I'm angry!

"I'm sorry. It was stupid of me." She does look kind of guilty. "Well, you see, that's exactly my point. You don't know. And you're afraid to make a mistake. So what do you do? You have two options: you can get to know him better and find out who he is, but there's a chance you'll get hurt, or you can just forget about him, and then you won't make a mistake for sure, but in this case you can miss out on something good."

She sounds so reasonable, but where does it get me? I'm still not sure how to behave around Nick.

"Thanks, Mom," I say, and end the conversation.

Two options. It's easy for her to say.

We go to the kitchen to eat. We talk some more. Suddenly I realize how late it is.

Omigod! I still have to do my homework! I feel so tired. It was such a long day.

"Good night, Victoria," says Mom. "I'm tired. It was a long day. I need to go to bed."

Here goes that psychic thing again.

"Good night, Mom."

I slowly crawl to my room.

* * *

It's the morning after. After our girls' fun day at the mall, I mean. It's the morning that will probably make history. Not the history of the world, but the history of our school. It's the morning everybody meets the new Tina Perelli.

Tina keeps her word and emerges, projecting a new image and a new style—normal hairdo, lighter makeup, and tasteful new clothes. She looks hip and trendy. She stops traffic. It takes a while for some people to realize that it's not a new girl walking by, it's just the new Tina. Eyes open wide in astonishment, jaws drop in surprise, and shoulders shrug in disbelief.

Some people make comments like, "You look great, Tina" or "I like your new image" or "Hey, Tina, I didn't know you could look that good."

Teachers say things like, "Now you look like a normal girl" or "Now you look decent, Tina."

The mean and snobby *Jewels*, on the other hand, point at Tina, whisper something, and laugh, but Tina's so ecstatic that she doesn't even notice or care. She talks to people, smiles, even laughs. She's never done that before. Today Tina seems more secure, more confident. She's absolutely glowing, and it makes the five of us very happy, too. We did a great job. A few more days like today and Tina's self-esteem might surface.

"Tina, you look great!" Jackie exclaims when we see her.

"Thanks," Tina says shyly.

"You look totally un-freaking-believable!" Liza declares.

"Do you mean it?" Tina asks.

I think she believes it, but wants reassurance.

"Are you kidding? Totally!" I say. "Abso-freaking-lutely! Tina, you're a show stopper!"

"Honestly, Tina," Chloe adds. She's so excited, like she's the one getting all the attention.

"We're very proud of you," Alex states, speaking for all of us, but she's right.

"You wouldn't believe what happened this morning," Tina says. "I come to the kitchen to get some cereal and milk, and who do I see? My parents! I never see them in the morning. If they see me when they come home, they just pass me by. And today, of all days . . . it's like it's been scripted especially for *this* morning."

"So tell us what happened!" Chloe exclaims impatiently.

"At first, they just froze and looked at me in silence. Then they said, 'Good morning, Tina.' Then my mom jumped from the chair and *served* me a bowl of cereal and milk. Then Dad told me I looked very pretty and offered to take me to school. I've been trying to get their attention for so long by looking freaky, but to them I've been invisible. Yet this morning, when I look all nice and proper, they suddenly notice me. Isn't it weird?"

"Not really," says Jackie. "I think they did notice you before, but *that look* upset and scared them. You were a different person, and they didn't know how to deal with you, so they pretended to ignore you. It was wrong, but they didn't know how to act around you. But today they got their Tina back, so they didn't have to pretend anymore."

"Jackie, please don't become Vicky," Alex says, and after Tina leaves us, our mother-slash-teacher concludes, "I must say guys, I'm very proud of all of us for the job well done."

* * *

I come home and see a note from Mom. Right away I remember that she mentioned going to Nora's friend's house. The note says, *Victoria, Nora is picking me up, so you have the car. Please go to the supermarket and get only the things on my list. Charge it. See you later. Thanks. Love, Mom.*

She actually underlined the word *only*. Mom knows me. She knows I tend to go overboard when shopping. There is a shopping list next to the note. I go to the store and buy *only* the things on her list.

* * *

I return an hour later. Mrs. Garner, our next door nosy neighbor sees me through her window and comes out.

"Hello, Vicky," she says. "Where were you?"

"Hello, Mrs. Garner," I answer. "I went to the store, if you must know. Why?"

"Your friend came over, the pretty Jewish one. She said you knew she was coming over."

Jackie! Omigod! I completely forgot that she told me she was coming over after school. *Why didn't she remind me today? Bummer!*

"Thanks, Mrs. Garner, but why did you say she was Jewish?"

"Isn't she? Doesn't she have a Jewish last name—Millman or something?"

"It's Millerman, not Millman, but it doesn't matter. Why did you have to mention it at all? I'm Jewish too, you know, but you don't greet me by saying, 'Hello, my Jewish neighbor,' do you?"

My tone of voice gets higher and louder.

"But you're only half Jewish, dear, on your mother's side, you have your father's last name, and you don't even look Jewish."

She doesn't get my point, and that pisses me off.

"And *your* name, Mrs. Garner, is it Christian?" I almost shout. "You *look* Christian."

"What is that supposed to mean?" Mrs. Garner asks, astonished. "What does religion have to do with my name or the way I look?"

"That's exactly my point," I reply, satisfied, but to my surprise, she still doesn't get it.

"You're losing me, Vicky. You're not making any sense," Mrs. Garner says, looking really lost.

Poor, silly woman. *I'm not making any sense! What a moron! Should I explain?*

That's another thing that pisses me off. Another pet peeve of mine. Let's analyze. If Judaism is a religion, how come then people say, "You look Jewish" or "It's a Jewish name" or "You're only half Jewish, on your mother's side?"

Imagine someone saying, "You don't look Protestant," or "It isn't a Catholic name," or "You're only half-Christian."

Maybe I'm not an ideal example of what God had in mind for his *chosen people*, but I'm not stupid either. It simply doesn't make any sense to me, and if something doesn't make sense, it doesn't work; and if it doesn't work, I don't want to accept it.

"I'm Jewish on my *mother's* side, and that makes me Jewish. Oh, by the way, Mrs. Garner, did you happen to notice if any of my Christian friends came by?" I ask sarcastically.

I think that now she *does* get my point, judging by the expression on her face.

"You don't have to be so rude and defensive, Vicky," she says, offended. "I didn't mean anything by that."

Mrs. Garner is upset with me. I can see it. But I don't care. *Let her think first before she speaks next time.*

"I know you didn't mean anything. You just had to point that out. Nobody ever means it, but it's always a Jew who gets mentioned," I say angrily.

"Are you accusing me of something? I don't like your attitude, young lady. It's arrogant and insulting. I won't stand for it. I'll talk to your mother about the way you speak."

"You can do whatever you want. Goodbye, Mrs. Garner," I say and walk toward my door.

As I'm about to open it, I hear Mrs. Garner's door open and see a tall young man.

"Vicky, wait!" he calls.

Omigod! It's Jamie, Mrs. Garner's grandson. He used to come and stay with his grandmother every summer and then he stopped coming. Mrs. Garner told us that her son's family had moved to another country. (Her son, Jamie's father, is in the military and was stationed in Germany.) When we were younger, we used to have a crush on each other. Jamie gave me my first kiss. We were watching *French Kiss* at my house once and pretended we were in Paris. We kissed. It wasn't a wet, inexperienced French kiss. We didn't just exchange saliva. We *really* kissed. It was kind of soft and tender kiss, the one you always remember. I was twelve years old then, and Jamie was fifteen.

"Jamie!" I exclaim, genuinely happy to see him. "I can't believe it's you! You're so tall and handsome. You're so . . . grown up."

"It's me, all right, and I'm a grown man. What did you expect? I'm twenty. And I can see that you're . . . well endowed, as my granny would say. You're hot! But you've changed so much. You used to be feisty, free-spirited, and opinionated, but you were still nice and sweet. Whatever happened to that sweet girl I shared my first kiss with? From what I just witnessed, she turned into an angry, bitter, rude, and offensive old woman with a major attitude problem." He shakes his head and asks, "Did you have to tear my poor granny to shreds?"

"What? First of all, I'm not bitter or angry. Second, I've always had an attitude, but I don't consider my attitude a problem." I pause to catch my breath. "And finally, no offense, but your grandmother had it coming to her. She got exactly what she deserved."

"Please forgive me. I'm completely wrong. You're an ultimate Miss Congeniality," Jamie says with sarcasm in his voice. "But seriously, you're talking about my grandmother, you know. So be careful."

I can see that he's a bit pissed off. *What did I say?*

"Sorry," I say and then add, "Miss Congeniality, huh? Yeah. And don't you ever forget it! I'm a nice and decent girl, and modest at that," I joke.

We both laugh. It's great to see a dear old friend after years of separation. Suddenly I realize that I don't have the same feelings for Jamie I used to. Why? He's even more handsome and muscular than he was before. *Is it because of Nick?* I wonder.

"Listen, Vicky," Jamie says. "Who was that girl that came over earlier? I saw her through the window, and I must say, she's the most beautiful girl I've ever seen."

"She *is* unbelievably beautiful, I agree. Her name is Jackie, and she's one of my best friends. Wait, haven't you ever met her?" I ask and then answer myself, "Of course, you haven't. She went to stay with her grandparents in Florida every summer. And Alex and Chloe went to summer camp. You've only met Liza."

"I remember Liza very well. She always talked about clothes. How is she, by the way?"

"She's fine. Still talks about clothes all the time and thrives on shopping. So Jamie, if you like Jackie so much, does it mean that our love affair is over? Are you dumping me?" I joke, sticking my bottom lip out, a la Chloe, and blinking fast, pretending that I'm hurt.

"I'm not dumping you. I'm just moving on to the next pretty thing. But don't worry, kid. We'll always have Paris and that almost-French kiss." We both laugh. "No hard feelings?"

"No hard feelings," I reassure him, "and as for Jackie, you'll meet her later, I promise."

PART II

Growing pains and other Aches

"By the time I'd grown up, I naturally supposed that I'd be grown up."

—Eve Babitz

Blast From the Past

"The past is not dead. In
fact, it's not even past."

—William Faulkner

I keep my promise to Jamie. As soon as I get inside, I put the groceries where they belong and dial Jackie's number. *She must be so pissed off. I would be if I were her.*

"Jackie, hi," I say in a sneaky-sweet voice when she answers the phone. "Mad at me?"

"I'm not mad, but you'd better have a very good reason for standing me up."

She doesn't even sound mad. She's so good-hearted.

"Would you believe me if I told you I broke my leg on the way home and was taken to a hospital? And of course, it's a known fact: they don't allow using cell phones in a hospital."

"What? Are you okay?" Jackie sounds concerned.

She actually buys that shit.

"Chill, I'm kidding, but I'm touched that you care and trust me so much," I laugh.

"It's not funny, you jerk!" *Now* she sounds pissed off. "Where were you, then?"

I explain why I wasn't home, and she understands. She's so groovy!

"Listen, can you come over now? Mom's not home, but there *is* someone right here I want you to meet."

I try to sound very convincing and hope she says yes.

"Does it have to be today? It's getting late." She sounds annoyed, but I hear a touch of curiosity in her voice. "Who is it? Do I know this person?"

"You don't, but I want to fix that. Let's say it's someone from my past who's dying to meet you. Aren't you at all intrigued? Believe me, you won't regret it," I say, too fast.

"Oh, I don't know. I wanted to come so we could talk. I wanted to make you feel better. I'm not sure I'm up to socializing right now. I have so much homework."

"Please, Jackie, just for an hour or so. Pretty please!" I beg.

"Okay, maybe just for a little while," she finally agrees. "I'll be there in a few."

As soon as I hang up, I go outside and ring Mrs. Garner's doorbell. Thank god Jamie answers it. I wouldn't want to see Mrs. Garner at the door after our encounter earlier today.

"Jamie, come to my house, quick! Jackie's on her way. See, I'm keeping my promise."

"That was fast. Thanks, Miss Congeniality," Jamie says, laughing. "How do I look?"

"Like a grown man that verbally abuses teenage girls by calling them names," I joke, as I lead him inside.

We come in and Jamie looks around, admiring the changes Mom has made to the house.

"I haven't been here for five years. Wow, your house looks great!" he exclaims.

"Thanks. It's all Mom. I think she's got a real talent for it," I say, starting to believe it.

"So what's up with you, with your life?" Jamie asks me.

I don't feel like informing him of what's going on in my life right now. Not yet at least.

"Nothing much. School, home. Home, school. Same old, same old, you know. What about you? You didn't tell me how come you're here. Did you leave Germany? Are you home for good? How long are you going to stay here?" My curiosity takes over.

"My parents are still in Germany, but my father is retiring from the Army soon. I'm back in New York for good. Right now I'm in the process of transferring to Columbia University."

"Wow! You must have really high grades if they've accepted you at Columbia."

"I do. I have a long way to go, though. I'm pre-law," Jamie says as he continues to wander around, his eyes darting everywhere. "Then I'll have to go through law school. I'm majoring in Business Law," he says proudly.

"So you'll be a corporate attorney then, huh? You'll be dealing with capital, investments, acquisitions, et cetera. Money, money, money. I love it! " I exclaim, smiling to myself.

Jackie will be thrilled! Jackie's a complete opposite. She's more into social issues and helping people. Takeovers aren't her thing.

We hear the car pull into the driveway. It's Jackie. I open the door just before she has a chance to ring the doorbell. She looks gorgeous, as usual, without really trying.

"Come on in, Jackie. I'd like you to meet someone," I say, pointing at Jamie and hoping she likes him. *Let's get it over with.* "This is Jamie. We used to be friends when we were younger. Jamie lived in Germany for five years, but now he's back for good."

"Hello, Jamie. I'm Jackie. Nice meeting you," Jackie says and smiles, holding her hand out to Jamie and looking straight into his eyes.

"Happy to meet *you*," Jamie replies, too eager to take her hand in his, smiling and looking into *her* eyes.

Well, I believe my job here is done. The love connection has been made.

"Listen, guys, you get acquainted while I go to the kitchen and get us some snacks and drinks," I announce. I think it's time to leave the lovebirds-to-be alone. "Coffee? Tea?"

"Tea for me, please, or juice," Jackie requests politely, looking at Jamie, not me.

"Me, too," says Jamie, not taking his eyes off Jackie.

They're a match made in heaven.

"Okay, suit yourselves, stay healthy," I say. "For me, it's coffee. I'm bad. I need my caffeine."

I walk to the kitchen, hoping that their chemistry kicks off. I'm surprised that I'm not even a little bit jealous. *Does it mean my ego isn't that colossal? Am I content with the fact that I'm not the one Jamie chose? Or is it because Nick is the only one who interests me right now? Am I really that into him?*

In a few minutes I decide it's time to get some feedback from the new duet.

"Hey, Jackie! Could you give me a hand?" I yell just as Jackie and Jamie walk in.

"Jamie, go back to the living room," I order. "Jackie and I can manage without you."

Jamie smiles understandingly. He obeys and leaves us.

"So, what do you think?" I ask Jackie as soon as he's out of the kitchen.

"About Jamie?" Jackie asks. "I like him. I like him a lot. He's so handsome and charming. "And he's so intelligent!

We have so much in common. Well, except that he wants to be a corporate attorney and I don't."

It doesn't seem to bother her, though. She seems totally excited and happy.

"But wait," she suddenly says. "Isn't he the same guy you used to like years ago? I remember you telling me stories about your neighbor's grandson or nephew."

"Right, grandson. Relax. I don't like him *that* way anymore. And besides, he apparently likes *you* now. I'd rather be in love with someone who loves me back."

I put Jackie's mind to rest. I'm actually glad that she and Jamie like each other so much.

"Really? How did you know he liked me and wanted to meet me? Did he tell you?"

"Yeah. He saw you through the window, when you came over the first time, and you swept him off his feet," I assure her and see her face light up. "He said he's never in his life seen anyone as beautiful as you. It's obvious that he's totally smitten."

"He obviously exaggerated, but I'm glad he did," Jackie says, pleased. "I like it."

We go back to the living room, carrying all kinds of goodies and drinks, and settle everything on the coffee table. After a long, nice conversation and a few lusting looks between Jackie and Jamie, Jackie announces that she has to get back home because she has "tons of homework to do."

"Well, thanks for coming. See you tomorrow," I say and kiss her on the cheek.

Jamie walks her to her car as I watch through my window. They talk for a few minutes, and then Jackie's car starts and Jamie walks back to his grandmother's house. He sees me and gives me a thumbs-up. I see his lips mouth, *Thank you*. I nod and wave.

*   *   *

Mom's not home yet. I decide to wait for her to ask if we can order Chinese and watch a Woody Allen movie. It's been a long time since I've eaten Chinese food, and I crave it. *It's not that expensive, is it?* As for Woody Allen movies, I could watch them every day. Mom has every movie Woody has ever made, and she made me watch them with her since I was really little. That's how her love for Woody transferred to me. Same with jazz. Mom loves it and has the most extraordinary jazz collection anyone could have. We play jazz in our house all the time. Mom and I have a lot in common, and we like many different things, but there are those three things we *really* share a love for: Chinese food, jazz music, and Woody Allen movies.

I go to my room and start on my homework. It takes two hours to finish. I fantasize about Nick. Suddenly my daydreaming is interrupted by a phone call. *Jackie! She probably wants to dish about Jamie. Or maybe it's Mom, wanting to tell me she's on her way.*

"Hello?" I say when I pick up the phone.

"Hello. Good evening," a deep woman's voice says. It doesn't sound familiar. "Is this Elizabeth Benson?"

"No, it's not. This is her daughter, Victoria," I reply.

I should've asked the woman who she was first. Why did I say my name to a stranger?

"Hello, Victoria. This is . . . umm . . . your grandmother."

The voice is not stable anymore—it's quivering. *Is this some kind of joke? Who is this lunatic?*

"Was that supposed to be a joke?" I inquire. "It's not funny. I know my grandmother's voice, and you're certainly not her."

I'm infuriated! *Who does she think she is to joke like that? What right does she have? What's going on here?*

"Of course not. That was inconsiderate of me. How could you have known?" she says softly, as if speaking to herself. "I'm Amelia Benson, your father's mother."

I feel my jaw drop and my stomach flip. I feel like I've been hit on the head with a heavy object. I just stand there, frozen and speechless, my mouth ajar, my head pounding. *Boom! Boom! Boom! Amelia Benson . . . Your father's mother . . . Your father's mother . . .*

"Victoria, dear, are you still there?" my long-lost grandmother asks.

"Yes, I'm here," I reply coldly. "What do you want?"

"I understand I don't have the right to ask anything of you," she starts.

You're damn straight you don't!

"But I need to see you. It's extremely important."

What nerve this woman has! What right does she have? She must be crazy to ask me for anything.

"Important to whom? You or me?" I ask angrily.

Can't wait to hear what she wants.

"It's not for me. I'm asking for your grandfather, Tori. Or is it Vicky?"

Huh? Tori? That does it! Nobody calls me Tori. Your grandfather? That's it! I've had enough! I'm going to stop it right here and right now.

"I don't mean to be rude or anything, but I have to say this before you go any further: you are *not* my grandparents. I already have two wonderful grandparents I adore and who adore me. I don't need another set. Please remember that." I say it firmly and definitely, and then add, "And for crying out loud, please don't call me Tori."

Don't call me at all. Ever!

"Of course, Victoria. I'm sorry. Please hear me out," she's begging.

I doubt she sounded the same way during her last conversation with Dad. I bet she sounded all mighty and powerful. In fact, I'd bet my life on it.

"May I call you Vicky? And you can call me Amelia."

I hear desperation in her voice.

"Victoria's just fine. What do you want, Mrs. Benson?" I demand, getting even angrier.

"I need to see you. Can we meet? Whenever and wherever you want."

"That's the thing: I *don't* want. Listen, Mrs. Benson, I'm not meeting with you. Not now. Not ever. So if you have anything to say to me or to ask me, do it now, over the telephone." I feel the blood boil inside my body and outrage just jumps out of me. "No more options, Mrs. Benson. Take it or leave it."

God, I didn't know I could be this tough and cruel! Well, she was asking for it. And she deserves it! She's had it coming to her for a long time.

"All right then. I didn't want to say it over the phone, but I'll take what I can get," she starts, her voice quivering again. "Your grandfather . . . I mean, Richard Senior, is terminally ill. All he wants is to see his only grandchild before he dies."

I didn't expect to hear that. Still, I'm not moved. *And where was he before he got sick? Wasn't I always his only grandchild? Why did he wait so long? If he could live without me for so long, he can certainly die without me.*

"I'm sorry to hear that, Mrs. Benson. What's wrong with Mr. Benson?" I ask, trying to sound compassionate, but honestly, I don't feel a thing. He's someone I don't even know.

"He has lung cancer. They tried to operate. They even opened him up, but then closed him right away. It didn't matter anymore. The cancer had spread to other organs too fast."

It sounds tragic and scary, and I'm sorry, but still I feel as if she's talking about a stranger.

"I'm very sorry, Mrs. Benson," I say softly and mean it, "but I can't help you. I just don't understand why he'd want to see someone he didn't want to know in the first place."

"That's why I wanted us to meet, so that I could make you understand—"

"I can't," I interrupt. "And I will never understand. Ever."

"I'm sorry you feel this way. It's very unfortunate. Listen, my number is . . ." She tells me her number, but I don't write it down. "Perhaps you'll reconsider."

I hear hope in her voice.

Never! You can hope all you want. I realize that I unconsciously memorized the number.

"I won't. Sorry again," I say and hang up.

And then I write my newly-found non-grandmother's number on the phone book's cover. *Just in case.*

*   *   *

"Victoria! Are you home?" Mom yells when she walks in. "Where are you?"

"I'm here, Mom, on the couch."

I'm still shaky from the phone call. I just can't get it out of my mind. I hear the words in my head, *your grandfather . . . dying . . . his only grandchild . . .*

"Why are you sitting in the dark?" Mom asks, turning on the light.

"Am I? I haven't even noticed."

"Are you okay? Have you eaten yet?"

Mom sounds concerned. *Should I tell her about the call right away? Should I wait until after we eat? I don't know what to do.*

"No, I haven't, actually. I was wondering if we could order Chinese." I don't feel like watching a movie any longer, but a girl's got to eat. "It's not that expensive, is it?"

"Don't worry about it. I think it's a great idea!" Mom exclaims. "I'm tired and don't feel like making anything right now."

"So how was your day?" I ask, trying to be polite and show that I care at the same time.

"Great! Nora's friend, Helen, wants me to do her house as soon as possible. She's not going to pay me a lot, of course, because it's my first professional job and Nora is the only one who vouched for me, but it's a start, right?"

Mom sounds so excited and enthusiastic.

"Right. I hope everything turns out the way you want, Mom."

I really do.

"Victoria, what's wrong? You look like you've just seen a ghost." Mom sounds worried.

"I have. Seen and heard. Two, actually. Well, the first one was more like a nice surprise. Jamie Garner is back from Germany and he—"

"Yes, I know," Mom interrupts. "I just saw Mrs. Garner and she told me. By the way, what happened today? She says you were rude to her. What's up with that?"

I tell Mom about the entire episode from this afternoon. She doesn't look too pleased.

"Listen, Victoria," she says. "I understand how you feel and I happen to agree with you, but it doesn't mean you need to be rude to a poor woman just because she doesn't analyze things like you do. I won't tolerate or encourage this kind of behavior, young lady. Understood?"

Mom sounds absolutely serious. She means business.

"Yes, ma'am!" I exclaim, saluting her like a good, disciplined soldier. Understood!"

"Good. Issue's closed. So what about Jamie?"

She snaps out of her *mother* mode and steps into her *friend* mode.

"He looks great, and he's got the hots for Jackie," I report matter-of-factly.

"Aren't you jealous? Don't you like him yourself?" Mom sounds curious and suspicious.

"Nah! I don't look at him the same way I used to," I respond, shaking my head.

"Right. Because of that guy in school. Am I warm?" Mom asks, raising one eyebrow.

"Nick. His name is Nick. I don't know if it's because of him. I just know that he's so . . . Well, every boy wants to *be* Nick, and every girl wants to be *with* Nick."

"Including you?"

She raises one eyebrow again and looks me straight in the eye.

"Mom, please. I don't feel like talking about Nick any more."

I really don't.

"I'm sorry. You mentioned two ghosts from the past. Who was the second one?"

She sounds intrigued. *Wait till she hears!*

"Someone called. It was Amelia Benson," I say quickly and look at Mom.

"You mean . . ." Mom says, her eyes opening wide.

"Yeah, Dad's mother," I confirm what Mom has already guessed.

"Wow! I don't know what to say. That's something I never would've expected." Mom looks shocked and distraught. "What did she want? What did she say?"

"Well . . ."

I repeat the entire conversation to her. I stand up, then sit again. Stand, sit . . .

"The old man is dying, huh? It's too bad. I feel so sorry for him. His son most likely doesn't even know about it. He can't even say goodbye. It's tragic and very sad."

"I think she hopes I'll reconsider and meet with them. Would you believe it?"

I start pacing back and forth, which obviously annoys Mom.

"Sit, relax," she says. "Honestly, I don't want to talk about them. They're not *my* problem, but as your mother, who cares about you and *your* problems, I say don't rush to say no. Think about it."

"Whaaat? What do you mean? What's there to think about?" I exclaim. "They rejected me *then*. I'm rejecting them *now*. What goes around comes around."

"It's not that simple. He's on his deathbed, and it's his dying wish to see you. You need to think, Victoria."

Mom sounds as if she were determined to make me surrender.

"Mom, can Grandma and Grandpa come over?" I suddenly ask. "I think we need a family meeting."

I feel like I need as many people as I can get to reassure me I don't have to go.

"Of course, but can you imagine your grandmother's reaction to this?"

Mom's surprised at my request. I'm surprised by Mom's reaction.

"I really want to talk to Grandpa, but I can't do it behind Grandma's back, can I?"

"You'd better not, because if you do, she'll never forgive you. Very well then, I'll call."

Mom dials my grandparents' number. I hear her talking to Grandma.

"Hi, Mom. Have you and Daddy had dinner yet? Great! Come over. We're ordering Chinese. Please, let's not argue now about who's going to pay for it. I invited *you*, so I'll pay. Don't worry. I'll order some steamed stuff for Daddy. I remember about his heart. No, nothing happened. What do you mean by *so soon*?" Mom presses her hand over the receiver and whispers to me, "She thinks something happened. She doesn't buy that we'd invite them to dinner so soon after Thanksgiving."

"Tell her the truth. Tell her that we need a family meeting," I whisper back, knowing that my grandmother won't give up until she knows what's going on.

"Mother," Mom says, following my advice, "we need a family meeting. No, it's not bad. I swear."

She hangs up and sighs loudly, as usual, after a conversation with Grandma. We go to the kitchen, find the menu, and order food from our favorite Chinese place.

* * *

My grandparents arrive just as our food is being delivered. We set everything on the kitchen table. Right away, my grandmother wants to know what the meeting is all about, so after several minutes of stalling, I finally repeat my telephone conversation with Amelia Benson. As expected, Grandma is furious. She can't believe that Amelia had actually called after all these years.

"I'm flabbergasted!" she exclaims. "How could she have the nerve, that woman? I understand that she doesn't have any conscience, but she's got to have some decency not to remind us of their existence. And to ask the poor child to meet them after they rejected her and her mother? Unbelievable!"

The drama queen is on a roll! She's outraged. Her face is all flashy-red.

"Mother, you can talk and eat. Everything's getting cold," says Mom.

"Libby, how can you even mention food at a time like this? Who can eat now?" Grandma wonders.

She can't actually believe that we should starve because of Amelia Benson's call.

"Well, *we* can. We're very hungry, so let's eat," Mom answers calmly, but firmly.

"What do *you* think of this preposterous debacle, Libby?" Grandma asks, ignoring Mom's order. "I'm sure you agree that we have to ignore the call."

"Honestly, I didn't even want to talk about it at first. However, Victoria's my daughter and she has to deal with a dying man's wish, so I believe she needs to think about it."

"There's nothing to think about. She goes there when hell freezes over! Over my dead body!" the drama queen proclaims her verdict.

"Yes, Grandma. I'll go when hell freezes over your dead body," I attempt to joke.

"We all know you're sharp-tongued, Victoria. You think you're so smart, huh? It's nice making fun of your grandmother, huh?" I think that Grandma is really offended. She looks hurt. "Go right ahead and dig the knife deeper into my heart."

"Rose, wake up!" Grandpa intervenes. "A man is dying, for god's sake, and you want to keep score? Yes, they weren't good parents, but it's all in the past. All's done and gone."

"Damn straight I keep score. All's done, but not gone, and not forgotten. Everything has its repercussions. If you do something bad, it comes back to you, and you have to pay for it."

Payback's a bitch, I think to myself. *Especially when it comes from my grandmother.*

"If you're talking about revenge being sweet, you're wrong. Revenge is a trap because anger creates more anger, and more anger. It's a never-ending loop. Do you really want Vicky inside that loop? Because *she's* the one who will suffer along with the Bensons. Someone needs to stop and break the chain. Let it be Vicky. If she wants to, of course. And Rose, you don't do revenge against a dying man."

Grandpa's sooo wise.

"I'm not talking about revenge, but I think that if we have the opportunity to pay them back, we pay them back," Grandma persists, still mad as hell.

"Rose, please can you not make things more difficult than they are?" Grandpa asks. Vicky told you what happened. She hasn't asked for your opinion or your advice, and I agree with Libby. Vicky should think about it long and hard and decide what *she* wants to do. Ultimately, it has to be *her* decision, and if you ask me, they've already been paid back in full. *They're* the ones who lost because they missed out on a chance to get to know two wonderful and beautiful girls like our Libby and Vicky."

"Excuse me, please. For what it's worth, I meant well. I wanted to help. I didn't mean to interfere," says Grandma, acting as if her ego has been hurt.

"Oh, puh-leeze!" Mom exclaims. "You *live* to interfere, Mother. You *thrive* on it. Daddy's right. We didn't call you here to tell Victoria what to do. We just wanted to inform you about it because you're family. Victoria's the one who makes the decision."

Grandma looks at all of us, lifting up her chin high (a sign of dignity and pride) and presses her palm over her lips, meaning, *I'll keep my mouth shut.* Then she makes another gesture: she moves her index finger and her thumb, pressed together, along her lip line, meaning, *I'll zip it up. You won't hear a word from me.*

I've heard three different opinions, and each one of them made a lot of sense.

"Well, you're both right, Mom and Grandpa. I have to think more about what I'm going to do, and then decide for myself. I shouldn't have expected you all to do it for me. I think I can handle it," I say, absolutely *not* sure that I can.

"Of course, you can. You're *so* self-sufficient," says Mom sarcastically. "Believe me, darling, even the strongest people need a little help and support from a family sometimes."

*   *   *

After my grandparents leave and Mom retires to her room, I call Liza and ask her if she could pick me up a little early tomorrow morning.

"I need to tell you something important," I explain to her.

"Tell me now," she insists, sounding anxious.

"No, tomorrow. I'll ask the others to come earlier, too. I'll tell you all at the same time."

After making the calls, I go to the bathroom to brush my teeth. *Hello, bed, here I come!*

I can't fall asleep. I think about my non-grandparents.

*   *   *

When we meet in the morning, I tell the girls the whole story—about the call, about the family meeting, about everybody's feelings, et cetera. Just as my family, each girl has a different reaction to the situation and a different opinion.

"I didn't sleep a wink last night. I kept thinking about that stupid call," I say.

Chloe, as usual, tries to be supportive and sympathetic. She nods to every word I say.

"Poor Vicky, I can't even imagine how you feel," she says, empathizing with me.

"If you ask me, I say screw them," Liza claims. "I'd never have thought I'd say that, but I actually agree with your grandmother. They're not worth you worrying about. Let them pay."

"Yeah, they're not worth it. Let them pay," Chloe agrees with Liza.

"Do you know what the great Confucius said?" Alex asks suddenly.

"No, I don't, but I'm sure I'm about to find that out," I respond sarcastically.

"Things that are done, it is needless to speak about . . . things that are past, it is needless to blame," Alex quotes and then asks, "Do you get my point?"

"Let bygones be bygones? Is that what you mean?" I ask.

"Something like that," she replies. "You're angry with them, I understand. You want to punish them, to pay them back, but how? The man is dying, for crying out loud. What are you going to do? Kill him faster? Just go see him and let him die in peace."

"Yes, Vicky. Go see him. He's dying, after all," Chloe says seriously, supporting Alex's theory.

I can't believe the girl! Does she think it's her duty to agree with everyone?

"Lyndon B. Johnson said," Alex continues making her point, " 'We can draw lessons from the past, but we cannot live in it.' Same thing."

"I think he meant we should learn from our mistakes, let go of the past and move forward," I tell her, "but he never said that we should forgive and forget."

"That's *exactly* what he meant," Alex insists. "If you don't want to forgive and forget, then don't. Just leave the past in the past. Get over it and move on. Go see the man."

"I personally agree with your mother and grandfather," Jackie says. "You need to think long and hard. Don't listen to anybody. Listen to your mind and your heart. Then decide."

"Right, Vicky. Think long and hard before you decide what you should do," says Chloe, siding with Jackie now.

That does it! We all look at her in disbelief.

"Shut up, Chloe!" the four of us yell in unison.

"I can't believe you!" I exclaim. "Can't you have just *one* opinion at least once? Stop always agreeing with everyone and supporting everybody. Stop taking sides. We'll love you anyway."

I know it's useless. Chloe will never change. Agreeing with everyone and supporting everybody means to Chloe what scores and grades mean to Jackie, what fashion and shopping mean to Liza, and what lecturing and being in charge mean to Alex—everything.

"I'm sorry," Chloe says, sticking out her quivering bottom lip. She's almost crying. "I'm just trying to be a good friend. I won't say anything more, just don't be angry with me."

"No, *I'm* sorry I yelled at you, Chloe. It's just my nerves."
I lean over and give her a hug. "You *are* a good friend. You're
the best friend a girl could have. I love you so much. Forgive
me?"

I feel so ashamed.

"I love you, too," Chloe says and hugs me.

All is forgotten.

"Remember, guys, how you told me I should think more
about my mom and less of myself, and how I should consider
Mom's feelings? Well, I just thought of something," I say, to
get back to the case in point. "Suppose, just suppose, I agree
to see the Bensons. How would Mom feel? Wouldn't she feel
betrayed by me?"

"Apparently she doesn't think so if she's encouraging you
to think about it and make your own decision," Liza says.
"She wouldn't bother otherwise. She'd stay out of it."

"What if she's testing me?" I ask.

Could Mom really be testing my loyalty? I take a deep
breath and then let the air out. I can talk about it all I want,
but the ultimate decision will be mine. *Thank god I don't
have to make it right this moment.*

"Thank god I don't have to decide right now," I say out
loud.

We change the subject. New topic: the upcoming party.

Mirror on the Wall Has Two Faces

"Beauty is in the eye of the beholder and it may be necessary from time to time to give a stupid or misinformed beholder a black eye."

—Miss Piggy

It's Friday night. I'm in my room, in front of the mirror, getting ready for the party. *Mirror, mirror on the wall, who's the fairest of them all?* The mirror remains silent. I look at my reflection and like what I see. I know, *beauty is in the eye of the beholder*, and in this case, I *am* the beholder, but, god, do I look good!

I've just finished putting some last touches on my makeup, and I did a great job. I always do, I must say. Makeup is my forte. It's like a science project to me. I know all the brands and colors. I research and buy, mix and blend, test and analyze, conclude, and finally, apply. I never put too much on, and I know exactly how and where to put it. I know how I should look during the day, when I go to school, and I know what my going-out-in-the-evening look should be. Like tonight, for example.

Mom always gives me some tips on how to look my best, but there are six rules she taught me *always* to remember, and I always do.

Rule 1: Always look your best. You never get a second chance to make a first impression.

Rule 2: Accentuate the positive, eliminate the negative. Show your assets, hide your flaws.

Rule 3: Remember that makeup isn't what makes your look, but what makes your look complete.
Don't try to look like somebody else. Be you, only better.

Rule 4: Define your style, but change or add just a little something every time. Don't go too drastic, but make your look a fresh one each time and make people wonder.

Rule 5: When in doubt of the way you look, tell yourself: I'm every bit as beautiful as I think I am.
Remember that if you feel beautiful, everyone will see you that way.

Rule 6: If you get compliments, don't be afraid to brag a little. You don't have to be smug about it, but by all means, do brag.

It's not the first time people from school will see me, but it's the first time they will see me at a party, so I must look my best. *And Nick will be there . . .*

Liza says that I have the sexiest bedroom eyes she's ever seen and the most sensual and kissable lips a girl could have. (She likes my lips even better than Jackie's, and I consider that a huge compliment.) I smudged a smoky eye shadow over my top eyelid, outlined the bottom eyelid with a mix of grey and brown pencils, and applied plenty of mascara to my eyelashes to make my eyes look deep, expressive, and sexy. Then I outlined my lips with a dusty rose lip liner to make it look almost natural, and filled it with just a lip gloss. (Accentuate, but not too obvious.)

Another look in the mirror. I think I've achieved my goal—my face looks flawless.

Tonight I decide to have my hair look au natural. So instead of straightening it as I always do or gathering it in a pony tail, as I often do before school when I don't have enough time to straighten it, I let all the waves down. I just use a little mousse and hair spray and leave a few curls around my face to make my hair soft, playful, and flirty-looking.

Now I have to decide what to wear. You must think, nice outfit, and you're out the door. It's that simple. Wrong! It's not that simple at all. No matter how beautiful your clothes look, the trick is: they should look good on *you*.

I stare at my body, wearing nothing but panties and a bra. It's not a bad body. Not bad at all. I'm not fat, though I don't look as if I'm malnourished either. I have silky skin, nice long legs, and a small, narrow waist. Two things I *would* change, though. My butt is too big, and my boobs aren't big enough, so I wouldn't mind taking some flesh off of my ass and sticking it on my bosom instead.

I remember what Liza said about showing my legs more often, so I put on my thin, see-through black panty hose, high-heeled black leather shoes, and decide on a D & G black mini-skirt and my new green cashmere sweater. They fit together perfectly. Moreover, the skirt has an A-line shape, so my butt doesn't look like it sticks out. And a push-up bra does its trick: my boobs look high and round. I'm totally pleased with the way I look. I think I covered the first five rules very well. As for the last one . . . well, it remains to be seen.

I take one last look at myself in a whole gorgeous entirety as I hear a knock on the door. It's Mom. I tell her to come in. She does. She sees me, presses her hands together and sighs.

"Tada!" I exclaim and let her look at me for a moment.

"You look so pretty, darling, heads should roll," Mom says, smiling. "You'll be the hit of the party."

She wraps her arm around me and presses her cheek to mine so that our faces are next to each other. I see how much I look like her. Even without makeup, Mom looks very pretty. She's turning forty in June, but doesn't look a day older than thirty. She needs to drop a few pounds, but for her age Mom looks mighty fine.

"Don't hate me because I'm beautiful," I say in a kind of low, sexy tone of voice, and then, shaking my hair and fluffing it with my hand, add, "it's a gift."

"It's hereditary," Mom says, mimicking my gestures and emulating my tone of voice.

"And smart, too," I continue playfully.

"Runs in the family," Mom plays along.

"And I love beautiful and expensive things."

"Another family curse."

Mom sighs deeply, then laughs and kisses me on the cheek

"Mom?" I turn around. "Does my butt look huge or not?"

"It doesn't, but remember: a woman without a butt is like a house without furniture."

"I have a better one," I say. "A woman without a butt is like an old man without Viagra."

"As a mother, I'd have to say that you shouldn't be talking like this, but as a person with a sense of humor, I have to say, that's a good one," Mom says and we both laugh. "You look great, honey, honest."

"I know. I *am* amazing, even if I *do* say so myself."

"Will that boy . . . um . . . Nick, be there?" Mom suddenly asks.

"I suppose," I reply, looking at her. "Why?"

"I'm just wondering. If you want to get his attention, you must *work* the room."

"Huh? What's that supposed to mean?" I ask in open-mouth astonishment.

"When a woman walks into a room, she must walk as if she's the only woman there. If you look great and carry yourself properly, people will notice, and you'll get all the attention."

You must know. You always get all the attention. Mom really knows how to.

"Well, I like the aspect of the spotlight," I say and we laugh again. "And they say *I* have attitude! Now at least I know where I get it from. You're saying *I'm* self-centered—"

"Being the center of attention at a party," Mom interrupts, "and acting as if you are the center of the universe are two completely different things."

Okay, I get the point. I should've left it at that. It would've been a great night. But instead, feeling like Mom and I had just bonded, I think that maybe now is the right moment to bring up college tuition. So I do a stupid thing: I start the line of questioning that kills the entire bonding moment.

"Mom," I begin. "Do you have any leads on your job-hunting yet?"

"Victoria, it's been only ten days since I lost my job. I haven't even started looking yet," Mom responds, suddenly irritated. "I need to update my resume first."

"But did you at least try to see what's out there?" I persist.

"It's a jungle out there. The job market is not great right now."

She looks and sounds sad.

"But, Mom," I keep pushing.

"Victoria, stop it, for god's sake!" Mom interrupts me. I can see and hear that she's pissed off because I started this conversation and don't know when to end it. "I think I've been very clear about my career options."

She's really angry now.

"You have, and that's wrong. I totally disagree. I object!" I exclaim.

"What?!" Mom exclaims in disbelief. "You object, do you? We're not in a court of law, Victoria, and the last time I checked, I was still the boss around here."

"Mom, I'm not trying to tell you what to do," I say, trying to justify starting this conversation, "but it concerns college. I have to know where I belong."

"But I thought you've already applied where you wanted to."

"I have. That's not what I mean. How will we pay tuition?" I ask.

"First of all, I have a little money saved for college tuition. Second, there's financial aid to apply for. If it's not enough, you'll do what other people do: you'll apply for a student loan," Mom says matter-of-factly, as if she's been there, done that, and has done it all her life.

"Student loan?!" I exclaim. "Do you know how much tuition is now at a school like NYU? Can you imagine what the total of my student loan will be by the time I graduate? The interest's accumulating, you know."

Now I'm furious!

"It's okay. Other people do it. My co-workers told me about their children and how they started repaying their student loans six months after they graduated and started working. And you know me. You know I'll help you to pay it off."

Mom sounds very confident. I'm not.

"Or maybe you should go back to work and provide for your child!" I yell at her.

I can't believe her! What kind of mother is she? College tuition is her responsibility, not mine!

"Provide for my child? You've got to be kidding!" Now Mom is furious. "I think I've been providing very well for you. What about your food on the table, and eating out? What about our house mortgage? How about our trips to resorts in the winter and to Europe on your spring breaks? Have *you* been paying for all that? And what about all your expensive clothes? Did you get them for free? Granted, your grandparents helped with paying for your dancing and tennis lessons, but who's been paying for your private schools and your fancy summer camps all these years? And you have the nerve to blame me for not providing?"

"Yeah, yeah, I know. Blah, blah, blah . . . " I start, but see Mom's glare and stop.

"I think we'd better stop now, before we regret what we say to each other," Mom says.

"But, Mom, you don't realize the gravity of the situation. It can't get any worse."

"There's no situation that can't get worse," Mom snaps. "A parent can get sick, for example, and unable to provide at all anymore, so a child has to suddenly grow up and provide for both of them. Things happen that are much worse than what we have right now."

It seems as if she just blabs it out unconsciously because as soon as she says it, she presses her hand over her mouth. Her face is pale. I see tears in her eyes. *What does she mean? Who is she talking about? Is she sick? What's happening?*

"Mom, what do you mean?" I ask, fretting about hearing something I wouldn't like. "Who are you talking about? Are you sick?"

"Never mind. Forget it," Mom says and starts to walk away.

"Mom, wait!" I grab her sleeve. "Please don't walk away from me. You can't just leave after you say something like that."

"Let it go," Mom says softly. "Please let it go."

So she *is* talking about herself.

"Please, Mom, tell me what it is," I beg. "You're making me worry."

"Sorry. I didn't mean to tell you," Mom says quietly. "It was just a slip of the tongue."

"Tell me!" I insist. "You're scaring me."

"I'll tell you after the party. Go enjoy yourself."

"Tell me now or I won't go," I don't give up.

Enjoy myself! Is she kidding?

"I think I found something under my arm," says Mom.

"Found what?"

I don't understand at first, but feel in my gut it's not good.

"You know, something like a little ball, a growth . . . "

Omigod! What if she has cancer? As soon as I think that, I feel that familiar flipping in my stomach and pounding in my head. *Cancer!*

"Mom, what are you going to do? We have to do something!"

"*I* have to do something. I've already made an appointment with a doctor. You, on the other hand, need to go. It's time to go to the party. You may take the car."

"Jackie's picking me up," I say automatically. "I won't go."

I don't want to go.

"Yes, you will. I won't hear of it!" Mom insists. "Otherwise, I'll feel guilty."

"Guilty? What are you talking about? I'm the one who should feel guilty for thinking only about myself. You're right. I'm selfish and self-centered. I'm such a bitch!"

"Victoria! Stop it! It's not your fault that I have this ... thing. When people get sick, it's nobody's fault—and we don't even know yet if it's something serious."

We hear a car horn. *What do I do? I can't leave her now, can I?* Another horn. Mom pushes me out the door.

I kiss her on the cheek and say, "We'll talk more later, okay?"

"Okay, I promise. Now go conquer the world," she tells me. "Have a great time at the party, sweetheart."

I put on my black wool maxi-coat, grab my purse, and run outside where the girls, with Jackie as the designated driver, are waiting for me in the car.

You Want to Play, You've Got to Pay

"Partying is such sweet sorrow."

—Robert Byrne

"Hi," I say to Jackie, Alex, and Chloe, settling down on the backseat of the car, next to Chloe. Alex rides in the front, with Jackie. "You picked me up before Liza. Why?"

"She wasn't ready when I called," Jackie responds. "Are you okay? You look upset again. I hope it's the same thing and nothing new."

"Oh, no! Not again!" Chloe cries. "Not tonight. Please, Vicky. Let's have fun."

"I second that. Let's forget about all the shitty stuff and enjoy ourselves," Alex says.

"I'm totally fine, honest," I lie. "We'll have fun, don't worry."

Thank god it's dark in the car and they can't see my face.

We stop by Liza's house ten minutes later and honk. Liza comes out, giddy and excited. She looks like a million bucks—very chic and classy—too good for this party.

"Let's dance our asses off!" she exclaims, plopping down next to me after Chloe and I move a little. "And let's do things that are bad for us and we shouldn't do, like smoking and drinking. Let's just be badasses tonight."

121

"You're a quintessential badass, Liza," Jackie says. "I think it's wrong to be drinking, not to mention smoking."

"Oh, come on, Jackie, don't be such Miss Perfect tonight," Alex says. I can't believe she's changing her mother-knows-best attitude to this careless-bad-girl attitude just for tonight. "You know I'm against smoking because it can kill you, but as for drinking, well, everybody does it. A few beers haven't killed anyone yet."

"Yeah, that's right. Sometimes a drink can help you to loosen up," Liza claims.

"I don't think you need any help in that department, Liza," Jackie chuckles.

"I, for one, want to drink *a lot*, much more than a few beers," Chloe announces. We all stare at her, astounded, as Liza turns the rear light on. "Why are you looking at me like that? Alex said we need to unwind, didn't she? So . . . "

What does she think should happen at the party? What does she expect from it? Should we worry about her?

"I think we should watch over our baby tonight so she doesn't do anything stupid," Alex says. "I don't like what she says and I hate how she looks when she says it."

"Well, I still think it's totally wrong," Jackie states, meaning drinking. "That's all I'm going to say."

"That's why we elected *you* our designated driver. You don't want to drink, so you shouldn't worry," says Alex.

"Let me remind you that I volunteered," Jackie laughs. "I worry about *you*, not myself."

"Well, don't," says Liza. "We're big girls and can take care of ourselves. Vicky, you're awfully quiet tonight." She turns to face me. "As a matter of fact, you haven't said a word since I got in the car."

"I'm okay," I lie again. "I'm always sleepy when I'm in a car and I'm not the one driving it."

Oh, darkness! Bless you for protecting me. You bring me comfort and serenity.

"Listen," Chloe suddenly changes the subject. "I'm thinking that maybe we should've asked Brianna if we could bring Tina to the party with us. What do you think?"

"I totally disagree." I get involved in the conversation this time. "I'm glad we didn't. Let's take things slowly with Tina. She's just starting to come out of her shell. She needs some time to adjust to her new image. This party might be too much for her."

"I'm with you, Vicky, on this one," Jackie supports me. "I don't think Tina's ready for a party yet. I'm not sure *we're* ready for this crowd."

"I think we're here," Alex interrupts. She looks at the piece of paper with Brianna's address on it and points at the house. "Yeah, that's it. That's the house."

As we pull into the driveway, we see lots of expensive cars already there. We can hardly squeeze ours in. Two cars, following us, have to park on the street—there's no more space in the driveway. Jackie shuts the engine off and we get out of the car.

"Don't forget the stuff we brought," Alex reminds us. The girls got an assignment from Brianna to bring some snacks, so we all pitched in and bought plenty of crackers and chips. "Brianna's planning to order pizza later. As the hostess, she's paying for it herself."

"The guys are responsible for the alcohol," Chloe declares, all excited. "I hope they bring loads of it."

We look at her and glance over at each other. I think we have reason to worry.

As we approach the door, carrying the food, we don't even have to ring the doorbell—it's ajar. More and more people continue to arrive. It seems that there's no end to it. Inside, it's so crowded that we can't see Brianna, but she sees us.

"Hi, girls," she greets us as we hand her the goodies we brought. "Thanks. You all look great. Welcome to our castle. I'm so glad you could make it. Don't be shy. Feel at home. Have a drink and enjoy yourselves." She gives us a big smile.

"Thanks, Brianna," we all say, and then Chloe adds, "Oh, I'm sure we will."

"By the way, Brianna, you look fabulous!" Liza exclaims. "Trendy, hip, and very posh."

"You really do," I second, and it's the truth.

Brianna always looks good, but I've never seen her look *this* good. Her short red hair and deep green eyes already make a beautiful combo, and by putting on a brown suede mini-dress, she knew she couldn't lose.

"Thanks," Brianna says and smiles again. "Everybody looks their best tonight. Would you like me to get you some drinks?"

"No, thanks," Alex replies for all of us. "I'm sure we can manage. You go mingle with the other guests. I don't think you'll have enough time tonight to tend to everyone."

"Okay," Brianna says. "Enjoy. See you later."

She walks away. We look around and see that some people have already been drinking up a storm. We get ourselves some beers. Jackie, of course, gets a soda.

Immediately, Liza and Alex start mingling, and soon I see them dancing with some guys I don't know. I also see Chloe dancing with Ted McAlly.

When did that happen? Chloe was just standing next to me. Actually, they make an odd, but cute couple—a perfect example that opposites *do* attract. He's big and tall and she's short and chubby. He's holding her as if she's a fragile damsel in distress and he's protecting or rescuing her—careful and tender. I'm sooo touched. I suddenly see McAlly in a different light. *Maybe he's not that bad after all.*

"Look at Chloe and Ted. I think he really likes her," I tell Jackie.

"I hope so, because she definitely likes him," Jackie says. "I'm glad Heather isn't here tonight. Right? We'll see what happens with those two."

"Yeah, but we have to watch Chloe. You know how she is. I believe she might do something crazy, and I'm concerned."

"Like what?" Jackie now also sounds and looks concerned.

"I don't know," I shrug, "but the way she was talking in the car—"

"I know. Let's keep an eye on her," Jackie says. "Listen, I'm going outside for a few minutes. I promised Jamie I'd call, and it's impossible to hear anything inside."

Suddenly I see Nick, talking to Amber, Bridget, and Ruby. I see Ruby follow Jackie with her eyes as Jackie steps outside. Actually, I've noticed before that Ruby sometimes stares at Jackie in class. *Is there something about Ruby we don't know? What if . . . omigod!*

Nick tries to take the glass away from Amber, gesturing with his hands. There's so much noise in the room that it's impossible to hear a word he's saying to her. Finally, Nick succeeds and *does* take the glass away. He goes to talk to Jordan. I don't think he saw me.

Nick looks so good in his new jeans and black silk shirt. It compliments his thick dark hair and his dark-blue eyes. I look at his angular cheek bones, his almost-square jaw, and the cleft in his chin, and my heart stops. Several top buttons of his shirt are unbuttoned, revealing the Adam's apple on his manly neck and the top of his chest. I feel that familiar warm blood wave rushing through my body. *Does he have to showcase his intoxicating physique?*

As I watch him, Liza, who's now back, joins me and moans and groans like a sex maniac.

"Mmm . . . He's so yummy," she says. "Yum, yum, yum . . . Psst . . . " She presses her index finger to her tongue first and then to her butt, meaning *he's hot.* "Why don't you dance? Go get him," she whispers and then leaves again.

How many drinks has she had?

I get myself another beer. Then a glass of wine. Then another. I need it. Otherwise, I won't be able to stop thinking about Mom. I don't feel anything. *Is that real alcohol?*

Alex comes back, carrying two glasses with something red. She looks like she's already had a good share of alcohol, but seeing her so loosened-up, so calm and relaxed—is priceless!

"Here, have some of this stuff. It's delicious!" she yells because of the noise and hands me the glass. Then she drinks hers with one gulp. "Isn't it, though?"

"This punch's spiked, of course. You know that, don't you?" I ask. "Do you hear me, Alex? It's spiked with alcohol. Go easy on it."

I've never seen her like this.

"Oh, puh-leeze! Live a little," she says, dancing in her place.

Whaaat? Hello-o-o!

"Please don't give me any lectures. It's *my* job. Vicky, I love you."

She kisses my cheek.

"I love you, too," I say. "But you're not Alex. A-lex, come ba-ack!" I yell, giggling.

"Wha-at do-o you-u me-ean?" she asks, surprised. "I'm r-ight here, but wh-ere's Jackie?"

She's so tongue-tied, she stumbles on every word. I think she's had enough for tonight.

"Jackie's outside, talking to Jamie on the phone. Alex, listen to me," I yell, grabbing her by the shoulders and shaking her. "You've had too much to drink. Stop it. Let's sit you down somewhere so you can sleep it off."

I start looking around, but Alex won't stand in place. She keeps dancing, a silly smile on her face, her eyes half-closed.

"I don't want to sit down and sleep it off. I want to dance it off. Not enough guys, though," she says with a frown. "Look at Liza. See how many guys are all over her? Of course, she's blonde and pretty, but in case you haven't noticed, *guys don't make passes at girls who wear glasses.*" She laughs, but sounds bitter. "Well, I'm going to dance."

As soon as she walks away, I start to feel the effects of the alcohol. I like it. My head feels light for the first time in weeks. I feel warm and relaxed. *I'm sure that everything will be fine. Mom will be okay. She'll get a new job and I'll have the money to shop again. Then everybody will be happy. I'll forget all about the Bensons. Nick's so hot. And his body . . . What a display! I think I'm in love with him. What's taking Jackie so long, anyway?*

Nick finally sees me and waves. I respond with the same gesture. Unfortunately, Jordan sees me too and approaches first. *That's all I need. Where's Tiffany?*

"Va-va-va-voom!" he exclaims. "You look hot tonight. Not that you're not *always* hot, but tonight . . . "

I feel like he's undressing me—his eyes slipping down from my face to my breasts, hips, and legs. They're all over my body, and it makes me feel very uncomfortable.

"I think we're connecting here. I feel passion igniting between us," he continues to annoy me. Well, he's being his typical jerk self. "Let's do it before we disconnect."

"You wish!" I exclaim. "Like that'd ever happen. Let's disconnect now. I don't want to keep you from your real passion. Where is Tiffany, by the way?"

"Who cares?" he replies with a question and grabs my arm. "Let's go upstairs."

"As soon as you iron your shoelaces and starch your ears," I say and pull my arm away. "Go away, Jordan! Go harass Tiffany. I'm sure she wants you to. I don't."

"Why? Aren't I good enough for you?" Jordan persists, leaning closer to my face. I can smell his breath and realize that he's already quite drunk. He notices me watching Nick and Amber and says, "Oh, I see. It's not me. You just want somebody else."

"No, it's you. The only way someone would have sex with you or even kiss you would be as a mission of mercy, or if you were a charity case. Oh, right . . . there's also Tiffany."

"And what's wrong with me? Most girls would be happy to be with me."

"Well, I'm not most girls. I guess you're just not my type," I say and hope that he leaves me alone, but he doesn't get the picture and continues to bug me.

As I think that, I see Tiffany, and she sees us. Her expression isn't a happy one.

"I'm not your type, huh? And who is? Carson, I bet," Jordan says, not giving up.

He looks at me with narrow eyes and a devious smile.

"Nick has nothing to do with it. I don't like you. Period. We just have different minds and personalities, that's all. Tiffany suits you much better. By the way, she's watching us right now." I'm so mad at him! *Who does he think he is, telling me who I want and who I don't want?* "Leave me alone, Jordan!"

"You mean I'm stupid?"

He doesn't sound at all offended. He also ignores what I just said about Tiffany watching us. "I can change to suit you."

He touches my face, and I hate it. I slap his hand.

"Don't go changing to try and please me," I say with sarcasm in my voice. "Besides, what do you need me for if you've got Tiffany? She loves you just the way you are."

"Listen," he persists, breathing in my face. "I'll be whatever you want me to be. Come on, baby, work with me here."

"Unfortunately, I don't think there's anything to work with in *that* area."

God, I think I'm doing it again—I insult people. Well, it's just Jordan, and he's asking for it.

"Don't breathe in my face, Jordan," I say, waving with my hand in front of my nose. "Get away from me!"

"Here goes that attitude again." Jordan doesn't give up. "I told you, it's a turn-on."

He tries to wrap his arms around me, but doesn't succeed. *How can I not insult him?*

"And how does no-way-in-hell sound?" I ask and push him away with one hand. "Is that clear enough for you?"

I hope it is. *He just doesn't get another language.* I'm sooo irritated.

"Go away, Jordan! Don't make me hit you."

God, I need to get rid of him!

"Come on, don't be a party pooper," Jordan cries and grabs my arm again.

It hurts!

"Let go!" I suddenly hear Nick's voice and see him grab and shake Jordan's hand. "You know you're beating a dead horse, right?" Nick turns to me and asks, "Are you okay?"

I nod. It feels great to have Nick protect me from Jordan, his friend. It means he cares.

"Oh, I see. The knight in shining armor comes to the rescue," Jordan says sarcastically.

"I guess it makes *you* the odd man out," says Nick. "So cut your losses and go away."

"Okay. I get the picture. She's all yours, since she wants *you* anyway," Jordan says bitterly and walks away. "And I thought we had a *moment* there," he puts in the last word.

"Are you all right?" Nick shouts over the noise as soon as Jordan leaves.

"I'm fine," I answer loudly and nod. "Thanks for calling me a dead horse."

"You know what I meant," he says with a smile, and I melt.

"I'm kidding. Of course, I know what you meant. I hope Jordan does." We both laugh. "Thanks for getting rid of him. It's sad that there are so many perverts all around the world."

"Well, you can't blame the guy for trying. It's hard to control yourself when you look like this. And besides, he's not that bad, just shallow," Nick says about his friend.

"I don't care, I just find him repulsive—personally and physically. I can't help it."

"Come on! You don't mean it." Nick laughs.

His laugh is divine!

I don't answer. I just reach into my purse for the compact and stroke my face with a powder pad. After Jordan touched it and breathed on it, I feel like freshening up.

"Don't," Nick says and grips my hand. As I raise my brows, giving him an inquiring look, he explains, "You can't improve on perfection."

Does he mean it? Is it a pick-up line? Whatever it is, I like it. It makes me feel good about myself. *Am I blushing?*

"Nobody's perfect," I say and immediately remember the *sixth rule*. "But when you've got it, you've got it, and green is my color. Thanks for the compliment."

"You're right. Green becomes you. It makes you like . . . a breath of fresh air."

Aww . . .

"Keep going. I love flattery," I yell, giggling.

"It's not flattery," Nick shouts back. "It's a fact. Listen, let's stop yelling and dance. Can I have this dance?"

"Sure. Why not?"

I feel my heart pounding. I feel his hands on my body. *Is it hot in here, or is it just me?*

The dance is over. *Oh, no! Isn't it too soon? Wasn't it an awfully short song?* We dance again and again. One song after another. We lose track of time. I think the same thing is happening with Chloe and Ted.

Suddenly we see Tiffany crying and Bridget, Ruby, and Amber comforting her.

"Do you mind if we go check the situation out?" Nick asks, and before I can answer, he grabs my hand and drags me to where the mean girls stand. But I feel so safe.

As soon as we approach, we see Jordan. He's totally wasted, in a reclining chair, his shirt unbuttoned. His mouth is wide open, and he's snoring. It's not a pretty picture. I never would've thought I'd say that, but I suddenly feel sorry for Tiffany. Even she doesn't deserve this. First, he makes a pass at me, and now this. How humiliating!

"Relax," Nick says to her, his hands on her shoulders. "Let him sleep it off. He'll be okay by the time we leave."

"Get me some wine, please," I ask Nick when we leave his friends and get some pizza.

"Don't do it. You shouldn't be drinking," he says.

Huh? Is he joking?

"Why not?" I ask, surprised. "Aren't *you*? What's the point of the party, then?"

"I don't drink. I play sports and it's very important to me. Basketball is my past, my present, and my future, and you *can* have a good time without drinking, you know."

Suddenly we hear some commotion by the bathroom. It's Brianna, knocking loudly on the door and shouting. Then we see three guys and two girls come out. By the smell of the bathroom, we realize they'd just smoked pot in there.

"Out!" Brianna screams. "And don't come back. Ever!" She looks furious. "I warned everyone: I don't want drugs in my house. Those pricks brought grass and a bunch of pills."

"Calm down, Brianna," Nick tries to comfort her. "It's over. You did the right thing."

He always knows what to say to people and how to make them feel better. What a cool guy!

Liza, Alex and Jackie hear all the fuss and run over to me to hear the details.

"Girls," Liza starts after I fill them in. "I hope you won't be pissed off if I abandon you. Craig just called. He came home a day early from his trip because he missed me. He'll be picking me up in about twenty minutes."

Craig is Liza's boyfriend. He's twenty-one. They've practically known each other from childhood, since Craig's father is Jeffery Tollan's attorney. Liza always liked Craig and fantasized about him, but they only started dating last spring, when Liza turned seventeen and Craig saw her in a different light.

Alex looks at Nick and me and then at our hands. I just now realize that he's still holding my hand in his.

She turns to Liza and says, "I won't be angry with you on one condition: you and Craig take me home first and then go wherever you want to go. Deal?"

She looks and sounds much more sober now, and so does Liza. I, however, feel . . . sooo good.

"Umm . . . well . . . We're kind of going in the opposite direction," Liza says defensively. "Can't you go with Jackie?"

"Yeah . . . Listen . . . I have to meet Jamie right now," Jackie starts, "but when you guys are ready to go home, give me a call and I'll come and get you."

"Can you drop me off first, Jackie?" Alex asks, not looking at me or Nick.

"Sure," Jackie replies. "Vicky, you call me. I'll come and get you and Chloe. Where is Chloe, by the way?"

We look around, but don't see either Chloe or Ted.

"Don't worry, Jackie, you don't have to come back," says Nick. "I'll take Vicky and Chloe home. After we find Chloe, that is."

"Are you sure?" I ask, hoping he doesn't change his mind.

"Positive," he confirms it and smiles at me with such a beautiful smile that I can't help it but trust him.

Alex, Liza, and Jackie say their goodbyes and leave. I dance with Nick again, but remind him that we need to find Chloe.

Brianna asks everyone to be a little quieter because her next-door neighbors have already called twice and complained that there was too much noise, and she doesn't want any trouble with her parents.

"Do they have any kids?" Nick asks.

"They do. Why?" Brianna asks.

"What ages are they?"

"They have a little girl and a son around our age," Brianna answers automatically, still not understanding where Nick's going with this.

"Invite the guy to join us. You know what they say: *Nothing makes you more tolerant of a neighbor's party than being there.*"

"You're a genius!" Brianna exclaims. "What a great idea!"

Suddenly we hear some barfing sounds coming from the bathroom. We look around and see some people who managed to drink themselves into oblivion. They look like they have no idea where they are, what they're doing, or what's going on.

"Maybe not," Brianna says. "I think maybe it's time to wrap it up."

"I totally agree," says Nick. "Let's do it before your house is a total mess. We'll help you clean up. Is it okay with you, Vicky?"

How nice and considerate is he?

"It's fine, but first I need to find Chloe," I say, worried.

"Okay. Listen, let me make the arrangements for going home first. Ruby, who didn't drink, I hope, is taking Bridget, Tiffany, and Jordan home, and I'm supposed to drive Ted and Amber."

Oh, of course, I forgot about Amber . . . I become sober right away.

"Wait!" he exclaims. "I'll ask Ruby to take Amber. I'll be right back."

He goes to talk to his friends. Immediately I see Ruby, Amber, Tiffany, and Bridget pick up Jordan from the reclining chair and drag him out. Tiffany and Amber look incredibly upset. *I wonder why.*

"Now let's go find Chloe and Ted," Nick says as Brianna joins us, having just walked their friends out.

"Someone saw those two going upstairs," she says. "You two go look for them and I'll start cleaning up."

"Oh, no!" I cry as we run upstairs and start to open the doors to the bedrooms. *God, how many do they have in this house? Tell me it's not nice to be rich.*

"If that jerk does something to Chloe, I'll kill him," I say, scared to death.

Finally we hit the jackpot.

"Bingo!" Nick exclaims. "Here they are."

We open the door wide and see Chloe on the bed, wearing only a bra and panties. Ted, without his shirt on, jumps up from the bed as soon as he hears us open the door and turns his back to us.

"Don't turn on the light!" he cries.

Judging by the sound, he's zipping up his pants. After that, he puts on his shirt inside out and covers Chloe up. She doesn't move.

"She's totally smashed," Nick says, turning on the light. "I think she's unconscious."

"Omigod!" I shout at McAlly as I try to revive Chloe by lightly shaking her and slapping her cheek. "What did you do to her, you creep? If you hurt her, I'll castrate you!" I scream, and I really mean it at this moment. "You, no good S.O.B.!"

"I didn't do anything she didn't want me to do," Ted says. "We're two consenting adults here, and for your information, I wouldn't hurt Chloe. I like her."

"Consenting adults? Are you insane? She's not even eighteen yet. If you did something to her, it's statutory rape. Got it?" I yell at him, forgetting that he's not eighteen yet himself.

"Nothing happened. I swear," McAlly defends himself. "Look at her. She's dressed."

"Barely. No thanks to you. You moron!" I shout. "If we hadn't walked in when we did, she would have been naked in the next minute or so. Am I wrong?"

I continue to shake Chloe, and finally she starts moving. She opens her eyes a little, but the light bothers her.

"Vicky," she murmurs, squinting. "Where's Ted? I want Ted. He says it feels sooo good, it's like flying to the moon."

I can see she's still lost in the moment.

"See?" McAlly asks me. "She wants me."

"Sorry, baby. I'm afraid Ted's flying solo tonight," I say to Chloe, and then to Ted, "I'm sure you're familiar with self-service, so use it—or go home and take a cold shower."

"Listen, Benson, take your attitude and shove it!" McAlly throws at me.

"Ted, stop it!" Nick snips.

"I don't feel very well," Chloe says softly, interrupting us, fully aware now of what's going on. She looks embarrassed. "I want to get dressed. Help me, Vicky, please."

Nick and Ted leave the room as I help Chloe to put her clothes on in silence.

When we're done, I ask, "Are you okay?"

"I want to go home," she mumbles. "Let's go home, Vicky."

"Okay, baby. We're going," I assure her. "Can you walk?"

It doesn't seem so. Nick and Ted help me walk her down the stairs. We see that everybody has already left. The mess is almost gone. We say our thanks and goodbyes to Brianna and go outside.

Nick opens the front door of his car for me. I sit down, watching Ted tenderly hold Chloe. They're in the backseat, her head on his shoulder, his arm wrapped around her.

We ride in silence for a while, but suddenly Nick and I hear some commotion in the back. We turn and see that Chloe is a little restless. She doesn't feel well, it's obvious.

"You have to stop, Nick," McAlly says. "She's sick. I think she needs to puke."

Chloe does just *that* as soon as Nick stops the car and Ted opens the back door. I see him holding Chloe's head and think that he apparently really does care for her. *Aww . . .*

"Where to?" Nick asks after Chloe throws up everything, including her guts.

"Let's take Ted home first and then go to my house. Chloe will have to spend the night there. She can't go home in this condition. I'll just call her parents and I pray to God that my mom is asleep by now."

All I need right now is for Mom to see us like this.

"Your wish is my command," Nick says and starts the car.

Is he for real?

Soon, we drop Ted off at his house. He kisses a sleeping Chloe on the forehead, which is very touching. Nick and I exchange glances. *Who would've thought?*

"Take care of her, Vicky," Ted says, and I'm touched even more. "See you Monday."

"Let's go home," I tell Nick. "Make a right turn at the second light."

"Are you all right?" he asks. "You were pretty shaken up when we found them."

"Can you blame me? Of course, you're a guy. You wouldn't understand."

Would he?

"I understand. You were worried about your friend and you're blaming yourself for not watching her well enough. Am I close?"

He smiles at me with that killer smile of his, flashing his perfect snow-white teeth.

"That about covers it," I say, upset and mad at myself at the same time. "I can't even imagine what I would have done if we were too late. I totally screwed up!"

"Don't be so hard on yourself, Vicky. Chloe's a big girl. You're the same age, aren't you? It's *her* responsibility to act the way she thinks she should. *She's* the one who decides what to do and what not to do."

Nick sounds so . . . grown up.

"Yeah, you're right, but Chloe's different. She's so child-like, so naïve and innocent. We always watch over her and protect her. That's the way it's always been."

"Well, maybe it's time to change it. Maybe it's time for Chloe to grow up. She should take chances and risks. Let her make her own mistakes. That's how you learn and grow. You can't live her life for her, can you?"

He definitely sounds mature. Like he knows exactly what he's talking about—yet he doesn't sound at all like Alex. What he says doesn't annoy me. He doesn't lecture me, but puts things into perspective. I trust everything he says. I don't know why, but it just seems right and natural. I feel so safe with him.

"Maybe you're right, but I can't help it. I worry about Chloe. Anyway, all's well that ends well."

Has it really ended? Or is it just the beginning of growing pains?

"I don't think it's over for Chloe. I don't even think it's over for you. Tomorrow you'll find out the consequences of drinking and regret it, but you learn from your mistakes."

"Sometimes drinking helps you forget things," I say, suddenly remembering Mom and our problems.

"Forget things?" Nick asks, looking surprised. "I hope you're not talking about that animosity you have toward Heather and Tiffany and that tug-of-war of yours. Are you?"

"No, of course not. The furthest thing from my mind is that duo. I have *real* problems."

"Do you want to talk about it?" Nick asks.

He seems really concerned. *Should I tell him? I trust him. He's so easy to talk to, and I'm sure he'd understand . . .*

"Not really," I respond. "At least, not tonight."

"Listen, I don't mean to sound paternal and tell you what to do, so I'm just going to put it this way: drinking doesn't kill the pain, anyway. So why drink? Do you know what they say about soberness versus hangover?" He answers after I shake my head, "Heartache tonight or headache tomorrow. So you see, you need to have your priorities straight."

"Well, we're here," I say when we approach my house.

Why was it such a short ride?

"Vicky," Nick starts after he stops the car and shuts off the engine, "I need to tell you something." He takes my hand in his and I feel butterflies all over my body. "I like you. I like you a lot, but I'm sure it's obvious. And I have a feeling that you like me too. Am I wrong?"

When he sees me looking down, he lifts my chin up and looks into my eyes.

"No, you're not wrong, but I don't think you have the right to talk to me about feelings when you have a girlfriend," I say, irritated.

How dare he? What about Amber?

"I have a girlfriend, huh?" Nick says with a strange look on his face. "Care to enlighten me on who she is?"

"Please, don't pretend that you don't know who I'm talking about. Amber, of course."

"Amber? My girlfriend?" He starts laughing. "Why would you think that?"

"Aren't you joined at the hip?" I'm surprised. "You're practically inseparable."

"Okay, for your information, Amber and I are neighbors. I bring her to school and home almost every day because it makes a lot of sense since we live next to each other—it's ecologically correct. Listen, our families are friends, so I'm expected to watch over her, and I kind of feel overprotective toward her, but that's all there is to it, believe me."

Sounds convincing.

"Really?" I ask, pleased. I hope it's not that apparent. "Does *she* know that?"

"What do you mean? That she's *not* my girlfriend?"

Come on! How can he not know?

"Don't you know that she totally has romantic feelings for you?"

You've got to be blind not to notice!

"Really?" *he* asks this time, astonished. "Does she really like me *that* way?"

Men!

"Like? That's a major understatement."

How typical for a guy—totally clueless.

"Well, it doesn't matter. I don't have romantic feelings for *her*. I have them for *you*. So will you give me a chance, Vicky?"

He looks at me, waiting, but I don't know what to say.

"Give me one good reason why I should," I finally ask, flirty.

You bet! I'd love to!

"Hmm, let's see." He smiles. "I'm awfully handsome and terribly nice. I'm a prince!"

"And you're totally modest," I say seriously, and then giggle. "Prince Charming."

"No, seriously, Vicky, didn't you have a great time tonight?" Nick asks, looking me straight in the eye. "Be honest, please."

Not now. Mom needs my full attention now.

"Okay," I gulp out. "At first I felt like I was in shark-infested water or a rodent-infested cellar with no escape. But when you came over and we started dancing, it felt like I was in a royal palace. Now I feel like Cinderella, and the shoe fits, but I'm afraid that if I take that chance, the car might turn into a pumpkin, and I'm scared the crowd will talk and judge."

What am I saying? Royal palace? Cinderella? The shoe fits?

"It won't happen. You don't have to be scared. The car will stay as it is. And what happens in the palace, stays in the palace."

Again, he sounds very convincing.

"Why should I believe you? All guys are the same. They want one thing."

I believe him!

"Speaking from experience, are you?" Nick asks sarcastically. "You think I'm making you my sexual conquest, don't you? I can have any girl for *that*. They just don't have what I want and what I need. They're not you. Believe me, Vicky, I don't have an agenda. I really *like* you. I like you a lot."

Me, too, but I can't now. Now I have to concentrate on Mom.

"But how do I know it's not just small talk and that you really mean it?"

He doesn't answer. He just leans forward toward my face. *What is he doing?* I move closer to his face and close my eyes. *What am I doing?* We kiss. My head spins. Then everything stands still . . . *Wow! I've never felt this way before.*

As I sit there, speechless, my heart pounding, my pulse racing, Nick presses his index finger over my lips.

"You talk too much," he says, looking into my eyes. "I had to stop you."

I remember reading somewhere that Ingrid Bergman said, "A kiss is a lovely trick, designed by nature to stop speech when words become superfluous."

But I don't say it to Nick. I don't want to quote famous people all the time, like Alex does.

"So you found a way to shut me up. How nice," I say instead, sarcasm in my voice.

We stare longingly at each other. Neither of us says anything for a long time. How can I tell him that I'm so hesitant and cautious because of his friends? How can I tell him that I'm afraid of the gossip his friends are so good at? I wish I could tell him about Mom losing her job and discovering that growth in her breast, but I can't. Not yet. I just know that I can't be worrying about Mom and about Nick at the same time.

"You take my breath away and hold it hostage," Nick finally says, stroking my cheek. "It's too bad you don't want to give me the chance. Well, so be it. I can take rejection with dignity." He gets out of the car and helps me out, then says, "Let's get Chloe."

"So that's it? You're not going to ask me again?" I ask, astounded.

My ego's hurt! *Is he giving up so easily? Isn't he going to fight for me?* I can't believe it! *Isn't it what he wants?*

"What for?" Nick asks. "Would you say yes?"

He gives me an inquiring look.

"Probably not, but you still should've given me the chance to say no."

His move now. What do I want? I'm not sure myself. Maybe deep inside I do want him to insist. When I don't get any response, I help him pull Chloe out of the car and together we drag her to my door. She's totally out of it. *I have to say something. I need to explain.*

"Nick," I start, reaching into my purse for the keys, "listen, it's not you. It's just that it's not a very good time right now. I have so many problems, so many issues."

"Hey, don't sweat it," Nick says. "It's not a big deal." But I see that it *is* a big deal to him. "Don't forget to call her parents," he says, pointing at Chloe. "See you Monday. I did have a great time with you tonight." His voice trails off as he walks away.

I watch him, holding Chloe in my arms. As soon as he rolls off in his car, I think how stupid I was. *Why did I say no? I'll never get another chance with him.*

I go inside, dragging Chloe. What do you know? Mom turns on the lamp light. She's waiting for me on the couch. She looks at us and immediately jumps up to help me with Chloe. We put Chloe on the couch and cover her with a blanket.

"Nice party, huh?" Mom asks. She doesn't sound angry at all. "Bring a bucket or something. I'm sure she's going to need it tonight. She's sleeping here, right?"

"Right. I have to call her parents," I say, thinking how cool and understanding Mom is.

I apologize to the Wilmores for calling so late and explain that we came to my house after the party and Chloe fell asleep. (Needless to say, I don't mention the condition she's in.) I ask them to let her spend the night, and they don't object.

"How many drinks did she have?" Mom asks.

"I have no idea," I answer, and I really don't.

"And what about you?" she asks, carefully observing me.

"Mom—" I start, not looking at her.

"You don't have to answer," Mom interrupts. "I was your age once, and I also did what I wasn't supposed to do. I'm not a hypocrite. I'm not going to say, 'Do as I say, not as I do.' But it doesn't mean I want you to repeat my mistakes either." She strokes my hair and adds, "Well, I'm just glad you're okay. Go to bed. We'll talk tomorrow."

*   *   *

I was so sleepy, but now I can't sleep. I keep flipping and flopping, tossing and turning, twisting and rolling, huffing and puffing. I'm wide awake. I feel nauseous. My head's spinning. I need to vomit, but I can't get up.

When I wake up on Saturday, it's noon. I can't move. Everything hurts. My bed's so warm and cozy, and my blanket's so soft. I like to snuggle under the covers, as I usually do on weekends, but today I feel uncomfortable and sick. I remember what Nick said about experiencing the aftermath of drinking. Well, it doesn't do a body good.

Mom knocks on the door. I tell her to come in, but I'm afraid she'll start THE TALK.

"Good afternoon," she says. "Chloe's still asleep. The bucket is empty and clean, so she must've slept through the night. How're you?"

She smiles, seeing for herself *how* I am.

"Shh! Volume control, please!" I cry out, squeezing my head. "Kill me! I want to die!"

"That bad, huh?"

Mom makes a grimace, wrinkling her nose.

"Bad is a major understatement. I have a splitting headache. I feel like my head is going to explode. It hurts in places I didn't know I had."

I moan and groan, but it doesn't help.

"Well, there's a good explanation," says Mom seriously. "It's your body acting out. It's protesting against alcohol abuse. When you abuse alcohol, you abuse your body. It's that simple. Your body punishes you and teaches you a lesson at the same time."

"I'm sorry, Mom. I know I screwed up big time. Please don't give me a lecture about family values and virtues. Believe me, I've punished myself enough, and I'm destined to suffer after last night. I swear, it won't happen again. I mean it. I'll never have another drink as long as I shall live!"

God, I can't even say the word drink without nausea.

"I'm not going to lecture you. I see that you're suffering, and you shouldn't swear about anything that might or might not happen. I just hope that you've learned your lesson." She sits down on my bed and changes the subject. "Now tell me how it goes with Nick."

"It goes well, I just don't know where," I shrug, and that's exactly how I feel about it.

"Why? Tell me what happened."

She seems awfully interested in my love life.

"We danced a lot and had a great time. He brought us home. He told me he likes me. I believe him, I trust him, and I feel safe with him, but when we talked, I acted awfully skeptical and refused to go out with him. I don't know why." I catch my breath and ask, "Mom, he makes my heart beat faster and slower at the same time. Is that normal?"

"Yes, it's perfectly normal. You're in love."

Mom smiles and strokes my hair.

"Why does love have to be so painful?" I ask. "It's like a toothache, but in your heart."

"Well put," says Mom. "Love hurts, but it also makes you happy. Did he kiss you?"

"Mom!" I exclaim. "I'm not going to discuss this with you—but, yeah, we kissed."

"And?"

"Nothing else happened," I reply and try to end the conversation. "I can't talk anymore."

"By the way, in case you haven't noticed, Chloe has a huge hickey on her neck."

"So? What do you want me to do about it?" I ask, having no idea of what else to say.

Suddenly, I feel my guts demanding a release. I jump out of bed and, covering my mouth with my hand, run to the bathroom as fast as I can to throw up. I hardly make it.

After about fifteen minutes of repeat performances, I'm still sitting on the floor, my arms wrapped around the toilet. I feel like my body's a volcano that has just erupted.

Mom knocks on the door. I don't answer. Her knocking becomes more persistent.

"Victoria, are you okay in there?" she asks. "I don't hear you. Can I help? Let me in."

That's all I need! It's an individual process, not a team effort. Kind of a solo act.

"Can I have some privacy, Mom?" I ask. "I can handle it. I think I'm done here."

I clean the toilet and wash my face. Then I brush my teeth and gargle with mouthwash. *God, it feels good!* I feel like I'm reborn. I look in the mirror and come out of the bathroom.

"Feeling better?" Mom asks. "You're a little pale, but you look much better."

"My head's still pounding, but it's not spinning anymore, and the nausea's gone."

"Good. Chloe's mother called. I told her you talked all night and now you're asleep."

"Did the girls call?" I ask, wondering how Liza and Alex feel after last night.

"Jackie called," Mom responds. "I have a feeling the others feel the same way you do."

I remember how many drinks Alex and Liza had and think Mom's probably right.

"You mean you know that Jackie was the only one who wasn't drinking?" I ask.

"I suspect that's the case. I know Jackie," she says. "Call her when you feel like it."

"Okay," I reply. "What do we do about Chloe? We have to wake her up soon."

"Let's give her a few more minutes. Tell me who the hickey-leaver is."

What?

"Mom!" I exclaim. "It's not enough that you want to know everything about my love-slash-sex life. Now you want to know about Chloe's, too? Well, forget it!"

I turn away from my mother and walk out of the room.

The "L" Words, the Three "S's," and the Big "O"

"Love ain't nothing but sex misspelled."

—Harlan Ellison

"**I** don't understand why you're so hesitant to talk about sex," Mom says, following me to the living room. "When I was your age, all we talked about was boys, first love, and sex. I'm sure that you all think about it and talk about it. Am I wrong?"

"No, you're right, but now we also discuss 'paper or plastic,' " I try changing the subject.

"What is that supposed to mean?" Mom wonders.

"It's a joke we use. Some girls fill up their bras with tissues or toilet paper, and some . . . you know, nose jobs, boob implants, liposuction," I chuckle, seeing Mom's astounded face.

"You discuss plastic surgery? At your age?" She's in shock. "Unbelievable! But why?"

"Because everybody has something they want to change," I explain. "It doesn't mean we'll actually do it, so put your mind at ease. Maybe later, though," I laugh.

"Or maybe never!" Mom exclaims. "Let's continue our conversation about sex."

"Mom!" I exclaim. "You're not going to give me a lecture about the birds and the bees, are you?" *Why is she so obsessed with sex today?* "Please stop it!"

"I don't want to stop it! I worry about you." Mom doesn't give up. She looks anxious. "I know how those sex-crazed teenage boys with raging hormones are. I just want you to be very careful. Don't rush into anything. If you do—"

"I know," I interrupt. "I'll use protection."

"That's not what I was going to say, but it's a good point. I was going to say that your first time should be very special. It should be with someone that you love and who reciprocates your feelings. You know, pleasure from love only lasts a moment, but disappointment from love may last a lifetime. As you would say, it's a proven fact."

"Mooom! Please stop!" I exclaim. "Don't go there. It's too early for that."

"If I had my way, you'd be retired when you have your first sexual experience," Mom says sarcastically. "But you're in love with Nick, and he reciprocates your feelings. He said so, didn't he? So it's not too early for that."

"He did say so. And I feel it. I have no reason not to believe him. Liza, Chloe, and Jackie say it's obvious. They say he can't take his eyes off me."

"And what does Alex say?"

"I don't know, Mom. She has something against him." *Or maybe Liza is right about Alex having the hots for Nick herself?* "She doesn't say anything."

"I understand that Nick's proclamation of his feelings stunned you because it was sudden and unexpected," says Mom. "I think you have to give him his chance. Especially because he asked for one."

"I don't know, Mom," I shrug. "I was blown away by his words. But my reaction to it threw him for a loop. I think I lost my chance with him," I say with sadness.

"Don't give up," she says. "There's a good saying, 'If opportunity doesn't knock, build a door.' And you already have an opportunity—the door is open."

She speaks like an expert.

"Mom," I change the subject. "Let's talk about you now. You promised, remember?"

"There's nothing to talk about. I'll see a doctor, have a mammogram, and then we'll know," Mom says. "We'd better wake up Chloe. It's two o'clock already."

It's not an easy job to bring Chloe back to life. When we finally succeed, she relives my bathroom journey. While she's recovering from her "date" with the toilet, I place a call to Jackie and give her a thorough description of how Chloe and I are paying for our sins. She, in turn, confirms Mom's suspicions about Alex and Liza. Nick was right. It's not worth it to get so drunk only to feel like shit afterward. Well, you play, you pay. It's fair. Crime and punishment.

"You're so lucky, Jackie," I say. "You don't know how dreadful it feels."

"I'm not lucky, just smart," she says. "I hate to tell you I told you so, but . . ."

I tell her all about Nick, about what Mom had said, and that I'm afraid I blew my chance.

"I don't know, maybe he's my unattainable dream. Maybe I should just forget him."

"Don't think of him as your unattainable dream. Instead, think of him as your attainable goal," Jackie says. "Your mother's right. You've made a mistake. Now you should fix it."

"What do you think I should do?" I ask.

"What do *you* think you should do?" Jackie, the shrink, asks me a counter question.

"Right now I don't know. I have other problems, but I don't want to talk about them."

"Okay," Jackie says. "I'm not going to push. Better tell me what happened with Chloe."

"It's not my tale to tell. You're going to have to wait till Monday. Better tell me, did you have a good time with Jamie?"

"Grand!" Jackie exclaims. "He's unbelievable. Thank you for him. I think I'm in love!"

*   *   *

On Sunday we all feel much better. We're back to life and able to communicate. Alex calls first. We talk about the party and exchange our after-party experiences. She doesn't mention Nick at all, but when I say how nice it was of Nick to bring Chloe and me home, she interrupts and asks me what happened to Chloe. I tell her just what I told Jackie: she'd have to wait till Monday.

"The way we behave confirms that we're still children," I say.

Did I just admit it?

"Maybe not children, but we're still not mature enough," Alex claims. "Do you know what the difference between us and grownups is?"

Here we go again . . .

"Hmm, let's see. They have jobs, pay the bills, and it's legal for them to drink and have sex. Did I miss anything?" I ask. "If I did, I'm sure you're going to clue me in, Alex," I add sarcastically, "so knock yourself out. Tell me."

"One of the things about being a grown-up is learning how to act right, even when you feel wrong," she says, and then elaborates, "Sean Stewart said that."

How nice. I'm so happy she clarified it for me.

"Good for Sean. Even better for daddy Rod. He's a damn lucky father."

*   *   *

I call Liza and Chloe to find out if they've completely recovered. They have. Chloe still wants to sleep all the time, though. Liza, however, is her usual self. She wants to know everything about me and Nick. I know she won't let go, so I tell her what I told Jackie.

"Are you insane? You said no? Why would you do something like that?" she yells. "When I saw you two dancing, I said to myself, *He's hers!* The way you looked at each other and held each other . . . If that's not sexy, I don't know what is. What's your problem?" She sounds like it's something personal. "You need to have your head examined!"

"Don't shout, Liza. You sound like *your* life depends on it and I'm ruining it for you," I say, annoyed. "I'm acting like this because of his friends. I know already he's not *with* Amber, and he's nothing like Heather, Tiffany, or even Jordan, but he still hangs out with them. I don't need rumors and speculations. I don't want to be a subject of their gossip or an object of their smear campaign."

"Tell me something," says Liza. "Why do you care who he hangs out with? Do you want to *hang* out with him or *make* out with him?"

"I think that one's kind of inevitable because of the other," I reply, hesitating for a moment.

"Vicky, trust me, it doesn't matter. When you're alone, his friends won't matter. Nothing will. Come on, look at him. He's a poster boy for male gorgeousness—tall, dark, and handsome. And what about his eyes, those dark baby blues, and those abs? Phew! I'm getting hot." The funny thing is, she sounds serious. "He's intelligent charming, dashing, and yet intriguing and mysterious. It's such a turn-on. If I wasn't in love with Craig, I'd go for Nick myself—and I'd definitely get him."

"In your dreams!" I exclaim. "You're delusional, Liza. He wants me, not you."

"I rest my case," Liza says, and suddenly it comes to me what she was trying to do.

"Please tell me you didn't just—"

"I totally did," she interrupts and laughs. "As long as I got your attention."

"Okay, I got the point. Now tell me, how things are with Craig."

"He wants to have sex," she announces, just like that.

"Did he say so?" I ask. "Are you ready to have sex?"

"No, he doesn't say it, but his actions speak louder than words. He doesn't push. Not yet, at least, but you know, he tries. I think he's waiting for my eighteenth birthday, and I'm going to be eighteen at the end of March, remember? I'm the oldest of all of us. But I'm not ready yet, and I don't know when I'm going to be ready."

"Well, then, forget it. If he's got an itch, let him scratch it himself," I declare.

"What if he leaves me? I love him so much. I can't even imagine being without him."

"Listen, Liza. You have to understand something," I say with confidence, sounding so mature, like I'm speaking from experience. "Love can be eternal when you know it's there with you, but just because you touch something, it doesn't mean it's yours to keep. If you get something you want, it doesn't mean you *have* it. You can't just look at the moon to *be on* the moon. Am I making any sense? My point is: if Craig loves you, he'll wait until you're ready. But you can't make him *love* you just by *making love* with him."

"I got it. I know what you mean," she responds and changes the subject. "Now I want to hear everything about Chloe and McAlly. They looked so cute and sexy dancing together. Just like a comic version of you and Nick. So what happened? "

That does it! Why me?

"Oh, shut up!" I exclaim. "I'm so tired of all of you. Why are you asking me? Call Chloe and ask her! Or better, leave her alone till tomorrow. She's still very sleepy."

We hang up and immediately I start thinking about Mom. *What's going to happen?*

*   *   *

It's Monday morning. We meet early and go to the cafeteria for breakfast and chatting.

"I want to be briefed on current events," Alex states, "and I want it fast and thorough."

"Jordan made a pass at Vicky. Everybody saw it. That part I can still remember. Tiffany was extremely pissed off. Nick stood up for Vicky and got rid of Jordan. And then Nick and Vicky danced, and danced, and danced," Chloe says it all without a break.

"Chloe, Chloe, relax. Catch your breath," I tell her. "Yeah, I even felt sorry for Tiffany." I tell the girls how Jordan ended up. "Well, I guess it works out for them. She *loves* him, he *does* her. Mutual gratification. I looked at him and thought to myself, *And Tiffany still wants him, even like this. Is this her blonde ambition?*"

Oops! I did it again. I said the 'B' word. I made a 'blonde' remark. Liza will kill me.

"Sorry, Liza. Please don't kill me."

"Go to hell, asshole!" Liza says. "I stopped paying attention to you."

"Phew! It comes as such a relief to me," I say, waving my hand, and we all laugh.

Liza and Jackie, in turn, tell Alex and Chloe my story with Nick. Chloe is so excited, like it's *her* story.

She says, "I knew it! I told you he likes you. Why didn't you say yes?"

"Well, I was so tempted, but . . . maybe I just got cold feet," I reply.

"So Tiffany actually didn't spend any time with Jordan?" Alex suddenly interrupts.

"Well, she did. Some," I answer. "Blink-and-you-missed-it." We all giggle again. "At least with Jordan, what you see is what you get, but Ted . . . he's totally un-getable."

"Like you can't *get* him or can't *understand* him?" Chloe asks, and more laughing comes.

"I mean that one minute you think he's a jerk, and another . . . Well, he surprised and impressed me at the same time last night," I tell her. "Relax, baby, I think you've already got him."

"Really?" Alex asks, turning to me. "I saw them dancing very closely. What happened?"

"I can't wait to hear!" Liza exclaims, all excited, and also looks at me.

"Me, too. So?" Jackie says, giving me a long stare.

I glance over to Chloe and say, "Why me? It's your tale. You tell it."

"No, Vicky, you'll tell it so much better. Go ahead," she begs. "Besides, I don't even remember most of it."

"Well, what do you want to know?" I ask. "I can tell you what I know, that's all."

I tell them the entire story of Chloe and Ted dancing and disappearing, about me and Nick finding them, and how Ted took care of Chloe and impressed us.

"That's it. I don't know what happened in the room before we found them," I finish.

"Chloe," says Alex, and everyone turns to face Chloe. "I want vivid and precise details. So spill! Inquiring minds want to know."

"Is it necessary?" asks Jackie. "I'm afraid that in-depth description might make me sick to my stomach. Can she spare us *some* details?"

"Come on, Jackie! It won't kill you," Liza says. "We're curious. Go ahead, Chloe."

"You're pumping for info, guys," I say, "so be careful what you wish for. You might get more than you bargained for." I look at Chloe and ask, "Are you sure you want to talk?"

"It's okay, I don't mind. I only remember how he kissed me, and undressed me, and . . . touched me," she starts. "He was very gentle, but then . . . something happened."

"Ooh!" we all exclaim in unison. "What?"

"Spill all," Alex says. "Don't be shy and don't hold anything in now."

She looks like she's in the movies.

"I got scared. His . . . thingy . . . It's huge!" Chloe looks down, embarrassed, her face red.

"His penis, you mean?" Liza asks matter-of-factly. "Good to know."

"Whoa! Too much information. Even for inquiring minds," Jackie says and presses her hands over her ears. "No more! No more!"

"Ewww! Gross!" Alex exclaims and makes a grimace. "This is too much even for the curious and inquisitive. Jackie's right. Details like this one may be spared."

"I can see that it's over the top, even for nosy and meddling folks like you," I say, annoyed. "Didn't I warn you? But you just wouldn't let it go. You asked for it, you got it."

"I still don't want to let it go," says Liza. "It's not too much for snooping and fishing, which I am, and I'm okay with it. Well, Chloe, did you touch it?"

"I don't remember. I don't remember anything else," Chloe cries out. "I fell asleep."

"Leave her alone!" I insist. "Ted offered to fly her to the moon, if you get my drift, so I told him to fly solo or take a cold shower. Anyway, I think he's more talk than action. You know, his bark is bigger than his bite. I'm sure that at the last moment he wouldn't do it to her. He knows the difference between Chloe and Heather. Nick thinks the same thing, but who knows? Nick also says Jordan is harmless, just shallow. He stands for his men. You know, male solidarity at its finest."

"So Chloe, this was the first time you saw a man's equipment, huh?" Alex asks. "So what? I only saw it in pictures, too."

"So did I," says Jackie.

Me, too.

"Poor Chloe. She took a nice little peek and got frightened by a big, bad thing. And they say that size doesn't matter," Liza laughs. "I'm surprised Chloe went that far."

"Let's say it was a glimpse at what lies beneath," I say. "Chloe just got caught in the moment and began to unravel. Until she fell asleep, that is."

We all laugh hysterically as Chloe blushes even more.

"That's it. You can laugh all you want. I won't say squat anymore!"

She's angry with us, and who can blame her? *We're shameless pigs!*

"We're sorry, Chloe," I say. "We weren't laughing at you. If you want McAlly, you should have McAlly. I can tell you one thing: I'm sure he wants *you*. I saw it last night."

"Really?" Chloe asks. "Are you sure? Because I like him a lot. But that's not the only reason I want to be with him." She stops for a moment and looks at us. "Don't laugh, okay?" She continues after we all nod, "I'm afraid I'll never have a boyfriend."

"Why?" we all ask, surprised.

"Look at me. I'm not exactly a leading lady type," she says sadly and looks like a puppy.

"Baby, you're beautiful," I say and the others confirm it. "We love you so much."

"*You* love me, and maybe Ted *likes* me, but who else?" she asks. "I'm a *friend* type. Liza has Craig, Jackie has Jamie, Vicky can have Nick any time she wants, and you can all have other guys, if you want, but me . . . Who wants me? So if I don't get Ted, I might end up being alone for the rest of my life. See?"

"I think she's got a QBS—Quintessential Bridesmaid's Syndrome," Alex says. "She's afraid people will say, 'Oh, here comes that little Chloe, always a bridesmaid, never a bride.'"

"Is that what bothers you?" I ask. "It's sooo stupid."

"No, it's more like, 'Here comes that chubby little Chloe, a quintessential girl *friend* who never made it to a *girlfriend*, poor thing.' That's what bothers me," she says, looking gloomy.

"Come on, Chloe," says Alex. "Aren't you forgetting something? I also don't have a boyfriend. As I said, *boys don't make passes at girls who wear glasses*. So what? I'm not worried. There's someone out there for me, too, somewhere, and I'm on a quest to find him."

"You shouldn't worry, Alex," Chloe says. "Don't compare yourself to me. You're normal height and weight, you're cute even with your glasses, and you're so smart—"

"No matter what a woman looks like, if she's confident, she's sexy," says Liza. "I heard Paris Hilton say that, and I totally agree with her. The trick is: feel secure and confident."

"Paris Hilton is the highest authority, no doubt," Jackie interrupts. "Well, no matter how we look, we all want to love and to be loved. So we wait for something, and we look for someone. We don't know what or who exactly, but we should have hope," she adds seriously, but with a kind of a dreamy look on her face, and we all stare at her, flabbergasted. "Where there's hope, there's life, and as long as you have hope, life goes on."

She stops and there's a moment of silence.

"Wow!" Chloe exclaims first. "That was so beautiful, Jackie."

"It really was," I confirm. "Very well put. I think you've already found that someone. You know, they say that old maids live longer than married women. Now I know why. Old maids still have hope, but as soon as you get married, your hopes, dreams, and illusions vanish."

"Come on, Vicky, don't be so negative. Seriously. Marriage isn't always bad," Alex says, and then she says to Jackie, "I'm happy that you found Jamie. You're amazing."

"I think Ruby would agree with you," I say, flashing a mischievous grin.

"Ruby?" Jackie asks, lost. "What does Ruby have to do with it?"

"I know what Vicky means," Chloe says. *Does she?* "We've never seen Ruby with a guy alone. She's always in a group. She didn't even dance. Did you notice? Vicky means that Ruby should have hope, and she'll find love."

God, how naïve can you be?

"Maybe Ruby prefers imaginary men," says Liza. "Maybe she likes them best of all."

"Or women," I murmur, looking down.

"What?" my four friends ask in wide-eyed-open-mouth-dropped-jawed astonishment.

"When I said that Ruby would agree, I wasn't talking to Jackie. I was referring to Alex's comment about Jackie being amazing." I decide to share my suspicions. "I think that Ruby looks at Jackie *that* way."

I raise my left brow and wink with my right eye.

"What way?" Jackie asks, confused.

"Yeah, what way?" Chloe demands.

Liza and Alex just look at me, waiting for a reply.

"Come on! Don't you get it? Haven't you ever noticed? Ruby likes Jackie romantically."

"You mean she's gay?" Liza inquires, and everybody looks at me, astounded.

"I don't know. I'm not saying that. I just think that she might be sexually ambiguous."

"Sexually what?"

Chloe is so lost. Poor, baby. She's completely clueless.

"Sexually confused," I explain. "I saw what I saw, and I saw Ruby admiring Jackie."

"Well, I don't know if that's the case. I don't think so, and I don't care," Alex finally gives us her feedback. "Ruby mentioned at the party that she wants to have this end-of-school shindig at her house in June. Will we go?"

Wow! Alex's becoming a party animal, a social butterfly. What next?

"Well, it depends. Is it her coming-of-age party or coming-out party?" I ask, laughing.

"How very un-PC of you," says Alex. "I want so much to wipe that smirk off your face."

"Very un-what?" Chloe inquires. "What does it mean?"

"Politically correct," I explain to her. "Forget Ruby. Let's talk about something else."

"Vicky," Liza says. "*You're* the one who started this conversation about Ruby. And now you sound so . . . acidic. Stop being so cynical. It's not you. Not after giving me that heartfelt and touching *moon* speech yesterday when we talked about Craig."

"I'm not being acidic or cynical. What Jackie said about having hope was beautiful, so don't think of me as cynical, think of me as cynically hopeful," I joke with a serious face.

"What did you say about Craig?" Alex wants to know.

Liza and I, in turn, repeat our conversation to the girls.

"I told her not to have sex just to hold on to him," I say.

"Yeah, but she explained why so beautifully, just like Jackie."

Liza repeats what I said.

Alex thinks for a moment and then says, "Liza, I agree with Vicky. Don't give in to him. Where are you with him, by the way? Second base?"

"Oh, second base is so passé," Liza responds and looks away. "It's so three months ago."

"Well," Alex says. "So what do you want then? Of course, he's trying."

"And you're telling *me* what to do and what not to do?" Chloe asks angrily.

"There's one thing that bothers me, though," Alex continues, ignoring Chloe's protest. "If Craig can't . . . umm . . . deflower you, as they used to say, he's been probably smelling other flowers in someone else's garden, if you know what I mean. Are you okay with it?"

"Hell, no, I'm not okay with it!" Liza proclaims. "It bothers me a lot. Are you saying that if I don't want him to . . . smell other flowers, I'd better give him mine? Otherwise, I might lose him? You're contradicting yourself, Alex. Didn't you just say *not* to give in?"

"Listen, Liza," Alex says seriously. "Have you ever wondered why we have two ears and only one mouth? I think it's because we should listen more and talk less. With you—it's *in* one ear, out the other. Hello! Haven't you been listening at all? Vicky explained it to you. I explained it to you. What's your problem?"

"I don't get it," says Liza, confused.

Honestly, I think we all are. Only Alex knows what she means, but I'm sure it has something to do with sex.

"It's simple," Alex explains. "If he doesn't push, it means he does another girl—or girls. Or maybe he's just not that into you. You just need to decide what bothers you more— that he tries or that he doesn't push."

"And you say *I'm* cynical! Ha!" I exclaim. "I think Alex means that the difference between you and Craig is: to you he's THE ONE, and to him you're one of many."

"Something like that," Alex confirms. "Look, all men think about is sex. Every man. All the time. Otherwise, there's something wrong with him."

Hmm, how does she know?

"Now I'm even more confused," Liza says. "So what do I do with Craig? Now I feel like I don't mean anything to him and all he wants is sex. You've been a great help. Thanks."

"I'm confused even more than you are," Chloe says, though her reason is different from Liza's.

"Sex is not the answer," I say.

"Sex is not the answer. *Yes* is the answer, and I don't want to say it," says Liza.

"Liza, relax," I say. "You need to talk to Craig about it when he starts pushing. Then you'll know." I turn to Alex and ask, "How come you know so much about men, Alex?"

"I've heard a lot of stuff from people who know," she says. "Come on! Don't we all know that?" She looks at us, waiting for a response. When she doesn't get any, she goes on, "By the way, I got an instant message from some jerk last night. He had a lot to say about men's sexuality. Much more than I cared to know. I played along at first—"

"You're a virtual slut!" I interrupt.

Who would've thought?

"LOL!" Alex responds. "Anyway, after a while, I gave him a piece of my mind. He won't IM me anymore, I'm sure of that."

So am I.

"I agree," I say. "All men are pigs, Chloe. All they want is to get into your pants."

"My pants?" innocent Chloe asks.

You can't help but love her.

"Well, generally speaking," I answer. "It's all about the three S's."

"Three S's?" everybody asks in unison and Alex adds, "Elaboration would be nice."

"Sex, *sex*, and more *sex*," I say.

"LMAO!" Chloe exclaims.

"Oh, yeah? And what about Nick?" Liza asks me. "Except for that one kiss that was so nice, did he touch you? Did he mention sex to you? You said yourself he was a perfect gentleman, didn't you?"

"Yes, but—" I start, but Alex, not letting me continue, interrupts yet again.

"I'm sure he's the same as every man alive," she declares. "They're all the same."

"Come on, guys!" Jackie, who hasn't said a word in a while, suddenly exclaims. "You three are such a bad influence."

Of course, she means me, Liza, and Alex.

"I remember when it was so easy, and I wasn't thinking about having sex," Liza says. "Of course, it was B.C."

"Before century?" Jackie asks, looking and sounding surprised.

"No, before Craig," Liza replies seriously, but we all laugh.

"Well, I remember there was a time when I didn't even think about kissing and had no idea what sex was," says Alex. "It was, of course, B.S."

"Bullshit?" Chloe wants to know, as the four of us look at each other and start to giggle.

"Before Sam," Alex tells her. "Remember I told you about him? He's a boy I met in camp when I was twelve. We swapped spit, and I hated it. I never came near him again."

"Well, there's nothing wrong with having sex. It just has to be at the right time, in the right place, with the right person, and you have to be ready for it, that's all," Jackie says.

"You sound just like my mother," I say.

I tell the girls about my conversation with Mom.

"Beautifully put again, Jackie," says Alex, "but a man doesn't care about the woman, or the time, or the place, as long as he *has* a place for sex. And that's the difference between women and men. As Billy Crystal says, 'Women need a reason to have sex. Men just need a place.' It's totally right. Ask any man."

"Enough about sex," Jackie says, looking annoyed.

"Is sex dirty? Only if it's done right." I demonstrate *my* erudition this time. "Woody Allen."

"You know, the only time I think of sex as being dirty, and it's totally grossing me out," Alex starts, "is when I imagine my parents doing it. Ick!"

"Ewww! Gross!" Chloe exclaims even louder. "Tell me about it. It's disgusting!"

"Parents are people, too, you know," says Jackie, and then she makes a face and adds, "but I don't even want to go there."

We're all hysterical.

"What can I say?" I ask. "With the knowledge we all have just demonstrated, I only wish we could get credits in sex education. And if they could make sex an extracurricular activity, I'm sure everyone would participate."

"Well, there's a time for sex and there's a time for class," Alex says. "Let's go.

*   *   *

It seems that education is the last thing on people's minds today. Everywhere and all the time, people discuss the party. They whisper, tattle, and blab, especially the members of the *Jewelry Collection*. I don't even want to think about who the subjects of their gossip are.

Tiffany looks at me as if I'm an enemy of the state. Heather looks the same way at both me and Chloe—me for obvious reasons, Chloe because she was probably informed of Chloe and Ted's excellent adventure—but who cares? We certainly don't.

When Nick sees me, he smiles and asks how Chloe and I are, but nothing else. *What can I expect after the way I ended our post-party escapade?*

*   *   *

It's lunchtime and we reconvene in the cafeteria. Tina and Norman wave at us. I don't think they know about the party, or maybe Tina just pretends she doesn't know.

"I talked to Ted," Chloe says. "He was so nice. He said he was sorry if he hurt me in any way. I told him he didn't. He asked me out. Omigod! I can't believe it!"

"What did you say?" I ask.

"I asked about Heather, and he said they broke up for good. I said I'll think about it and let him know."

She sounds so excited that I admit, "I *am* a bad influence. Chloe, you're repeating my mistake. You're acting with Ted the way I acted with Nick. Don't overdo it. You can go out with him, but just be careful."

"Love is in the aaair," Liza sings, then adds, "You guys can double date!"

"Something's definitely in the air. I just don't know what," I tell her.

"You're forgetting the *Nick factor*," Liza says. "Where does Nick fit into all this?"

"He doesn't," I respond, "and love is extremely exaggerated. There are four 'L' words involved in this. Who knows what they are?"

"Location, location and location?" Chloe asks. "No, wait, that's three. I don't get it."

The four of us have a good laugh, and then I say, "No, Chloe, that's real estate. Think. You see a guy you like. You want him. You fall in love with him. And then you break up. So the four 'L' words are: like, lust, love, and loathe."

"Why loathe?" the girls ask in unison.

"You know what they say: there's only one step from love to hate," I clarify.

"Vicky and Alex, you're so negative," Liza says, and Jackie agrees.

"I'm only negative when it comes to sex," says Alex. "Vicky is negative about everything. I have nothing against love. I told you, I'm going to find my other half."

"Vicky, we need to find out what Nick and Ted think of you and Chloe," Liza proclaims.

"Well, that's where you come in," Jackie says. "You three are so good at it." She points at Chloe, Liza, and Alex, giving each of them an appropriate assignment, "Go fish! Snoop around! Eye like a spy!"

"No, thank you very much," Alex says. "I have better things to do with my time. By the way, talking about location, location, location, I just remembered a joke I read somewhere. What's the real estate heaven? *Life after death in a world full of angels.* Get it? Isn't it hilarious?"

She laughs, and I immediately think of Mom. *What if she dies? I have my closest friends with me and I need their support.* I decide to talk. Finally.

"Guys," I say quietly. "I need to tell you something. At first, I didn't want to, but now I do." I look at all of them, and see I have their full attention. "Mom found a lump in her breast. We don't know anything yet, but I'm afraid it might be something bad. She has to have a mammogram, and then we'll know."

I see the girls exchange glances and concern appears on their faces.

"Poor Vicky," Chloe says and strokes my shoulder.

Here comes that *abused child* face.

"I'm sorry, Vicky," Liza says. She looks really worried. "What can we do to help?"

"We don't know anything yet," says Jackie. "We can't do anything about it, but we can give Vicky all the support she needs."

Upset, she squeezes my hand, as she usually does.

"I'm scared to death," I say, looking down and fiddling with a napkin. Then I look at the girls and ask, "What if it's . . . you know . . . cancer? What if my mom dies? Oh, my god! I can't lose her. She's the only parent I've got."

"Vicky, you can't beat yourself up over things that can't be changed, and you can't change things or situations you have no control over," a wise, but distressed Alex says. "We just have to wait and see. The results will tell us what the problem is, or if there even *is* a problem. Your mother can't do anything unless she knows for sure, and neither can you. And besides, it's the twenty-first century. Nobody dies of breast cancer these days."

I realize that Alex is right: all we can do now is wait.

Not a Very Merry Chanumas or the Chanumas Blues

*"I merely took the energy it takes
to pout and wrote some blues."*

—Duke Ellington

Waiting is never easy, especially when you're waiting for something that might change your life. You try to be patient, but soon your patience wears out and you become desperate. And the fact that this period of nerve-wracking desperation coincides with the holiday season, your favorite time of the year, the time that's supposed to be jolly and joyful, makes it absolutely unbearable. You feel angry and bitter. You feel completely helpless and lost. That's exactly how I feel this holiday season.

It's been over a month since Mom lost her job and several weeks since she told me about the lump in her breast. She saw a doctor and, as we presumed, he referred her for a mammogram. She had it done a few days ago, but the results, of course, will be sent to the doctor after the holidays. Nobody wants to work between Christmas and New Year's. Do they care that Mom's life might depend on it?

Ever since I can remember, we've been celebrating both Christmas and Chanukah in our household. We light the menorah every night during Chanukah, and then we decorate

171

the biggest and most beautiful Christmas tree we can find. Mom and I love to do it together because it's fun and a good bonding experience. For my grandmother's benefit, we call it the Chanukah bush.

Mom started the tradition out of respect for Dad, but truth be told, both Mom and I love Christmas. We love the whole concept of it—the joy, the happiness, and the thrill— and what difference does it make what religion you are when it comes to holiday spirit? Both holidays are about love and kindness, and I always get plenty. Both are about loving and caring, giving and sharing. *Wow! I'm beginning to rhyme words! I wax poetic!*

But what I like the most about it is the *receiving* part. I've never been deprived of that. I usually get money for every day of Chanukah and the most beautiful and expensive gifts for Christmas. This is the time of the year I love most. In our family we call it Chanumas.

*   *   *

The joy of Christmas shopping is gone, but I still go from one store to another to buy presents for my family and friends. During Chanukah, I collected another four hundred dollars. That and the three hundred dollar reserve I have left from our last shopping spree make my resources a respectable capital.

For my grandparents, I get matching his-and-hers slippers that are warm, cozy, and quite expensive. Well, there's no couple in this world that deserves it more than them.

I spend around fifty dollars on each of my friends. I get a beautiful sexy tank top for Jackie (she'd never get it herself), a leather glasses case for Alex (she's got a plastic one), and a leather wallet for Liza (she needs a bigger one). I think about getting the same one for Mom, but then decide against it. She might think it's a hint to go back to work and fill it with money. I have no idea what to give Mom. So I decide to leave it for later.

In the meantime, I go to the arts and crafts store to get a gift for Chloe. Soon I find a beautiful art set (she mentioned she wanted a new one). As I proceed to the cashier's desk to pay for it, I see a huge book on a stand. It just came out. *Everything You Want to Know About Interior Design and More*, I read on the glossy cover. Wow! It has lots of beautiful illustrations and comes with a set of adorable little cards and envelopes in a box. I think I just found a perfect present for my mother. It will show her that I do listen to her and respect her wishes. The book costs almost a hundred bucks, but I don't care. It's worth every penny if it makes Mom happy—and right now that's exactly what she needs.

I end up spending about four hundred dollars (my Chanukah stash) and still have a little over three hundred left. *I'd better keep it. I'm going to need so much for the prom.*

I meet several people from school, including Tina. She looks well-groomed, happy, and excited. She's genuinely glad to see me and stops to chat for a moment.

"Hi, Vicky," she says. "Christmas shopping? Me, too. I'm buying gifts for Norman and my parents. It's been great at home lately. You were right: talking does help. We had a long talk, and now they try to be home more often—thanks to you guys. You made it happen."

"I'm happy for you, Tina. Glad we could help," I tell her. "You said you're getting a gift for Norman. I didn't realize you were so close. Good for you. He's a great guy."

"He's a wonderful *friend*. He always helps me with my homework and projects," she replies. "Oops! It's late. Got to run. Nice seeing you, Vicky."

Well, I'll be damned!

I'm glad I don't meet any of the *Fab Five*. I don't want them to see what I got for them.

On the way home I recap everything that happened these past few weeks. Let's see. Chloe went to the movies with Ted a few times. They play a lot of tonsil hockey, but when he tries to get to second base with her, she stops him. He doesn't push, and she's happy.

Jackie and Jamie also kiss a lot, but talk even more. So far, the subject of sex hasn't come up. They're perfect for each other. The problem is he's going home after the holidays.

Liza and Craig are still on third base, but she knows that as soon as she turns eighteen, he'll want to move to the next level, and that scares her.

Alex now acts like two different people. One is still very much in charge, but the other is careless and loosened-up. She continues to interrupt anyone who brings up the *Nick factor.*

Our SAT scores came back. We all did well. Jackie, of course, got the highest score, Alex came in second, and I was the third. Liza's score was close to mine, and Chloe came in last, but even her score passed the minimum requirement. However, we applied to several more colleges, just in case NYU doesn't accept us. (Jackie, of course, has nothing to worry about.) We hope for the best, but you never know.

So the waiting game continues. Now it's all up to time, fate, and a little bit of luck.

*   *   *

I'm in my room, waiting for my grandparents to come over. Mom and I had dinner at their house several times recently, so today we're having an early dinner at our place, and later, my four friends will be coming over so we can exchange gifts.

It's not a very merry Chanumas in our home this year. I'm in a melancholy mood most of the time. First of all, I'm worried about Mom. I keep telling myself that everything's going to be fine. Then I start thinking, *But what if it's not?* Then there's also the *Nick factor* and a long line of what-ifs and maybe-I-should-haves. *This mental struggle is becoming a pain in the butt. It's got to stop!*

The only thing that makes it all bearable is school break. First, because I don't have to sit in class, pretending that I care about what's going on, or do my homework. (I'm totally lacking in concentration and stamina.) Second, because I don't have to see Nick every day and pretend like it's enough just to be civil and say a few words to each other, and that my heart isn't pounding every time I see him.

I turn on the TV. God, even today, on Christmas Day, they can't stop talking about politics. They talk about Republicans and Democrats, what they do right and what they do wrong, but all I can think about is that instead of being brainwashed, I'd like to hear poetry and music. Is that too much to ask? *Jazz!* I need jazz.

I go to Mom's room and take out some holiday CDs. Mom's got the most beautiful and romantic collection of Christmas songs. One of my favorites is Nat King Cole's rendition of "Chestnuts Roasting on an Open Fire." The beautiful melody, Nat's velvety voice with a touch of huskiness, and the rich sound of the saxophone reach so deep into my soul that time stops. I can't help but sing it along with Nat and hum along with the saxophone.

As I put on Mom's Kenny G Christmas CD, my grandparents arrive.

"Hi, Grandma! Hi, Grandpa!" I greet them. "Happy holidays."

We hug and kiss. I wonder why I don't see any bags. *Where are our gifts, mine and Mom's?* We go to the living room, where my grandparents admire the tree.

Grandma says, "I have to hand it to both of you. Every year when I see the tree, it looks even more beautiful than all the previous years."

She always says, 'the tree.' It's never a 'Christmas tree.'

I give them my gifts. My grandparents are thrilled. They put on their slippers right away. Mom gives them a gorgeous crystal vase. Of course, it's more for Grandma, but Grandpa doesn't mind. As long as she's happy—and she certainly is. She tries to give Mom something like a you-shouldn't-have-spent-so-much-money-in-your-financial-position speech, but not for long.

"Mom, yours is next," I say as I hand her my gift.

"Thanks," she says.

She unwraps it, sees the book, and just sits there with an open mouth for a while. I think she's so thrilled that she might've bitten her tongue or something.

But then she looks at me and says, "I don't know what to say, Victoria. I'm speechless! This book is something else. It must've cost a fortune!"

"Well, do you like it?" I ask, though I already know the answer.

"Like it?" Mom exclaims. "I love it! I can't tell you what it means to me."

I see tears in her eyes. She's all choked up. *Aww . . .*

My grandparents look at each other, confused.

Then Grandma asks, "What's so special about that book? The cover certainly looks very pretty, but—"

"Mom's interested in interior design. It's her thing," I interrupt. "You know how people always compliment our house? Well, Mom . . ."

I stop because I see Mom slightly shake her head and casually touching her lips with her index finger. I get it. She's giving me a sign, meaning, *Don't say anything.* I nod, letting her know that I got it.

"So I decided to give her this book so she could enjoy it, and she obviously loves it," I finish.

My grandparents are satisfied with my answer and we change the subject.

"Girls," Grandma says. "You probably noticed that we didn't bring any bags, right?"

"You didn't have to," says Mom. "You brought yourselves, and that's what matters."

"David," Grandma says as she reaches into the inside pocket of Grandpa's jacket.

She takes out two familiar envelopes and hands one to me and another to Mom. They're from Tollan's. In each envelope is a gift certificate for three hundred dollars. I'm thrilled! Now I can have another day in paradise. *Of course, if Mom's okay. Otherwise, I don't care.*

Mom, as usual, tries to express a protest against *her* three hundred dollar present.

"That's enough, Libby!" Grandma snips. "It comes from the heart, so please show us your gratitude and just enjoy it, for goodness sake."

"Sorry, Mother. You're right," Mom says. "Thanks to both of you."

She looks and sounds like a child being disciplined. Then she suddenly starts laughing. We look at her, lost and confused, but she gets up, walks to the bookcase, takes a little flat box off the shelf, and hands it to me.

I open it and see . . . a two hundred dollar gift certificate from Tollan's! We all laugh.

I thank Mom and she says, "Last time you went shopping with the Girls, you only bought a pair of boots. I figured you saved the rest of the money you got from your grandparents for Christmas shopping, and that deserves praise. That's why I got you this. Now you can buy a nice dress. I know you need one.

I wish I could have that little black dress I tried on at Tol-lan's the other day, but it's too late now, isn't it?

"Guys, I love you all so much!" I announce.

"When people say you can't buy children's love, they lie," says Mom, looking serious, "because you absolutely can. Big time! I love you, too, Mom and Dad."

We all laugh again.

During dinner, Mom tells my grandparents about my SAT scores. They're pleased and proud. We discuss school and college. We talk a lot and laugh a lot. But what makes it all so difficult is that Mom swore me to secrecy about the lump. She doesn't want them to worry unless there's a reason, so I have to pretend everything's just peachy, and that's kind of hard, considering that I think about it all the time.

As we are about to start on dessert, my friends arrive. I warn them to act as if they don't know anything about Mom. They nod in agreement and hand me the goodies they brought—apple cider, vanilla-and-chocolate-frosted cake with cream and nuts, and of course, gifts.

The girls gladly accept Mom's invitation to join us at the table (dessert is the *Fab Five's* greatest weakness). I put the cake and apple cider on the table and take the gifts to my room.

We spend another hour on pigging out and small talk, and then my grandparents leave. The girls help clear the table. Then, after thanking Mom, we take the rest of the cake and apple cider, pick up five champagne glasses, and go to my room.

"A menorah and a Christmas tree," Liza says. "What a charming family tradition. How cute is that? Well, Happy Chanumas!" she exclaims as we raise our glasses.

"Why are you so blue, Vicky?" Jackie asks. "Come on, give us a big smile!"

"Someone said," says Alex, "a smile is contagious; be a carrier."

"How come you don't know who said that?" I ask. "I can't believe it!"

"I don't. So sue me," she replies. "That's not the point. Why are you so gloomy?"

"You didn't get what you wanted from your mother and grandparents?" Chloe asks.

"No, they did good." I show them the gift certificates. "A month ago I would have been thrilled, but now . . . this year I don't even care. I just want to stay in bed and never get up."

"Is this major depression or annual winter hibernation?" asks Liza, giggling.

"You've never been that scroogy during the holidays," Alex says. "Is this a new development?"

"That would be so funny, if it weren't so sad," I mutter. "Don't you know how I feel?"

"Sorry, Vicky," Liza says and hugs me. "Of course, we know. That's why we're trying to cheer you up."

"Poor Vicky," Chloe sympathizes. "Are you worried about your mom?"

"You think?"

How could she even ask that question?

"I can appreciate that you're concerned, but you shouldn't worry in advance," says Jackie . "You don't even know what she has or if she has anything at all."

"I know you're right. I shouldn't worry ahead of time," I say softly, "but every time I think about it, I can't help it but imagine the worst. I see Mom going through this ordeal . . . you know . . . chemotherapy and stuff, and it makes me sick to my stomach."

"You've got to chill," Alex tells me firmly. "Your mother is going through this I-hope-it-is-not-cancer period because she's got a reason, but you're going through this what-if-she-has-cancer-and-dies thing *without* a reason."

"Alex is right, Vicky," says Chloe. "I'm sure everything will be fine."

"I wish I had your optimism," I say.

"Maybe that's your problem," says Alex. "You're too negative. You're a typical pessimist. You should always be optimistic."

Here we go again. You should always have positive attitude.

"As Colin Powell said," she continues proudly, "perpetual optimism is a force multiplier."

"Alex, please stop quoting," I snap, "and please don't tell me to be optimistic. I try. I really do. Over and over. Again and again. But what good does it do me? It's been one bad thing after another. First, Mom loses her job; then there's that thing with Dad's parents; and now this. It's like having a dark cloud or a fog hanging over me; it's like an endless black stripe invading my life. I sense that there's no light in the end of *my* tunnel."

I feel the tears filling up my eyes. My four best friends try their best to console me. I'm so lucky to have them.

"Vicky, it happens sometimes," Jackie says. "Black stripe isn't endless. It will pass." She strokes my shoulder and adds, "It will get better, you'll see."

"Problems should be solved as they come, not all at once," Liza adds.

"If you can't let go of the situation, sooner or later the situation will let go of you," Alex claims.

Is she kidding me? Is it her expression or is she quoting someone else again?

"Better a horrible end than horror without an end," Chloe proclaims.

"Is that supposed to be black humor or something?" I ask, shocked. "It would be very amusing if it weren't so pathetic."

"I'm sorry," Chloe cries and makes her *abused child* face again. "I meant well."

We all look at her in astonishment and Alex says, "Chloe, we know you're trying to help, and we love you for that, but please don't. Believe me, you're *not* helping."

"Oh, yeah? You wanna bet?" Chloe asks, squinting. "Maybe I actually know exactly how to make Vicky feel better."

We all look at her, then glance over to each other, and then give Chloe another long stare.

"Well," Alex interrupts the silence. "Start talking. We're waiting."

"Okay, listen to this," Chloe starts, excited. "Last night, at the movies, Ted and I met you-know-who. He was with Amber and her brother. He asked about you, Vicky. He's got it sooo bad for you! Ted says Nick's in love with you. He says that, and I quote," she makes a quote gesture with her index and middle fingers of each hand, "every time he sees you, he feels you attracting him like a magnet."

Wow! He told me that he likes me, but in love with me? I attract him like a magnet?

"Well, if that doesn't get your heart beating faster, you might need to check with a cardiologist," Jackie states.

"And if that doesn't go into your brain, you'd better have your head examined by a neurologist," Liza adds. "Don't you want to feel the difference between looking into his eyes and falling into his arms?"

"Cut it out, Liza!" I shout. "Why are you doing this? I'm trying to be strong, but you're making it so much more difficult." She just doesn't know when to stop. "Stop torturing me!"

"Sorry, but there's a difference between strong and head-strong. And you, dumb ass, are pig-headed." It seems that Liza's as mad at me as I am with her. "Don't you see that I'm just trying to wake you up? You can have it so good, so why are you sabotaging yourself? You can insist on trying to prove that you can do without Nick; you can scream your lungs out till you're blue in the face; you can even die celibate, but you can't deny the obvious: you want him as much as he wants you."

"Listen, Vicky," Jackie starts. "It's your prerogative to have a great guy who loves you and wants to be with you. Why don't you use that prerogative?" She stares at me for a moment and then continues, "Nick's drop-dead gorgeous, but that's not all he is. There's so much more to him. He's so much more than just a pretty face—"

"And hair . . . and eyes . . . and lips," Liza cuts in, "and chin . . . and broad shoulders . . . and pecs . . . and abs . . . and that cute, firm butt . . . Ooh! I'm getting hot again."

"Shush!" I moan. "You're a sick bitch! I've always suspected that you have a sadistic streak in you. You've just confirmed it."

Is it the goal of her life to make me suffer?

"Vicky, chill," Jackie intervenes. "You said yourself that when Nick professed his feelings to you and asked for a chance, you were tempted. You kissed him back, didn't you? You acted on impulse, right? So do it again. Act on impulse. Don't think, just let go."

"But I don't want to let go!" I snap. "I need to deal with it. Sometimes you just have to ignore even a well-intended impulse or temptation because it might be destructive if you act on it and might bring you disappointment and grief." I pause for a moment. "I explained to you: I don't want to be under the scrutiny of those sanctimonious bitches. Well, anyway, I've decided that it's better this way. Right now I don't have the strength or the energy for all this shit. My only concern is Mom. Nick is the furthest thing from my mind right now."

"You're such a good liar, it's scary. Scary-good," Chloe suddenly gives her input. "*It's* scary-good, or *you're* scary-good. I'm not sure which." She shrugs, shakes her head, and goes on, "Nick is a typical leading man, and if you're not smart, he'll be the leading man in someone else's movie. Think about it."

Since when did she become so wise?

"Well put, Chloe. I couldn't have said it better myself," I react. "As a writer though, I would say he might be a hero, but not of my novel. I'm totally aware that it's going to be too late if I change my mind later, but I can't help it. That's how I feel right now."

"Right now you make the most beautiful non-couple. Just contemplate the idea of becoming an item, okay?" Jackie asks softly.

"Seriously!" I snap. "If you want to make me feel better, let's not mention you-know-who anymore."

I look at one girl at a time, and every one of them, except Alex, nods in agreement. I realize that Alex hasn't said a word during this entire conversation about Nick.

"Vicky's right," Alex changes the subject. "It seems that we all forgot the purpose of our visit. I think that if we start doing what we came here to do, *that* will definitely make her feel better and cheer her up."

"Right!" Chloe exclaims. "The gifts!"

"Well, Vicky, do you think you have the strength and energy for that?" Jackie jokes.

"Piece of cake," I reply, laughing. I feel better already. "Who goes first?"

"I will," Alex responds. "And speaking of cake—"

She points at the cake they brought.

"Later. Gifts first," Jackie interrupts, "and since my bag is the smallest, I'll go first."

She puts her bag in the middle and takes the gifts out. They're all thin and flat, but beautifully wrapped and tied with a satin ribbon, and each has a little name card on it.

Chloe unwraps hers first. It's a DVD—*The Sisterhood of the Traveling Pants*. It's about four friends, just like us, who are always there for each other. If one's in trouble, the other three drop everything and rush to be with her. Chloe loves the book and the movie. She says that when she watched it, she thought about us and our friendship, so she's ecstatic.

"I thought you might want to watch it more often if you owned it," Jackie says.

Alex gets a *Now and Then* DVD. It's also about four friends who promise each other one summer that if and when one of them needs the other three, they'll return, no matter what. They reunite in twenty years. We've rented that movie many times, and we all love it, especially Alex. She says it's one of the best movies ever made. Now she owns it.

"We can watch it together now any time we want, along with Chloe's," says Jackie. "Liza, you go next."

Liza unwraps her present, and we see a book. It's called *The Guide For Shopaholics: How to Control Yourself Without Going Crazy*. It's humor, and every chapter is someone else's experience. We all laugh hysterically, and Liza just shrugs, meaning, *I know I need it.*

"It's hilarious," Jackie says. "There's a sequel in the works. It's called *Shopaholics Anonymous*. I'm just kidding. No offense."

We giggle again. *It feels great for a change.*

"None taken," Liza says. "I know, I know. The hint is right on the money, but . . ."

Finally, I unwrap my square little box. It's a CD. I can't believe it! It's *Mystery Lady: Songs of Billie Holiday*, performed by Etta James. Again, she's right on the money.

"I thought both you and your mother might enjoy it," says Jackie.

After we all thank her, she sighs heavily and says, "I know, guys, it's not much, but that's all I could afford."

We all tell her that she's crazy, that we love the presents, that it's the thought that counts, and in her case, there was a lot of thought put into it. Most of all, her gifts all came from the heart.

"I'm next! I'm next!" Chloe yells.

How can you say no to that?

Chloe can hardly pick up her huge bag. Inside are four identical, flat, and quite big packages, beautifully wrapped in different paper. Each package is adorned with a handmade satin flower. We all unwrap them at the same time. They're sketches of us! Every one of us gets a sketch of herself in a beautiful, hand-crafted wooden frame. Wow!

"Chloe, you're a real artist!" I exclaim, and the others agree. We're flabbergasted!

"I didn't make the frames, though, just the sketches," Chloe says seriously.

"No kidding! Of course, we understand," Alex says, imitating Chloe's tone of voice and mimicking her face expression.

I imagine those frames cost a small fortune.

Alex goes next. She takes her bags (she and Liza have two bags each) and starts taking out huge packages, strangely shaped. We unwrap them. All of us get identical baskets of body stuff, but in different aromas. Each basket contains a bubble bath, a shower gel, a bar of soap, after-shower body splash, body lotion, a scented candle, and an aromatherapy oil.

"This stuff relaxes and soothes you," Alex claims. "I think we all need it now."

We all agree and thank her. I notice that Liza doesn't volunteer to claim the next round, so I decide to take it instead.

"I'm next," I announce.

I hand the girls their presents all at once and wait for their reaction. They unwrap the gifts and express their gratitude by hugging and kissing me. They can't believe I paid attention and got all of them just what they needed and wanted.

Finally, it's Liza's turn. It was her choice to go last, and I know why. I'm sure that her presents are the most expensive. She knew that if she presented first, anybody else's gifts would pale in comparison. *How clever and considerate is she?*

Chloe, of course, is the first one to open her gift. It's a leather portfolio.

"For your sketches," Liza declares, "so go ahead, sketch away, knock yourself out."

After Chloe stops screaming, expressing her delight, and jumping up and down in ecstasy because she has a new art set and a new portfolio, Liza tells Alex to open her gift.

Alex does. It's a purse from Coach! It scares me even to think of how much it might have cost. No wonder Alex is so pleased.

"And now, Vicky and Jackie, open yours at the same time," Liza demands.

Jackie and I glance at each other and do what Liza asks. We're both stunned! Inside my box I see . . . the notorious little black dress! As for Jackie, not only does she get the infamous red sweater, but the whole enchilada: a matching set, including a hat, a scarf and gloves! (Just like my grandparents gave me on Thanksgiving.)

We're speechless!

Finally, I regain my composure and ask, "How did you manage that . . . unless . . . *you* were the one who bought it? That's when you went back to supposedly say hi to some people . . ."

I say it more to myself than to her.

"Yeah, just before you changed your mind and ran back to get it, so they told you the dress was already sold."

"You mean you knew all along?" I exclaim.

"I totally did. As soon as I saw Jackie and you wearing those things, I knew they should belong to you. And as soon as you decided not to buy them, I knew exactly what to give you for Christmas. So I went back and told the sales girl to put them away for me. I picked them up the next day."

"But Liza, how can we accept them?" Jackie starts. "They're so expensive."

"Easily," Liza claims. "Daddy won't even notice. Besides, I get a family discount."

"Well," I start, "you shouldn't have." Everybody stares at me in disbelief. "But I'm glad you did," I add, and we all laugh.

I call Mom in to look at the presents. She loves them all.

She snaps a picture of the five of us with my digital camera and announces, "It's a great picture."

We all agree.

"I'm so happy!" Chloe exclaims suddenly after Mom leaves the room. "To be here today, with you."

Sweet little Chloe. It doesn't take much to please her and to make her happy.

"What do you suppose happiness is?" Alex asks with a dreamy look in her eyes.

"I think I know," I respond. "It's when there's no pain—physical or emotional."

My four best friends look at me for a long time, and then Jackie breaks the silence.

"You'll be happy soon, Vicky. You'll see," she says quietly, patting my back.

"Sweetie, turn on the CD player, please," I ask Chloe, sitting next to the entertainment center. "Let's all be happy today."

My eyes are wet. I'm waiting for the music, but there's no sound coming out.

"Chloe?" we all look at her inquisitively.

"I'm trying!" she cries. "I can't find the button."

"Chloe, are you technologically challenged?" Liza asks sarcastically.

"No, I think I'm mentally challenged," Chloe snaps at her.

I go to the player and turn it on.

Then I say to Liza, "Look who's talking! Domestically disabled. You're not even able to put an egg in water to boil it. You'll burn yourself."

"Are you kidding?" Alex asks. "She can't even boil *water* for tea."

"And what do you call yourselves?" Liza asks. "What about your obsession with control, lectures, and quotations that annoy everyone, Alex?"

"Annoyingly Obsessive," I answer for Alex, "and I'm Cynically Hopeful, as you know."

Then the four of us turn to face Jackie. We're trying to think of something that we can call her, but can't come up with anything.

"Shamelessly Perfect," I suddenly announce.

Jackie insists that nobody's perfect, but everyone accepts what I call her.

"Wow!" Alex exclaims. "Don't we make a nice group? Technologically Challenged, Domestically Disabled, Annoyingly Obsessive, Cynically Hopeful, and Shamelessly Perfect. We should call ourselves the *Bizarre Five* instead of the *Fab Five*."

"Bizarre or not, we love each other anyway," I say. "Thanks, guys. I feel so much better with you here."

I'm all choked up, my eyes teary, my chin quivering. I'm overwhelmed with emotion.

"It should always be like this," Chloe proclaims. "Let's do it every year, no matter what."

"She's right," Alex states. "Let's make a pact. From now on, no matter where we are and what we do, every year during Chanumas we find at least one day when we drop everything and meet, and be there *with* each other and *for* each other."

"Even when we're married, with kids," Liza adds.

"No matter what. Always," states Jackie.

"Agreed," Chloe and I say in unison.

"Do you know what we need?" Chloe asks. "We need a song. *Our* song."

"Right," Liza supports her. "Something that only *we* can know and sing when we meet."

"It should be about us, our friendship," says Alex, "and it should be happy."

"Yet a little sad at the same time," Jackie adds.

"Blues!" I, the jazz lover, exclaim. "We'll call it 'The Chanumas Blues.' Wait!"

Right away I mentally sing "Summer Time." Again, and again. It's stuck in my head, but then suddenly a new melody, in a similar rhythm, begins to emerge as I ad-lib it, gliding through the notes in my head. Soon, I hum the theme to the girls. They love it.

Now we need lyrics. Well . . . Okay . . . Umm . . . Let's see . . . It's not coming to me!

"Well," Alex says, looking at me. "How long should we sit here in silence?"

"I don't know," I reply. "I think I have a mental block or something. Nothing comes to mind, but you can go ahead and speak. I don't mind. Just ignore me."

"Writer's block, you mean," Jackie says.

"Whatever," I say. "I think I have both. Shh!"

I sit there for a awhile, totally useless, but suddenly I remember the DVDs and what we talked about, and the words just start coming. It goes like this:

> *Wherever I am, whatever I do,*
> *You'll call for me, I'll come to you.*
> *All for one, and one for all,*
> *Together forever—that's our goal.*
> *We'll travel through life hand in hand.*
> *Alone we fall, united we stand.*
> *No matter what happens, we'll call it a truce.*
> *Chanumas, Chanumas, Chanumas Blues.*

"Okay, listen to this," I start. "We don't have the music, so clap you hands, or better yet, snap your fingers—it's blues, after all."

I sing for them, snapping my fingers, and they snap along.

"What can I say?" Alex says when I finish singing. "It's—"

"Tacky?" I ask, grimacing.

"No, it's not tacky. Let's just say it's not the greatest literature ever written."

"Well, what do you want from me? I'm a writer, not a poet, and it was a kind of spontaneous, spur-of-the-moment sort of thing. I improvised, okay? The tune is good, though, isn't it?" I defend myself. "Who am I, the Gershwin brothers?"

"Well, I, personally, like it," states Jackie.

"Me, too," Liza claims, "and didn't we say it's for our ears only?"

"I love it, Vicky," Chloe declares. "Let's all sing it together."

"Thanks, guys," I say. "Let's do it."

We sing the song several times until it's stuck in our heads and everybody remembers the melody and lyrics.

"Now when we meet, we can have a profoundly poignant reunion," Alex announces.

"What kind of reunion?" Chloe wants to know. "Alex, can't you speak like normal people?"

We all chuckle. *Good point.*

"She means emotional, moving," I clarify.

"I'm already moved," Chloe says. "Let's have a toast."

"Liza, pour the cider, and let's have cake already, for crying out loud!" Alex exclaims.

When we hold up our glasses, filled with apple cider, I say, "To you guys. To all of us. To our love and friendship. To always being together. And to our families. Let us all be healthy and live long and happy lives."

PART III

Life As We Live It

"You have brains in your head; you have feet in your shoes.
You can steer yourself any direction you chose."

—Dr. Seuss

To Be, or Not To Be? What a Question!

"It's not that I'm afraid to die, I just don't want to be there when it happens."

—Woody Allen

Happy life or not, we don't want it to end. We all wish we could live forever. And if you don't, there's something seriously wrong with you. When people tell you they're not afraid of dying, don't believe them: it's a lie. It's just that we tend to think that tragic things don't happen to us; they happen to other people—and we always wish we're not there when death comes.

I once saw a movie when I was younger (I don't remember the title), and there was a scene at the funeral where they were lowering the coffin down into the grave.

People looked very sad and some even cried, but then one old lady suddenly said, "Life stinks, and then you die."

I remember thinking then how unfair it was—two bad things happen at once. It should be: *Life stinks, but then you live,* or *Life is wonderful, but then you die.*

So when I got older and heard people say, "Life's a bitch, and then you die," or "Life's a bitch, but then you don't die," I tried to make sense out of it. By that time I was already deep into my analytical phase. So after thorough analysis, I came to a conclusion: if life is wonderful, you want to live forever, but if life stinks, why would you want to go on? I honestly saw logic in it. But later, when I tried to put myself in the shoes of someone whose life was a mess, I realized that no matter how bad life was, I still wouldn't want to die. So, truth be told, I want to live, no matter what.

In the beginning of *Annie Hall*, there's a monologue by Woody Allen. He tells a story about two elderly women at a Catskill resort.

One says, "The food in this place is terrible."

The other woman adds, "I know, and such small portions."

Then Woody says, "That's how I feel about life—full of loneliness, and misery, and suffering, and unhappiness, and it's all over much too soon."

That's how we all feel about life. We complain and whine, we get annoyed and frustrated, we get angry and bitter, but we still want to live. How often have I said that I hate my so-called life, that I want to vanish, disappear from the face of the earth? How many times have I said that I wish I was dead? But the truth is: I don't mean it. I say it because I'm mad at the moment. Of course, I don't want my life to be over.

William Shakespeare asked one of the most infamous questions through one of his most notorious characters, Prince Hamlet, who said, "To be, or not to be: that is the question." The answer is . . . to *be*, because being means living.

That's deep, I decide as I write all of these thoughts in my journal.

*   *   *

I think about Mom all the time. It's hard to imagine what she's been going through. It's been over a month since she had a mammogram. The report showed something out of the ordinary—but they couldn't make out exactly what it was. They recommended a sonogram to see whether the thing was a cyst or a solid mass.

The sonogram identified a lump, so an MRI was recommended to detect whether it was benign or malignant. The MRI results were inconclusive, so Mom needed to have a breast biopsy—a procedure where they remove a piece of skin tissue or cells from a suspicious mass to see if it's cancer.

*   *   *

In school everything's the same. Classes are boring. We can't wait to get out and go to the Indulgence Café or to someone's house to hang out and, in the big picture, to go to New York and start our new, exciting adult lives.

Jackie and Jamie talk on the telephone ten times a day. They don't care about going over their limit of minutes. They're in love, and people in love don't watch time. Jamie promised to visit one weekend, and Jackie can't wait to see him and talk more in person.

Liza is truly, madly, deeply in love with Craig, and a) is excited about her upcoming eighteenth birthday because she officially becomes an adult, and b) dreads it because she knows in her mind and feels in her gut that moving to the next level is inevitable.

Chloe went out with Ted a few more times. Though she doesn't admit it, we all suspect that they've already made a transition to third base. She doesn't volunteer the information, and we don't nag. We saw Ted talking to Heather, and we didn't like that.

Alex and I still don't have boyfriends. For me the timing is wrong. As for Alex, I suspect that guys are scared to approach her. I also can't help but suspect that the object of my affection might be an object of her affection as well—and I like that fact even less.

I see Nick less and less in the company of Heather and Tiffany, and I definitely like *that* fact a lot. There's nothing between us, though, except a few friendly hand wavings, head nods and, of course, constant dreamy and lustful looks at each other.

Tiffany, Heather, and some other members of the J & J club continue to bully and terrorize Norman Fixx, but do their mocking quietly, without making a big deal out of it. Nobody wants to be called to the principal's office and get detention, or even a suspension. Everybody wants a clean record.

*   *   *

Time flies! It's already the middle of March. The weather is wonderful. It's still a little cool outside, but it's sunny and much warmer than it was just a week ago—but guess what? I still manage to catch the flu and get sick! It doesn't go away, so it's blown into a week-long-stay-at-home sabbatical. It's bad, but I'm not distressed—I need some time alone.

The girls call every day, but I tell them not to visit because I'm contagious, so they provide all my homework assignments via email, and school news briefs over the telephone.

On Friday, Liza calls and announces, "I want to come over. I miss you so much, and besides, I'm sure you're no longer contagious."

I think she wants to tell me something.

"Don't!" I exclaim. "Let's give it a few more days. I don't want you to get sick as well. I don't have a fever anymore and feel much better, so I'll probably be back in school on Monday. Can't you wait till then?" I hear hesitation. "Okay. What is it? Spill!"

"Listen, Vicky," she starts after a long pause. "I'm going to tell you something about Chloe and Ted, but if Chloe decides to tell you this herself, pretend it's the first time you're hearing it. I don't want her to get pissed at me because, as you say, it's her tale to tell, not mine. You have to promise, okay?"

"Okay, I got it," I reply, curious, but concerned. "I promise. So what happened?"

"There's a rumor going around that Ted slept with Heather again. He says it's not true, but Chloe doesn't believe him. I told her to forget about him because *once a man-whore, always a man-whore.*"

Later, Jackie and Alex call, respectively, and give me the same news. They also make me promise not to tell Chloe I heard it from them. I promise, just like I promised Liza. Finally, Chloe calls and lays it on me.

"I should've known! As soon as I saw that he had started talking to that bitch again, I should've known."

I hear her sniffle.

"Chloe, are you crying?" I ask, feeling bad for her. "Stop it. No man's worth it!"

"He's a man-whore!" she declares, sniffing and then exhaling.

"He's a man. Period," I elaborate. "Just a man, and that's what men do. But maybe it's not true. What if it's just a rumor?"

"What do you mean, it's not true? It's totally true! Everybody's talking about it. People saw them leave together yesterday," she assures me, sounding bitter.

"It doesn't mean anything, Chloe," I try to calm her down. "Did you talk to him?"

"Yeah, I did. He tried to deny it, of course. He said there's only one girl for him, and that's me. Then he gave me a kiss, but I stiffened, as though he was kissing a total stranger, or a statue." She stops for a moment and then proclaims, "My life is over!"

"No, it's not!" I exclaim. "Come on, Chloe, it's probably just a rumor, but even if it *is* true, your life is far from over. There'll be a hundred, no, a thousand Teds in your life. Trust me."

"Oh, by the way," she suddenly changes the subject, "they were on Norman's back again today. Heather and Tiffany, I mean, and a couple guys from Jordan's team. We yelled at them to stop, and Nick let them have it. He told them that he didn't want to be friends with them anymore. Even Ted was on his side and said enough is enough. Poor Norman, he just can't stand up for himself at all."

As usual, she just says it all in a patter, without even stopping to catch her breath.

"What?" I exclaim. "Why didn't anyone but you bother to mention it to me? I can't believe it! I think I've been home too long. I need to go back to school and pick a bone or two with those natural-born bitches and juvenile delinquents."

"No! Don't do it, Vicky!" Chloe yells. "You see, that's why the others didn't want you to know about it. They're afraid you'll do something drastic. They warned me not to say anything to you, but I did it anyway," she cries out. "You didn't hear this from me, okay?"

Aha! That's why they didn't tell me. They're scared I'll get into another fight.

"Don't worry, Chloe, I won't say anything—and I know exactly what to do," I assure her.

* * *

On Monday I feel healthy and renewed, so I go back to school. I'm not planning to get into another fight, but I have every intention of having a talk with my friends, Tina and Nick. We have to figure out what we can do together to protect Norman from the dregs of society. We need to stop the scum. They're poison, toxic waste that is contaminating our school. People like Norman are here to study and learn. They don't have time to be afraid of jerks.

"Can we talk during a lunch break?" I ask my friends. "It's about Norman."

"You know what happened on Friday?" Alex inquires. "Who squealed?"

"I've heard," I reply. "This meeting is important, long overdue, and can't wait."

I ask Tina to join us, not mentioning Norman, but I have a feeling she gets an idea.

Nick approaches me himself, saying, "I missed you. How do you feel?"

"Much better," I answer, smiling at him. "Thanks for asking."

We flirt for a while, and then I ask, "Are you available later, during lunch, to meet with me and a group of people for a little discussion?"

I hope he doesn't ask what it's all about. I don't feel like explaining now.

"Sure," he says, no questions asked.

I notice that Norman isn't in school today, and I think that's even better. Otherwise, he'd see us talking and might ask Tina what it's about, and she'd have to lie to him. *Yeah, it's definitely better this way,* I assure myself.

But our discussion never takes place and Norman will never have the chance to ask Tina any questions. Something happens, and our lives will never be the same—changed forever.

It all starts with an announcement during the first class, telling us that we all have to go to the gym. It's strange that a class has been interrupted in the middle, and why the gym? But everyone obliges and teachers lead their classes to the place indicated.

A voice from the loudspeaker asks us to sit down and wait for the principal to arrive. There's some commotion going on. People wonder what's up and why we're here.

"What do you suppose it's about?" Jackie asks quietly.

Alex, Liza and I just shrug.

"I have no idea," Chloe murmurs, "but I feel it's not good."

I hear a few whispers here and there, but other than that, we're pretty organized and do as we've been told: we settle down and patiently wait in silence.

Finally, our principal, Mr. Leighton, comes in, and by the look on his face, we can tell something terrible has happened. He just stands there for a long time, looking exhausted and crushed.

Eventually, he picks up the microphone, coughs to clear his throat, and says softly, his voice unstable, "Thank you all for coming and for being patient. Unfortunately, I have to be the carrier of very sad and distressing news. A terrible tragedy has happened. We've lost one of our students. Norman Fixx has died."

Mr. Leighton pauses for a moment and then, his hands shaking, takes his glasses off and rubs his eyes. He puts his glasses back on and then continues, "It shouldn't have happened. Norman's death was needless and pointless—and could've been prevented."

I hear word combinations like, "sad news . . . terrible tragedy . . . Norman Fixx . . . died . . . death was needless," but nothing makes sense. *What is he saying? It's a mistake! Norman's not dead! He can't be! No! I want this pounding in my head to stop.*

Then I hear a lot of ahs, ohs, and omigods, and people asking questions like, "How did he die?" or "Was he sick?" or "Was it an accident?"

My head is all messed up and I don't understand what's happening. *Is everybody insane?*

Principal Leighton looks around and says, "We have somebody here today who wants to speak to you about something very important."

He looks at someone in the first row, and then walks over and helps a woman to her feet. I get the shock of my life when I see her. She's tall and skinny, wears glasses, and . . . she's a female version, though much older, of Norman!

"This is Norman's mother," Mr. Leighton says. Then he turns to the woman, hands her the microphone, and adds, "Please, Mrs. Fixx, go ahead. You've got the floor."

Mrs. Fixx looks tired, but her voice is stable and loud when she speaks.

"You probably wonder how I can be here when I need to make arrangements to bury my son. I wonder myself, but I had to come. I had to see the people my son had to spend every day of his short life with. I'm strong. I can handle it. So I'm here. Norman, unfortunately, was not that strong, and that's why he's not with us today. He's dead. He took his own life because he couldn't go on living."

She stops for a moment to swallow the lump in her throat, but there are no tears in her eyes.

"Norman loved school, but I noticed that lately he wasn't eager to go there and always came home depressed. I should've known that something was terribly wrong, but I didn't want to pry and I thought he was just tired because he studied so hard."

She goes on about how on Friday Norman came home looking crushed, went straight to his room, and locked the door. He didn't come out for dinner that night. She couldn't sleep—maybe it was a premonition or something—and wanted to take a sleeping pill.

After realizing that her sleeping pills were missing, she ran to Norman's room. His door was locked, but she forced her way in, and that's when she found Norman. He was dead. Next to him was an empty pill container. He had taken all of them.

I mentally record everything I hear and it finally begins to sink in: Norman had committed suicide! I feel my stomach drop and my chest squeeze. *Norman Fixx killed himself!*

It's so quiet, it's scary. I look around and see many familiar faces, troubled, anxious, and disturbed, but no one dares to speak.

"Principal Leighton says that Norman's death was needless, pointless, and preventable," Mrs. Fixx continues. "I have to agree and disagree at the same time. Needless, preventable, yes, but pointless—no. Losing your only child is the biggest tragedy possible. Parents shouldn't outlive their children. There's a saying, *Everything happens for a reason.* And if something good *does* come out of it, it is making a *point* that my son's death was needless and could've been prevented."

She takes a deep breath, lets the air out, and goes on, "Norman was writing in his journal on the computer before he died. Normally, I'd never invaded his privacy by reading his personal thoughts, but it doesn't matter now, so I did, and I wish to god I had done it sooner. Sure, he would've been angry with me, but his life might've been saved.

'It's better to die on your feet than to live on your knees,' he wrote. At home he was on his feet, but in school he felt like he was always on his knees." She pauses for a moment and looks at the audience, her eyes wandering around the room. Then she clears her throat and starts again, "I found out that my son was subjected to severe mockery and scoffing. He was tormented daily by his schoolmates. Constant insults and humiliation by his fellow students—that's what he had to go through every day. On the night he ended his life, he made a very short entry in his journal. I think he meant for me to see it so I could understand what he was about to do.

'Napoleon Bonaparte said,' he wrote, 'Death is nothing, but to live defeated and inglorious is to die daily.' His last sentence was, 'I don't want to die daily anymore.' "

She finally stops. There's a long pause. It's still so quiet that I can hear people breathing.

Norman's mother slowly looks around the gym, her eyes darting from face to face, and then continues, "My son was a good and gentle boy who would never hurt a fly. His only fault was being brilliant and peaceful, so he couldn't stand up for himself. I don't want to blame anybody for Norman's death. The people who contributed to it will have to live with it on their conscience for the rest of their lives. If anything, I'm blaming myself for not seeing the signs and not preventing it from happening. I didn't come here to make accusations. I'm here today to make a point. I hope I've made it and got through to you. And I hope and pray to god that another mother won't have to lose a son or a daughter for the same reason I lost my Norman." She sighs heavily and adds, "By the way, I've already made the funeral arrangements. It's tomorrow. We don't have any relatives, just family friends, and Norman had only a few friends here in school. Whoever cared for my son and wants to attend his memorial service, you're welcome. I'll leave all the details with Mr. Leighton. Thank you all for listening."

Finally, she turns to face the principal and says, "Thank you for letting me do this."

Then she slowly walks out, accompanied by Mr. Leighton, who gestures for us to stay where we are. We do as we're told. Nobody moves or speaks. He returns shortly and goes through the same routine again: takes off his glasses, rubs his eyes, and puts his glasses back on.

Then, very slowly, he picks up the microphone and says, "Norman was a remarkable young man. He was the brightest and the most intelligent student I've ever known, and he had an outstanding personality. I'm sure he'll be sorely missed, but now we all need to deal with his death. There will be grief counseling available and a hot line you can call. It's for everyone who's lost a loved one—a relative or a friend. There also is a hot line for people like Norman, who need help if they're thinking of . . . ending their lives. You don't have to do it. You can get help. There are people who love you and don't want to lose you. I'll write all the numbers along with the funeral information on the board. And now, of course, you can all go home. Thank you."

He leaves, and after a long silence, some people begin to leave, but others stay and start talking.

Chloe speaks first.

"Omigod, omigod," she cries. "I can't believe it. Norman's dead."

"Why? Why did he do it?" I hear Jackie ask. "He should've talked to someone."

"Because of those bitches. That's why," Liza answers.

"They *are* bitches, but nevertheless, he shouldn't have done it. It was stupid and useless," smartass Alex states. "They're not worth it. How could he do it to his mom? Poor woman." She turns to me and asks, "Vicky, are you all right? You haven't said a word. Vicky, do you hear me?"

I hear her, but it sounds like an echo, mixed with a per-
sisting pounding in my head. I feel queasy. I feel sick to my
stomach. I don't want to talk to anyone. *Stupid? How can
she say that? Doesn't she understand?* Suddenly I realize that
there *is* one person I want to talk to, who *does* understand.

As soon as I think that, I see Tina standing next to me.
Her face looks pale and tired. She doesn't say anything, but
I know she wants to talk to me, too.

I wave my friends off and growl, "Later."

They look at each other, not sure what to do, but Jackie
gestures that they need to leave.

"Hi," Tina says as soon as the girls leave. "You don't look
so hot."

"Neither do you. By the way, I didn't see you earlier. I
thought you were out today."

"Actually, I came late, with . . . his mother," she explains.
"I found out on Saturday."

"I see," I murmur. "You were close to him. How are you
holding up?"

"I'm not going to cry, if that's what you mean," she replies,
her chin quivering. "I never cry. It's my iron-clad rule."

"Maybe you *should* cry. You'll feel better," I say, but do I
believe it myself?

"Why didn't he talk to me? We talked about everything.
I just don't understand why," Tina says, more to herself than
me.

Reality bites, I think to myself.

"He just snapped, I guess. Nobody's invulnerable, you
know. Maybe he felt embarrassed talking to you about it,
considering how he felt about you," I speculate, noticing that
we both refer to Norman as *he* or *him,* instead of calling him
by name.

"What do you mean?" she asks, looking confused.

"He liked you, I mean."

"What? I told you, we're just friends!" she exclaims and then corrects herself, "*Were* friends. He didn't like me *that* way. He liked you."

What? I'm flabbergasted! I'm shocked! *What the hell . . . shit! I need to close my mouth.*

"What are you talking about, Tina?" I ask. "Did he tell you that?"

"He didn't have to." She shrugs. "I know him better than I know myself. Knew, I mean. It'll take a long time to get used to the fact that he's gone."

She shakes her head and gulps.

"I had no idea he felt that way about me," I say, not looking at her. "Was it because I stood up for him the other day?"

I feel tears filling up my eyes so I move my jaw to stop them. I find it very hard to do.

"No, he always liked you." She pauses for a moment and then goes on, "You know, I feel responsible somehow. How could I not know, not notice the signs?"

"I was just thinking that same thing. I feel partially responsible for his death. Can you believe that today I was going to talk to all of you about doing something to stop those nothings from torturing him? Why didn't I do it sooner? Why wasn't I in school on Friday?"

I stop to catch my breath. *Why didn't I write about it?*

I breathe deeply for a moment or two and then shout, "I'm going to kill those worthless bastards! But not today. Today's about him, not them."

I swallow the lump in my throat. It's getting more and more difficult not to cry.

Suddenly, we hear some noise outside the gym. We look at each other and go see what this is about. There's a group of people gathering around, arguing. I see the residents of the

J & J club there and my four friends. They all yell at Heather for something she apparently did or said about Norman— and little Chloe's in the middle of it all.

"Norman was so much *taller* than you are," Chloe shouts. "And I don't mean your height, if you get my drift. It's a figure of speech, in case your air head doesn't get it."

"What did I say?" Heather asks with an innocent look on her face, like nothing had happened. "I'm just stating the fact that he had a humongous ego for a loser to compare himself to Napoleon. And to kill himself? Who does that? He lived as a freak and he died as a freak."

"My god, how nasty and mean is that? Do you get off on torturing people or something? Norman's dead because of you! And you're making fun of him?" Chloe screams. "You're evil, Heather. You're totally malicious in everything you touch, and you're not going to get away with it. I don't know when or how, but you *will* pay, you'll see." She clenches her teeth and proclaims, "An eye for an eye, a tooth for a tooth!"

Way to go, Chloe! I'd like to join in, but I'm not going to do it today.

"Spoken like a woman scorned," Heather says with a smirk, looking at Chloe and Ted.

"I'd like so much to wipe this smirk off your smug and disgusting face," Chloe screams.

"And I want so much to take a rope and tighten it up around her worthless, lying, sanctimonious neck," Ted adds and then goes after Heather, but Nick and Jordan stop him by grabbing and holding his arms.

"Everybody, stop!" Jackie, the diplomat, commands. "It's neither the time nor the place for fighting. We can't bring Norman back, so let's at least respect him enough not to do this today."

Chloe stops and others nod in agreement.

"Don't pretend like you all care. At least I'm being honest," Heather claims, standing there, still smug and spinning a keychain ring around her index finger.

"That's it! I'm so fed up with you!" Alex exclaims as she grabs the keychain. "I'm going to shove this down your throat."

"Go deeper," Liza adds. "Shove it down her esophagus."

"Why stop there? Go all the way. Through the empty space in her heartless chest. Right where a heart's supposed to be," a familiar voice says.

It's Brianna!

"Shut up, Brianna!" Heather yells. "Whose side are you on? Some friend you are!"

"Cut it out, Heather!" Brianna shouts back. "You're so full of it! I've wondered for a long time if you had a heart, considering how much pain you've caused people, and not just Norman. God knows I'm no angel myself, but at least I totally understand that. You set him off! You sent him over the edge, and we just looked on. I'll always regret not stopping you in time and not preventing Norman's death." She stops to breathe and then continues, "Chloe's right—you *are* evil and malicious. People are trying to have a normal conversation here, and you're acting like a heartless bitch. Nick was right to stop being your friend. Right now I don't want to be one, either, and if I have to choose between you and Nick, you lose. I'm sure that Ruby, Amber, and Bridget feel the same way."

She stops and glances over at the three girls she just named, and all nod in agreement.

"Who gives a shit? Traitors!" Heather exclaims. "I don't need friends like you, and I don't have to stand here and listen to this crap. Come on, Tiff, let's go."

"I'm not going anywhere with you anymore," another familiar voice says, a voice I hate.

It's Tiffany's voice! *I'll be damned!*

"Tiff? What are you saying?" Heather asks her partner in crime and shakes her head in disbelief. "You're supposed to be my best friend. We're the same, you and I."

"I know. Guys, we did a terrible thing, Heather and I," Tiffany says, ignoring her. "I don't know what to say to make all of you believe me, but I swear that I'm very sorry. I wish I could go back and make it up to Norman, but I can't, so I'll live with it for the rest of my life. I'll never forget what I've done."

Tell it to the jury.

She turns to face Heather and, as others look on in shock and astonishment, says, "You're wrong. We're not the same. I don't want to be anything like you."

"You should be so lucky!" Heather says and then, proudly lifting her chin, walks away.

God, I need some fresh air.

I can't stand it anymore. Another time I'd be happy about what was happening between Heather and Tiffany. I'd enjoy it so much, but not today. Today I just want to be alone, so I turn away and run outside.

Breathe . . . Breathe . . . Breathe . . .

My four friends, Tina, and Nick run after me, asking if I'm okay, but I don't answer. I don't want to see anyone right now. I need to take a refuge in silence. *I can't breathe.*

Everybody wants to take me home, but Nick insists that he should have the honor.

Suddenly it gets dark and gloomy. It looks exactly the way I feel. Almost immediately we hear the sound of a thunderstorm and see the lightning. The rain starts pouring. *It's like the earth and the sky are crying for Norman.*

We run to Nick's car. I follow him automatically and he helps me into the front seat, next to him. He starts the car and for a long time we ride in silence. Suddenly Nick pulls over, stops the car and shuts the engine off.

He takes my hand, and looking deep into my eyes, asks, "Vicky, are you all right? Would you like to talk?"

When I don't answer, he gently takes me by the shoulders and says, "Come here."

As I lean toward him and put my head on his chest, I start feeling protected and safe. Nick holds me tight, strokes my hair and murmurs words of comfort in my ear.

"Tell me how you feel," he says. "Talk to me. You're in shock, and I want to help you."

"It's the worst," I say.

Suddenly I trust him completely, so I start expressing everything I feel.

"My chest's so tight, like someone's squeezing it. And I feel something heavy inside, like a huge rock. It's like carrying a tremendous weight around—you want to drop it, but you can't." My throat feels dry, but I can't stop talking. "I have this lump in my throat and it's choking me. If I hold it in, I can't breathe, but if I let it out, I know that I'm not going to be able to stop crying. I feel helpless and lost. Please tell me what to do."

"Don't hold it in. Let it all out," he says—and that's when I break.

I start weeping so bad that tears dripping from my eyes and rolling down my cheeks and lips.

"Why didn't we do anything to stop them from hurting Norman? Why didn't we do anything to help him? He was a person. A real, live person. He had feelings, and they got hurt. He had a heart, and it got broken. And now he's dead."

I let it all out, just like Nick said I should, and my chest begins to feel lighter and I start to breathe easier.

"You'll feel better now," Nick says when I stop sobbing, and wipes the tears off my face with his handkerchief. "Shh!" he says, stroking my hair, cheeks, chin, lips.

Then he takes my head in his hands and starts kissing me, gently at first, but then his kisses become more persistent, more passionate. I kiss him back. *What am I doing?* I can't stop. My head is spinning, my heart's pounding. *How can I feel so bad and so good at the same time?*

"I love you, Vicky," Nick whispers. "I really do."

"I love you, too," I whisper back and break away.

I suddenly remember that Mom's doctor should call today or tomorrow with the biopsy results. I feel shivers going through my body.

Mom! What if she's got cancer? What if she dies? Omigod! I can't handle so much. Norman, Mom . . .

"What?" Nick asks, confused. "Did I do anything wrong?"

"No, no. You didn't do anything. It's me. I can't explain now," I blubber. "I'll tell you later, I promise, but now I need to go home. Please take me home."

"Sure," Nick says, looking disappointed. "Whatever you say."

*   *   *

Mom's in the kitchen, cooking. She's surprised to see me home so early.

"Did the doctor call?" I ask.

"Not yet," she answers. "Honey, what's wrong? You look like something—"

"Norman's dead," I interrupt.

Then I sit down and tell her everything. It feels better talking about it, especially to Nick and to Mom.

"Mom?"

"Mmm?"

"I'm devastated about Norman, but I can't help thinking, was his life really so bad that he couldn't go on living anymore? Would it make a difference if people who cared about him, like his mom, and Tina and I, paid more attention to him and showed him that he mattered?"

Then I think, *Would he have done it anyway if he had positive attitude?*

"Nobody could answer those questions except Norman," Mom responds.

"How does it work, Mom? Who's in charge of people's lives?" I ask. "I mean, who controls who should live and who should die?"

"Well," Mom says, slowly sitting beside me. "Sometimes we do, like in Norman's case, and sometimes it's out of our hands and we have no control over it. Then it's not up to us; it's up to fate."

"Like in your case?"

"Exactly," she replies, and we both look at the telephone, but it doesn't ring.

*   *   *

The girls call, all four of them. They want to know why I ran off like I did and what's happening to me right now. I don't feel like talking or explaining, so I make some excuse and find out when they'll pick me up tomorrow for the memorial service.

Then Nick calls.

"I got your number from the phone book," he says. "I hope it's okay. I wanted to know how you were. I'm worried about you."

Awww . . . How nice.

"It's fine," I say, touched. "I'm better now, thanks to you."

"Would you like to go together to the funeral tomorrow? I can pick you up."

"No, thanks. I'm going with my friends, but thanks for asking. And thanks for calling."

I hang up. Despite everything that's been happening, it feels really great that he cares.

In my room I try everything—reading, listening to music, even watching TV, but nothing helps. I can't stop thinking about Norman's death and Mom's test results. I take my journal and start writing. It helps.

It's already late at night. I can't fall asleep for a long time. When I finally do, I have a dream, or rather a nightmare: I see Norman in the coffin, but when I come closer . . . it's not Norman. It's Mom! I scream, but there's no sound coming out of my mouth. I try to run away, but my feet won't move. I wake up in sweat, shaky, with chills going down my spine and my heart beating fast. I'm relieved that it's just a dream and that Mom isn't dead, but then I remember that Norman *is* dead, and it's very real. When I fall asleep again, I keep seeing the same dream, over and over again, so I get up and start pacing back and forth.

In the morning I feel sleepy and completely worn out.

*   *   *

There's a huge turnout at the funeral home. It seems as if the entire school is here for the memorial service. All the jocks, led by Jordan and Nick, are here, and even the *Jewels* (minus Heather) have found the time in their busy schedules to pay their respects.

The crowd gets bigger and bigger. *Where were they all when Norman was alive?*

Tina, who never talks to the right-siders, begs me to ask Tiffany and her gang to leave. I don't mind doing just that, so we go together over to them.

"Tiffany, you shouldn't have come," I say politely because it's neither the time nor the place to start a fight. "You don't belong here. So please take your sidekicks and leave."

"I can't blame you for saying that, Vicky," she says, "but please don't make us leave."

Mrs. Fixx hears us talking and says, "It's okay. Everyone who wants to say goodbye to my Norman is welcome to stay."

Then she wraps her arms around Tina and me and takes us aside.

She gives me a long stare and then asks, "You're Vicky, aren't you? I feel like I've known you for a long time."

"Yes, I am," I respond. "Nice to meet you, Mrs. Fixx. I only wish we could meet under different circumstances. What did you mean when you said you feel like you know me?"

"I read my son's diary, remember? He described you perfectly. You must be a wonderful person if Norman liked you so much, especially when you stood up for him like you did. He wrote about that day, and Tina told me about it. I want to thank you for that." She squeezes my hand and says as we approach my friends and I introduce them, "All of you girls, thanks for always being nice to my son."

She then takes Tina's hand and leads her away.

There's a eulogy delivered by a family friend, and then some left-siders remember nice things about Norman. It's the first time they're not afraid to speak up, and the first time nobody makes fun of them.

At the cemetery, when they lower the coffin into the freshly dug grave, I repeat in my head, *Life stinks, and then you die . . . Life stinks, and then you die . . . Life stinks, and then you die . . .*

Two bad things happened to Norman: he lived on his knees and died on his feet.

* * *

At home, I tell Mom about the memorial service, but all I can think about is the dream I had last night. Of course, I don't tell her about that.

"A life was lost," she says.

Yes, and Norman made his own decision how to dispose of it.

At that second, the telephone rings. We both freeze for a moment, then Mom slowly gets up, walks to the telephone, and answers it.

It's her doctor, but I can't make anything out of their conversation by looking at her expression.

Mom hangs up the telephone and sits down. *This is the longest pause in my life.* I see tears in her eyes and my heart stops.

She brushes the tears away and quietly says, "It's benign. I don't have cancer."

Yes! Thank goodness fate made a decision in Mom's favor.

"Yes!" I exclaim, making a fist and jumping up and down.

Then I hug Mom and we both start crying—tears of joy for Mom and tears of sorrow for Norman.

"I wish we could celebrate," I say, "but I don't feel like celebrating today. Today is . . . Mom, you *do* understand, don't you?"

"Sure, I do. We have plenty of time, and Victoria, please don't mention anything to your grandparents. About me, I mean. What they don't know won't hurt them."

"Okay, Mom. I won't say anything," I assure her and go to my room.

"And Victoria, remember: what doesn't kill us, makes us stronger."

I call my friends and tell them the good news. They're all happy for Mom and me, and it makes what happened to Norman a little easier to deal with. At least now it's the *only* thing I need to deal with.

Tonight I have the same dream I had last night, but instead of seeing Mom's face, I see a faceless old man in a coffin. *Who is it?* I wake up, scared and confused.

Suddenly I think of something, and I get an idea. Why not share all of my thoughts about living and dying with others in my editorial for this issue of our newspaper? I won't mention Mom, of course, but I have to write about Norman's death. It's a story that must be told. As his mother said: his death was needless, but it shouldn't be pointless. So I get up and turn my computer on.

I call my article "Whose Fault Is It Anyway?" I take my journal and copy some stuff from there, and then go on writing.

I write about Norman and what kind of person and student he was. Then I write:

Victor Hugo said, "To die is nothing, but it is terrible not to live." Nobody's invincible, and there is a limit to how much a person can take. Norman reached that limit, but he didn't have to die.

They say that everything happens for a reason. What was the reason for Norman's death? I think it showed us that we need to appreciate people more. It's so often that we don't treasure what we have, and after we lose it, we regret it and cry for it. We didn't appreciate Norman. He didn't feel loved or treasured enough to live.

Who's to decide who lives and who dies? Sometimes we do, ourselves, and sometimes it's up to fate. Norman decided for himself that he didn't want to go on living.

Norman Fixx had a good and kind heart. He never hurt anyone. He had a brilliant mind and a bright future. But most of all, he had his whole life ahead of him. Unfortunately, he decided to end it. Norman, the genius, could become the greatest scientist who ever lived. Norman, the man, could become a great husband and the best father in the world.

A mind is a terrible thing to waste, but to waste a life is a crime. Did Norman commit a crime by ending his life? Or the people who made his life unbearable and unworthy of continuing? Or maybe those who didn't do anything to stop them are guilty of this crime? Perhaps people that didn't see the signs of a preventable tragedy are responsible. Whose fault is it, anyway, that Norman is no longer with us? That's something for him to know and for us to think about.

There's an old saying, What goes around comes around. Let's start with being nice to one another. Treating people with respect doesn't cost a thing; showing that you care is priceless. So let's be more patient, more tolerant, and more considerate of each other's feelings. We need more eye contact, more handshakes, and most of all, more smiles. We'll get back what we give.

Remember: behaving nicely doesn't cost a thing; being human—priceless.

Samahria Lyte Kaufman, who has helped so many people with the power of love, said, "Person to person, moment by moment, as we love, we change the world."

Perhaps we can't change or save the entire world, but if each of us changes or saves just one life by being kind, thoughtful, and open-minded, we can make the world a better place.

*   *   *

Someone enlarges my article and puts it on a wall in the hallway so everybody can read it. I get compliments on how good it is, and how touched people are by it.

"You get rave reviews from us," Jackie says, and the others confirm it. "It's so powerful."

Brianna and Tina think my editorial is a real tribute to Norman, and it feels good.

I see Nick with Jordan and Ted, and they all tell me how much they liked the article.

"It makes a strong point and makes people think," Nick says. "I think it's the strongest piece you've ever written."

That means a lot to me.

Later, I pass Heather, standing by the wall, reading. She's all alone. When she sees me, she starts reading out loud the last lines of the article, "By being kind, thoughtful and open-minded, we can make the world a better place." Then she turns to face me, all smug and mighty, and with a disgusting smirk on her face, says sarcastically, "Lucky world. It's in good hands." She laughs and goes on, "I don't need you to counsel me on how to feel about people and to teach me how to treat them."

"Listen, Heather," I tell her quietly. "I'm not going to be dancing the same dance to the same tune with you. I just wish you could think long and hard about what's in that article, and I wish you could truly understand what it's about. Otherwise, I feel very sorry for you. What if people start thinking that *your* life is worthless? You're so screwed then."

With those words I leave her standing there, all alone.

I don't feel like fighting with Heather anymore. As I walk away, I remember something I heard a long time ago: *Fighting fire with fire only gets you ashes.* That's what my grandfather meant when he was talking about revenge. Then

I remember what Alex said about letting go of the past, and finally, I think of my own words about not appreciating what we have and crying when we lose it, and I know immediately what I need to do.

As soon as I walk into my living room that afternoon, I go straight to the lamp table, where the phone book is, and dial the number I wrote on its cover several months ago.

Where There's Smoke, There's No Fire

*"The here and now is all we have, and
if we play it right it's all we'll need."*

—Ann Richards

Amelia answers the phone and recognizes my voice right away. She doesn't sound surprised at all, like she knew I would call, so I tell her that I decided to meet with her and her husband, after all. She sounds happy and nervous at the same time.

"I'm so glad you changed your mind," she says. "I was hoping you would."

I ask for directions to their house on Long Island, but she wouldn't hear of it and says that it's hard to find the first time. She insists on picking me up at our house.

"How does next weekend sound?" Amelia asks. "I understand if you wouldn't want me to come in because it would make your mother uncomfortable, but I don't mind waiting for you outside."

I remember that Mom mentioned going to New York next Friday to spend the weekend with Nora Brickman and reply, "That sounds fine. Mom won't be home, so you may even come inside."

Suddenly, I think that I *do* want Amelia to see our house, our home, and realize what a wonderful and talented woman her son married. Then I'll ask, *Who's sorry now?*

Later, as I open my mouth to tell Mom about my decision, my grandmother arrives. She doesn't even apologize for not calling first, saying she was in the area and decided to drop in unannounced. *It's just as well*, I think. *I can tell them together.*

"I'm going to the Bensons next weekend," I announce, looking at Mom first.

Like Amelia, she's not surprised at all. Grandma, however, is another story.

"Is it your goal to put me six feet under?" she asks, squinting.

She shakes her head in indignation and looks at Mom, her eyes begging for support.

"It's my mission in life, Grandma," I reply seriously. "The entire world is against you."

"Go ahead, insult me," she says. "I know why you want to meet them. It's because they have money, isn't it? All malice and menace come from money. If money's that important to you, I'll give you money. Of course, we don't have as much as they do, but I'll give you everything we have. Just don't go, please."

"Mother, how can you say that?" Mom comes to my defense. "I'm not defending her, but I'm sure I know the reason." She sounds confident. "Victoria's just lost a friend from school. A boy committed suicide. I think his death had a profound affect on her, and I fully understand and completely support her decision."

Mom looks at me approvingly.

"Oh, my god!" Grandma exclaims in horror. "I'm so sorry. Poor boy! Poor parents!"

"Norman only had a mother," I clarify. Then I add, "He was her only child."

"Little children, little problems; big children, big problems," Grandma says and then sighs deeply and heavily. "Little children don't let you sleep; big children don't let you live."

The Drama Queen presses one hand to her forehead, and then, gesturing with the other, says, "Okay, go. Don't worry about me. I'll be fine. I'll have my meltdown afterward."

"Grandma, please, no melodrama. I want you to understand something. Despite all the animosity and hatred you have for the Bensons, they're still my grandparents, good or bad." I see her open her mouth, ready to object, but I gesture with my hand for her not to. "Let me finish, okay? What I'm trying to say is that they'll never become what you and Grandpa are to me, and I won't shed a tear when Richard Senior dies because he's a stranger to me, but I have to make his dying wish possible. Otherwise, I won't be able to live with myself. So you see, it has nothing to do with money.

"Mom's right. Losing Norman made me think long and hard, and it made me realize something: I don't want to live with maybes and sorrys, should'ves and would'ves. I don't want to ask myself in twenty years, *What if?* I don't want a life full of questions and regrets. I want what's here and now, and I have to try to make the best of it, because we don't know how long we have on this Earth."

I stop and take a deep breath.

"Do I make any sense at all?"

"Honey, you make perfect sense," Mom answers, "and I'm very proud of you for it."

"Thanks, Mom," I say, "and Grandma, don't worry, I'll be very cautious."

* * *

When I'm at home, I'm okay, as long as I don't think about Norman, but as soon as I come to school, everything changes. I can't concentrate. I think of Norman all the time. I look for him everywhere. I keep hoping that the door will open and he'll walk in, smile, and say, "It was a mistake. It wasn't me who died. It was another boy," but I know deep inside that I'll never see him again, and I feel miserable.

Will this ever go away? Will it ever stop hurting so much? I wonder. The weather doesn't help either. Ever since Norman's death, it's been raining nonstop, as if nature can't stop crying for him, either.

Tina and I talk about Norman all the time, without mentioning his name. I'm not sure that it's easier this way, but we do it anyway.

This pain in my chest is still strong. I don't know how to end it. I snap at my friends. I'm even rude sometimes. I still want to kill Heather and Tiffany. Well, I want to kill Heather and maybe just injure Tiffany a little (she did show some remorse, after all), but I don't act on it. It won't bring Norman back anyway. And Heather . . . she's all alone.

Nick checks on me all the time to make sure I'm all right. Today he even asks me out. Well, not exactly.

He says, "Let's go somewhere after school. We'll grab something to eat, and then we can talk."

"I'm not very hungry," I say, but when I see disappointment on his face, I reluctantly add, "Well, maybe some coffee and dessert." I don't want him to think that I'm playing hard to get. "How about the Indulgence Café?"

He gives me a happy nod.

As soon as classes are over, I tell Liza not to wait for me because I'm going with Nick. She makes a sound like "Ooh" and gives me a little wink as she leaves.

Nick's waiting for me outside. We walk hand-in-hand to his car and ride to the café. While there, I order a tall latté. Nothing edible. *What if I have something stuck to my teeth? What if I chomp or choke?* I don't want him to think that I eat like a pig.

"What about dessert?" Nick asks, confused. "You wanted to have some."

"Well . . . I don't know," I start. *As god is my witness, I tried to resist.* "An éclair maybe," I say to the waitress.

She nods, looks at Nick, and smiles.

As soon as she walks away, Nick takes my hand in his and asks, "So how are you, really?"

I shrug at first, but then suddenly think it's time to explain everything. I owe him that much. I tell him about Mom losing her job, her cancer scare, our money fights, and about the Bensons. I can't stop talking. It's like after a long constipation, in the speech department that is, I suddenly have verbal diarrhea. Nick listens to me carefully, with no interruptions.

"Oh, Vicky," he says after I finally stop. "I'm so sorry. You've been going through so much. No wonder you told me you've been having some problems and issues. I had no idea. If I only knew . . ."

"It's okay. My friends have been very supportive."

"And on top of everything, there's Norman's death . . . It's affected you so much."

I think he's now as gloomy and miserable as I am, and it makes me feel even worse. He offered me a shoulder to cry on, and I just laid all my shit on it. *Good job, Victoria Benson!*

"Don't worry, Vicky," Nick says, squeezing my hand. "It's just a little smoke, and it will disperse eventually. There's not always a fire where there's smoke." He looks so serious and sounds so mature! Sometimes I forget that he's a teenager, just like me. "I understand that you need time to deal with all this stuff, but I'm willing to wait for you for as long as you need. Just remember: now that I know, you can always count on me. Whatever you need . . ."

I can see he really means it, and I totally believe him. How can I not, when I'm absolutely, completely, totally in love with him? How can I not, when I'm sinking deeper and deeper in those big blue eyes of his? *I'm a goner!*

"Thanks for being so understanding and patient with me," I say, squeezing his hand.

*   *   *

I decide not to tell the girls about my trip to the Bensons. I don't want to hear different opinions and advice again. My mind has been made up. What if I change it? I'd better tell them when I come back. It's too soon since Norman's death for something fun this weekend, so I don't have to make any excuses.

Friday afternoon, as soon as Liza drops me off at my house, I call Amelia to confirm our meeting for tomorrow and tell her that she can pick me up at noon. I look for Mom around the house and find her in her room, getting ready for her trip to New York. She looks beautiful, all made up.

"Can't decide what to do with my hair," she says, looking in the mirror and frowning.

"Hmm . . . let's see. Do you want to look pretty and sexy or do you want to look sexy and pretty? That's a real dilemma," I joke. "I can understand that it puts you in a very interesting predicament."

"Ha, ha! Very funny," Mom says, slightly offended. "No, seriously."

"Okay, okay, I'm kidding," I laugh. "Do you want a fabulous updo or a bodacious blowout?" I start playing with Mom's hair. "Do you want it fancy, chic and classy?" I take her hair, lift it up, and let her look at it for a while. Then I let it down and fluff it. "Or do you want a young, hip, sexy, yet glamorous look?"

"Where do you get these things?" Mom asks and laughs. "You sound so confident."

"You betcha!" I say with a grin. "I get it from you. I just define it differently. Okay, tell me where you're going and I'll tell you what you need."

"Well, tonight we're going to see a Broadway show, and tomorrow we're meeting Nora's friends for cocktails somewhere near Central Park."

"Okay, question number one: Are those friends men or women? And if the answer is *men*, question number two: Are they married or single?"

"Answer number one: Both men and women. Answer number two: I have no idea. I assume they're married couples. She didn't say, and I didn't ask."

"And you're calling *me* clueless!" I exclaim, astounded. "Mom, wake up! Nora's obviously trying to set you up with someone. How naïve can you possibly be?"

I'm flabbergasted!

"No, she's not! Is she? I told her not to," Mom reminds me of Chloe now.

"Okay. Fabulous updo for the theater, bodacious blowout for the *friends*." I gesture quotes with my fingers. "And Mom, wear something low-cut to show your cleavage."

"Hah! You flatter me," Mom laughs. "As they say, *If you ain't got it, don't flaunt it*."

"Who says that?" I ask.

"I don't know." She shrugs. "People."

"Well, don't listen to them, and appreciate what you've got," I say, meaning that she could've easily lost her breasts not so long ago. Judging by her face expression, she gets the hint. "Come on, Mom! I dare you! Do something crazy, something drastic. Have sex with a younger man on a first date, for example. For you, it's taboo."

"Do you know how demented that sounds, Victoria, even for you?"

She looks shocked.

"What did I say?" *Seriously, what did I say?* "I mean, just let your hair down, loosen up, or in the words of my dearest friend, Alex, live a little!"

"It's such a cliché," Mom says, annoyed. "I live just fine. I'm happy with my life."

"Touché!" I exclaim to retaliate. "It's the twenty-first century! Think of female takeover, think of sexual revolution."

"The sexual revolution isn't my thing," Mom replies, hooking up her earrings.

"Why? Are you sexually repressed?" I ask.

Mom stares at me in jaw-dropping-wide-eyed astonishment and says, "Remember *Freaky Friday?* I feel like we switched bodies, and you're my mother in this conversation. Don't you think that this line of questioning is—"

"Are you sexually repressed?" I repeat the question, ignoring her comment and interrupting her in mid-sentence.

"Correct me if I'm wrong, but not so long ago you cringed when I tried to have a sex discussion with you. So now, when it concerns me, it's suddenly okay to talk about it, right? Double standard!"

"Answer the question!" I persist.

"Mmm . . . Let's say I'm on sexual strike."

"Okay, be that way. You don't have to have sex, if you don't want to. Just date."

"Really? Okay, Miss Know-it-all. I don't want to discuss it with you, but if you insist . . ." Mom turns to face me and asks, "I'm not your age, Victoria. Do you really think that men will take me out for dinner and drinks and waste their time on me without having sex? If so, you're delusional! There's an old saying, *Free cheese might be only in a mousetrap.*" Mom stops for a moment and then goes on, "Remember that guy, my co-worker, who used to show up all the time to help me with handiwork a few years back? You thought he was my boyfriend, and I told you that he *wished* he was, but I didn't feel the same way about him. Then, when he realized that, he stopped coming. Remember?"

"Yeah." I nod. "So what's your point?"

"My point is," Mom says, "men never do anything unless they want something in return, and they usually want one thing—we both know what it is—and if they don't get it, they still hope that someday they will. As their hope fades away, so does their help."

"Hmm, it's good to know. It was very enlightening," I react to Mom's speech. "However, it doesn't change the fact that you *do* need a man. You're not getting any younger, you know. Although you're very well preserved for your age, let's face it: you're no spring chicken."

Mom gives me a long stare and then shakes her head, meaning, *I can't believe you just said that.*

Then she says, "I know I'm no spring chicken, but I don't have a sign on my forehead, saying, 'Single and desperate,' do I?"

"My point is: find somebody before it's too late," I persist. *A rich husband would be nice.*

"Are you giving me advice or ordering me around?" Mom asks, staring at me strangely. "Why are you trying so hard to convince me that I need a man? Do you have a reason for that? Just the two of us isn't enough? Is there something I should know about?"

"There's only one reason, Mom. I want you to be happy," I say, and that's the truth.

And having money wouldn't hurt.

"Thank you, I think. I'm touched. But to get back to the case in point, there's too much talk about sex," Mom says. "In America, sex is an obsession, in other parts of the world it's a fact." She looks at me, waiting for a reaction, but doesn't get any. "The great Marlene Dietrich said that. That's the problem in this country. People are so into sex that they forget about love."

"Mom, how would you describe the difference between love and sex?" I ask.

"Sex is the passion of the body, but love is the passion of the heart," she responds. "And you need both to have a relationship."

"So basically you're telling me that unless you fall in love, you won't have sex or date, right?" I ask. "What's wrong with *like*? What about just plain physical, animal attraction?"

"What makes you think that you're the relationship expert?" Mom asks, agitated. "Attraction and sex, and even love, are not always enough. Well, I don't know how to explain this to you. Take your Dad and me, for example. We were so much in love, we couldn't imagine our life without each other. We were inseparable. We used to finish each other's sentences. When I itched, he scratched. There was no way to tell where he ended and I began. We completed each other. We were two halves of a whole. Well, I don't have to tell you how it all ended."

"Because you stopped communicating. I understand. You lost trust. Your faith's broken, but it doesn't mean that you should suppress your romantic feelings and—"

"It's not broken. It's mildly sprained," Mom interrupts. "But the point is, I don't just need chemistry. I need fire. I need a flame, not just smoke."

"And with Dad you had everything, right?"

"Yes, we did at first. How do I put it?" She hesitates for a moment, and then goes on, "Where there's smoke, there's not always fire. But where there's fire, there's always a flame. Sometimes you want to add some fuel to keep that flame going, and sometimes you feel it's better to put that flame out. So your father and I decided that it was time to put the flame out. Do you understand now?"

She looks at me with hope in her eyes.

"I think so. You mean that even if you like a man and then fall in love with him and have a wonderful physical relationship, that might be not enough. You have to *want* a relationship, and then you need to work on it to keep it going, and if there's a problem, you should feel that it's worth saving."

Do I want to keep the flame going between me and Nick?

"You got it!" Mom exclaims, happy that she doesn't have to go on. "After your father, I've never met a man I wanted a relationship with. You see, there's always someone to sleep with, but I've never wanted anyone to wake up with. Why bother, then?"

"Well, let's hope that some day the right man comes along and you'll open your heart back up," I state, and then, smiling as if talking to myself, say, "It's so strange."

"What is?" Mom wonders.

"I've already had this smoke-fire conversation today with Nick. He said the same thing, *Where there's smoke, there's not always a fire*, but you both said it about different things. And you both made a lot of sense."

"So you had a conversation with Nick today, huh? Interesting. What about?" Mom asks, looking intrigued.

"Mom, let's not talk about it now. You have to leave soon. It's a long drive to New York," I say, trying to end the conversation I started myself.

"Come on, Victoria. Tell me! That's not something I'm oblivious to," Mom insists.

"Well, we were talking about our problems and Norman. He's just like Jackie—he really listens, he doesn't interrupt, and when he says something, it makes me feel better. He totally gets me, Mom," I say, excited. "Even more than the girls. I feel closer to him every time we talk. He said he'd give me as much time as I need, but I don't think I need any more time. I'm sure I want to be with him."

"That's great, honey," Mom says, as excited as I am.

"Mom, seriously. You have to get moving or you'll miss your show."

Mom looks at her watch and exclaims, "God! You're right! You have to promise me, Victoria, that you'll be cautious and alert tomorrow at the Bensons."

"I promise, Mom. You look awesome! I love you. Bye, Mom! Go already!" I say, trying to push her out of the room.

"Are you trying to get rid of me?" Mom asks, looking suspicious. "First, you're trying to force me on men, and now you're pushing me out of my own house. What are you up to, Victoria? Anyway, thanks for your oodles of love and admiration. It's mutual."

*　*　*

I'm awakened by the sun, shining through my window. I can't believe it's finally sunny outside! I look at the clock. It's ten. I have to get up and get ready. Amelia will be here at noon and I need to make myself presentable. Not that I care what Amelia or a dying man think of my looks, but on the other hand, I want them to see that the granddaughter they rejected is a nice-looking girl. Well, a real knockout, actually. I'm just being modest.

After a nice long shower and a light breakfast, I put on my favorite jeans and a crisp white shirt. Then I gather my hair in a ponytail and apply just a touch of mascara and a little lip gloss. *In this case, less is more*, I think.

At noon, a black Lincoln pulls into the driveway and a woman gets out.

I open the door and say loudly, "Come on in, I'm all alone."

She smiles and walks toward the house. I didn't expect Amelia to look that good. I mean, my grandma Rose is pretty and looks quite young, but she's medium height and a little overweight. Amelia, on the other hand, is tall and slender. She's not that pretty, but there's something about her . . . I just can't put my finger on it. Nobility maybe, and class. Yeah, definitely class.

But how could a noble woman with class reject a daughter-in-law and her only grandchild? I try not to think about it right now.

She's tastefully dressed and is very . . . groomed and polished, I would say.

"You're very pretty, Victoria," says Amelia. "You don't look much like Richard, but I can definitely see a resemblance, and you're tall, just like your father."

And you.

I lead her inside, take her coat, and show her into the living room. As I expected, she admires it. I offer her a drink, but she doesn't want one. Instead, she asks for the tour of the house. I oblige and take her upstairs. I can see she's impressed.

"It's all Mom's doing. She's very creative," I say proudly. "I'm, however, more into clothes."

"So you like to shop, huh?" Amelia asks with a smile.

I nod.

"So do I," she says. "Your mother is apparently very talented. Is that her?" she asks, pointing at a framed picture of Mom and me on the piano. "Who plays the piano, you or your mother?"

"Yes, that's my mom," I reply to her first question, and then answer her second one with pride again, "I play a little, but you should hear Mom play!"

Like that's even possible!

"Well, no wonder you're so pretty. You've got two beautiful parents."

"Thank you," I say politely, and then add, "Actually, I've always had just one parent."

I can see that she gets it, but doesn't say anything. Instead, she looks around and says, "I love this house. It's not that big, but it has everything you need. Every room is perfect. Furniture, accessories, pictures . . . it's not just a house, it's a home. You must be very happy here," she says, and it pisses me off.

Mom made it a happy home, not her precious son!

"Yes, I'm *extremely* happy here," I say. "Mom always makes sure of it, and my grandparents help a lot," I say on purpose, "but you didn't come here to discuss our living arrangements, Mom's decorating style, or my shopping habits, right?"

I see Amelia's expression and it's obvious that I've just spoiled the mood. However, she doesn't respond to that. We sit in silence for a while. It's awkward. You can cut the tension with a knife.

"Shall we go?" she suddenly asks, smiling.

She could've been a good actress.

"Sure," I reply coldly. I can't help it.

*   *   *

We don't talk much in the car at first. Just small talk.

"How's Mr. Benson?" I ask, just to be polite.

"He doesn't have long. It's almost over," she replies, her voice shaky. I look in the mirror and see her eyes, full of sadness. Then she changes the subject. "Tell me about your school."

When I do, I see that she's surprised, but impressed that Mom sent me to a private school.

"Do you have a lot of friends?"

She seems interested.

"I have four best friends."

That's my favorite topic. I can't stop talking about the girls.

"I'm glad you have such wonderful friends," Amelia says. "Do you have a boyfriend?"

What? She wants to know if I have a boyfriend? What right does she have?

"Yes, I do," I answer.

It's not exactly a lie. I did decide to give Nick a chance.

"Tell me about him," she says.

She's really a piece of work!

"Well," I start. "He's nice, and smart, and handsome, and I like him a lot."

"Good. I'm happy for you." She sounds sincere. "Okay. We're home."

We stop by the beautiful two-story house. Amelia lets me look for a moment and then pulls the car into the garage. I see another car there, a Mercedes. She shuts off the engine and we go in.

"You have a nice house, Amelia," I say at a glance.

"Thank you. It does need a little renovation and remodeling. Please sit down and feel at home," she says, pointing at the couch.

This will never be my home!

"Can I offer you something to drink? Or to eat perhaps?"

"No, thank you. I'd like to see Mr. Benson first, if possible," I say quietly.

"Of course. Let me just go in first and prepare him, all right?" she asks.

I nod.

When Amelia leaves the room I start to look around, zooming in on things. I see a lot of antique pieces—furniture, lamps, vases, picture frames. Brown and beige colors dominate here. The room is beautiful, but a little too crowded for my taste. I wonder if everything was the same when my father was a boy, living in this house.

Amelia comes back and then leads me to a bedroom on the second floor, where my dad's father is dying. As I climb the stairs, I feel a little nervous, but glad to get it over with.

There's a huge bed in the room, and in the middle of it there's a very thin elderly man, with gray hair. The faceless man in my dream now has a face. His face is very pale, but a handsome one—my father's face in about twenty-five years.

There's a nurse sitting in the armchair next to the bed. Amelia asks her to leave us.

"Hello," I say softly and take a few steps forward. "I'm Victoria."

Richard Senior tries to reach out for me with his hand, as I move further forward.

"Sit beside me," he whispers, pointing at the bed.

"He can hardly talk," Amelia explains. "He wants you to be closer so you can hear him better. Go ahead."

I sit next to him on the bed and take his hand.

He tries to squeeze it, but can't, so he just holds my hand in his and murmurs, "Thank you for coming. You're very beautiful."

"Thank you," I murmur back, feeling very sad. "How do you feel?"

"Can't you see? I'm terrible. Thanks for asking," he whispers, then makes an attempt to laugh and says, "Soon, I'll feel no pain and be at peace."

I see tears in Amelia's eyes and I feel even worse.

"Please forgive me for everything. I'm so, so very sorry," he mumbles.

"I forgive you," I say, squeezing his hand.

He closes his eyes and I see something on his face that looks a lot like a smile. And then I see a single tear roll from his eye.

"He needs to rest now," Amelia says, wiping his tear away and then her own tears. "It's too overwhelming for him."

She calls in the nurse and we leave the room.

"He refused to be hooked to the tubes and machines," she tells me as we walk down the stairs. "He even tries to eat and to drink something as long as he doesn't have to be dependent on the IV."

I'm not sure what I feel, but I definitely feel uncomfortable. We sit down on the couch in the living room. We don't talk. There's that tension again.

"Well," Amelia breaks the silence. "Let's have something to eat, shall we?"

She gets up.

"I'm not hungry yet," I say.

"Then have something to drink," she insists. "What would you like?"

"I'd like the truth, straight-up." As soon as I say it, I regret it. "I'm sorry. I promised myself I wouldn't do this, but—"

"That's okay," Amelia interrupts. "I presume by the truth, you mean, how could we reject your mother and you, right?" I nod. "Well, I expected that. I just didn't know when you were going to bring it up."

She stops and looks at me, and when I don't say anything, she asks, "How much do you know? What did your mother tell you?"

"She told me that you didn't want your son to marry a Jewish woman and you didn't want a Jewish grandchild. Do you hate Jews so much that you thought it was worth losing your son and never getting to know his family?"

"But you see, it's not true. It's not that! If you think I'm anti-Semitic, you're wrong. I'm not! Our best friends, the Kleins, are Jews, and our attorney, Mr. Cohen, and his wife have been family friends for as long as I can remember."

"Did they know about what you said? Weren't they at least offended?"

I can't believe it!

"I told them, and no, they weren't offended. They know me. They were a little disappointed. Sometimes you do the wrong things for the right reasons. I thought I had one."

"What was your reason? Why did you say that?" I ask, giving her a long, piercing stare.

"Because I would have said the same thing if your mother had been Chinese, Italian, or anything else, for that matter. No matter who she was, she was the enemy who was taking my boy away from me. Don't you see? I didn't want to lose my son. I wasn't ready to let go. Not then. It was too soon— and my husband would say anything I want him to say."

"It sounds familiar. My grandpa also says whatever makes my grandma happy, but not when it counts. He's very wise, and if she's wrong, he tells her so," I say to Amelia. "A child isn't a possession. It's a part of you. You have to love it, support it, and make sure it's happy. If you thought about it, you could've had your son and his family with you now." I look at her and see that she agrees with me. "Anyway, Mom was a stranger who took your son from you, but what about me? Why didn't you accept me? I guess blood isn't always thicker than water."

I'm so frustrated, I could scream.

"It wasn't you," she responds. "When your father called and said they were expecting a child, we honestly believed it was a hoax. We thought he had made it up so we'd accept his marriage. If we only had known . . ."

She looks at me with such sadness in her eyes that I almost feel sorry for her.

"Actually, Mom made Dad call you. She didn't want to stand between him and you. She thought that if you found out you were having your first grandchild, you'd accept their marriage. You could've checked it out," I say, agitated. "Why didn't you?"

"It wasn't that simple," Amelia starts. As I'm about to open my mouth to object, she continues, "Okay, I'll tell you everything."

She stops and coughs to clear her throat, then goes on, "We tried to contact your father, but he didn't want anything to do with us. I can't blame him, of course, but when he graduated and moved away, we hired a private investigator to track him down. He did. My husband went to Richard's office and tried to explain and apologize, but your father was as hard as a rock. He couldn't forgive and forget. We kept track of him. We even drove by your house several times, but we never got to see you or your mother. We saw Richard a few times. We tried to talk some sense into him, but he was unbreakable.

"Then we found out that he had left without a trace. Our detective couldn't track him down. Richard never used a credit card, so he couldn't be located. We wanted so many times to contact your mother and beg for her forgiveness. We wanted so much to get to know both of you, but we were afraid. But ever since we found out that Richard was dying, he couldn't stop talking about it, and I knew that no matter how scared I was, it had to be done. So I called and luckily got you and not your mother, and the rest is history, as they say."

She finally stops and looks at me.

"Do you have any idea why he left?" she asks.

I tell her what I remember about our non-existent relationship, about my parents' marriage, and what Mom had told me last night about their love.

Then I add, "He suffered because he didn't know what to do, and she suffered because she couldn't help him. He said he didn't know who he was, so he left to find himself. I hope he did."

"It's too bad that he doesn't know what a beautiful and wonderful daughter he has," Amelia says. "Tell me how you feel. Upset? Angry? Hurt? Tell me everything."

"Am I upset? Am I angry? Am I hurt? Absolutely! Totally! All of the above!" I almost shout. "I'm upset and angry with you and your husband for rejecting me, and with your son for leaving me. You hurt me because you didn't care enough to get to know me, and my father hurt me because he didn't love me enough to stay."

I stop and look at her.

"That's how I feel. Well, you asked. I'm sorry for being so graphic. I'm a writer, and I like to express myself. Unfortunately, I can't press my internal *mute* button. Anyway, I'm willing to give you the benefit of the doubt. I'll trust that you told me the truth, the actual story."

"But can you forgive me as well?" she asks. "Remember, I'm not dying yet."

"Good. It means we have time. Everybody deserves a second chance, but I can't give it to you. Not yet, at least. I need more time. Maybe I'll be able to forgive you."

"Thank you," she says, swallowing the lump in her throat. "You don't know how much it means to me that you're even willing to consider it." Her eyes are full of tears. She wipes them off and asks, "Shall we eat now?"

She asks the housekeeper to set the table for two and tells the nurse to feed Mr. Benson.

The dining room is big and well-lit. The dinner is delicious: a light salad, a lobster-bisque soup, a mustard Dijon salmon with rice, and Crème Brulé for dessert. We move back to the living room and have coffee. Amelia mentions how impressed she was with Mom's decorating ability. I tell her that Mom wants to be an interior designer.

"She should. She's got a real talent for it," Amelia says. "Victoria, are you upset again?"

"It's not you, it's me," I say.

I don't know how and why, but I suddenly feel that I can talk to her. So, to my surprise, I spill everything, just like I did with Nick. I would never have believed that I would, but I certainly did.

"So you see, I'm not that good. I love money so much that I think only about myself and don't care about Mom's feelings."

"Stop it, Vi . . . may I call you Vicky?" Amelia asks.

"You may call me Tori, if you want. I know you like it more," I reply, and wonder at myself.

Why would I let her call me Tori? Nobody calls me that. Maybe that's why.

"Very well, then, Tori," she says with a smile. "You shouldn't be so hard on yourself. It's not easy to get used to one lifestyle and then suddenly be thrust into another."

"You understand, don't you? You know, I was so nervous about meeting you. I didn't know what to expect. I was even a little scared, but you're so easy to talk to that I feel comfortable with you."

It probably sounds corny, but I think she should know that.

"I'm glad to hear that," Amelia says. "You see, there's not always fire, where there's smoke."

I can't believe she just said that! This was the third time I'd heard this analogy in two days. Three people, meaning three different things, but they all made sense.

"Anyway, you should support your mother. Very soon you'll leave, and she'll be all alone in the empty nest. Let her do what she loves to do, what makes her happy, especially because she's so good at it."

She sounds so confident, so involved, like she really cares. *Does she?*

"You're totally right," I say. "At first I was a jerk about it, but then I tried to understand and even support her." I tell Amelia about the book I gave Mom for Chanumas. "But then I made a bad remark about her not making any money, and yesterday I told her to find a man."

I sigh and suddenly say, "I can't imagine what would've happened if she'd had cancer. I would've been lost without her. I have my grandparents, of course, but it's not the same.

Mom has always been both a mother and a father to me. I don't know what I would've done."

I look at her as if searching for the answer and she was the one who could give it to me.

"If, god forbid, it had happened, you would've risen to the occasion. If push came to shove, you would've stepped up to the plate. I'm sure of it. But thank god you didn't have to. That's the most important thing."

How can she be so sure? She hardly knows me.

"Thanks for your confidence in me," I smile. "Wow! Look at the time. It's almost ten!"

"So what? Are you an early bird or a night owl, Tori?" Amelia asks.

"I'm both, actually. I have to be. I go to sleep late because after doing my homework I like to read, to write in my journal, and then watch a little TV. Then I have to get up early to go to school. On weekends, though, I sleep in late. Why do you ask?"

"Because I think it's too late to drive you home now, and to tell you the truth, I'm enjoying our conversation so much that I don't want to let you go. Why don't you spend the night and we can talk some more? We'll have snacks and have fun, and tomorrow you'll sleep as late as you want. Then I'll drive you home. What do you say?"

She seems very enthusiastic.

"Well, I don't know . . ." *I do need some time with her.* I see her face, full of hope, and say, "Okay, I'm game!"

At that moment, my cell rings. It's Mom!

"Hi, Mom!" I exclaim and see Amelia tactfully leave the room. "What's up? How is it going? Having fun?"

"Where are you?" Mom asks, concerned. "I tried to call home a few times, but you weren't picking up. I'm worried."

"I'm still at the Bensons. I'm spending the night here," I announce.

"Oh? You must've been having a good time then," she says, sounding a little jealous.

I hope she doesn't feel betrayed, but I don't want to leave. Not yet.

"I have, believe it or not, and what about you?"

"I'll tell you when I see you," Mom says.

Suddenly, I get an idea and ask, "Mom, listen, when are you driving back home? Do you mind picking me up on the way so Amelia doesn't have to drive me back?"

"Actually, I do mind. To be honest with you, I don't want to be near their place."

"Please, Mom," I beg. "Call me when you're close by and I'll meet you outside. Alone."

Mom reluctantly agrees. I give her the address and we say goodnight.

I call Amelia. She walks in and I tell her that she doesn't have to drive me back home.

"You know, people say that grandchildren are the grand-parents' revenge and parents' punishment for the crimes they committed," Amelia says, "but it doesn't apply to you. You're a blessing. Your relationships with your mother and your grandparents can attest to that."

"Please, Amelia," I smile. "You're giving me too much credit. I can be a real pain."

"But look at you. You're so well-rounded. You're a great daughter and a wonderful granddaughter. You're beautiful and smart, and you're so mature for your age! You're articulate and you're a writer. I'd say you're very accomplished."

She says it with such pride that I start to believe it. *But even if it's true, she had nothing to do with it.*

We talk, and talk, and talk. We don't notice the time. Finally, at two a.m. we go to bed. The room I'm in is pretty and comfortable, so I fall asleep almost immediately.

* * *

I'm awakened by the knock on the door. It's Amelia. She apologizes and reminds me that Mom will be picking me up soon. *Omigod, it's eleven already!*

We have a yummy, mouth-watering breakfast and talk some more.

"Tori, before you go," Amelia starts, looking a little uncomfortable, "I want to give you something. Here."

She hands me a check for . . . a hundred thousand dollars!

I look at it, speechless. I'm not sure what shocks me more—the amount or the fact that Amelia presented me with it. *How dare she? Does she think she can buy my forgiveness or my love and affection with it? Think again!*

"Richard also wants you to have his Mercedes. He doesn't need it anymore."

I'm totally flabbergasted! I can't believe what she just did and said! *How could she?*

"Amelia," I start, "I had such a great time with you. Please don't make me think that I've made a mistake coming here. Please don't make me regret my decision to meet you. You can't compensate for all the years I've been out of your lives."

I tear the check up.

I can't believe I just threw away a hundred thousand dollars, but harboring a grudge for my non-grandparents is apparently much stronger than my love for money.

"But Tori, it's not what you think. I understand that we can never be real grandparents to you, but I was hoping we could become real friends. We can! Didn't you feel it last night?"

"Yes, I did, and that's why I can't accept your generous gifts. I don't mean to sound ungrateful, but that's the way I feel," I say firmly and definitely.

The verdict is final!

*   *   *

Mom calls at one o'clock. I go upstairs to say goodbye to Richard Senior, but I don't think he hears me. Amelia and I say our goodbyes and I promise to stay in touch. Then I go outside and think of the old dying man for about ten minutes while I wait for Mom.

"Hi, Mom," I say, quiet because of my thoughts, and kiss her on the cheek.

"What's wrong? Did something happen?" Mom asks, worried.

I probably look sad.

"No, it's all good," I reply, "except for the dying part, of course. I saw him. I didn't feel anything. Does it make me a bad person, Mom? Am I totally heartless?"

"Of course, not," Mom answers. "It's understandable. You don't know him."

"I actually had a good time."

I tell her about Amelia. I tell her almost everything we talked about.

"I told her that maybe in time I'll be able to forgive her, and then you won't believe what she did. She gave me a check for a hundred thousand dollars! And get this: the old man wants me to have his Mercedes!"

I look at Mom. She doesn't even blink.

"What did you say to that?" Mom asks calmly, looking at the road.

"Thanks, but no, thanks, and I tore the check up," I announce proudly.

"Well, I can't believe you turned down the money," says Mom. "It's so not like you, but I'm glad you did. It's one thing when people die and leave you an inheritance, but to give you the check . . . Well, you did good. I'm proud of you."

"Thanks. Now tell me how your weekend was. Did you do anything bad and dirty?"

"You wish!" Mom exclaims. "Well, you were right. Nora did try to set me up. We went to the Tavern on the Green to meet her imaginary friends, but instead, it was a party for singles. My god, Victoria! You should've seen those men. Ask me who attends those parties. Desperate people, that's who! Well, I'm not one of them. How could Nora do that to me?"

Mom sounds and looks angry. She keeps shaking her head in indignation. *Poor Nora. I can only imagine what my mother had to say to her!*

"That bad, huh?" I ask.

"Don't even!" she exclaims and sighs, shaking her head.

"I can imagine how angry you were," I state, knowing my mother.

"You can say that again," she says.

"Please tell me you didn't smoke!" I exclaim.

She does that when she's angry or stressed out.

"I did. Actually, smoking kind of saved me," Mom chuckles.

"What do you mean? You didn't like anyone so you had to smoke to ease the pain?"

"Have you ever noticed that there are fewer men who smoke than there are women? It's because men love themselves more, and most men don't like women who smoke. So at the party, every time I saw a man walking toward me to ask me to dance, I would light up a cigarette and he would turn away fast and ask another woman instead."

"Do you mean to tell me there wasn't a single man you wanted to dance with?" I ask, astounded. "Lot's of smokin', but no fire, huh?" I squint. "Come on, Mom! Not one?"

Mom gives me a glance, and flashing a naughty smile says, "Let's say I've never smoked so much in my life!"

We both laugh. *I had a much better time than she did,* I think.

*   *   *

Later that night I get a call from Jamie. He wants to know what to buy Liza for her birthday. *Shit! I completely forgot.* It's on Saturday, March thirty-first.

"Gee, I don't know, Jamie," I say. "What do you buy someone whose father owns a chain of department stores? Are you coming on Friday? We'll discuss it then. How's it going with you and Jackie? Love is in the air, huh?"

I want to hear what *he* has to say.

"Vicky, I can't explain how I feel," he starts. "You see, when I look at you, I feel smoke, but with Jackie, I'm on fire! Do you know what I mean?"

The smoke-fire analogy again!

"As a matter of fact, I do." *That's exactly what Mom meant.* "I'm deeply hurt, but I forgive you," I joke. "Watch it, though. Otherwise you might end up calling the fire department," I chuckle. "Bye, Jamie. See you Friday."

I hang up the telephone and think about a present for Liza.

Trials and Tribulations of a Teenage Drama Queen

*"Character is forged in the smallest of struggles.
Then when the big challenges come, we're ready."*

—Waiter Rant

With Liza's birthday on the way, I decide not to mention to the girls how I spent the weekend. It can wait. I'll tell them after the party, which promises to be very exciting since Liza's father took his girlfriend to some islands somewhere and we have the whole house all to ourselves.

I want to ask Nick to come with me. *Will he go? I'd love it if he did.*

"Hey, Benson!" McAlly interrupts my deep mental process. "Sorry, Vicky, can I talk to you? It's about Chloe." He presses his hands together and begs, "Please help me! Please tell her it's not true. I didn't sleep with that bitch. Well, not since I've been going with Chloe. Heather made it up. Ask anyone."

I give him a long stare. He looks and sounds sincere.

"But people saw you leaving together. What do you say to that?" I ask.

"Yes, we did leave together once. Actually, she followed me. She wanted me back. So I took her home, but on the way explained to her that I like Chloe and that it's all over between me and her. I swear, that's exactly what happened."

"I can vouch for that," says Nick as he approaches us. "Amber told me that Heather was complaining about it. She couldn't accept it, but the girls made it very clear for her. It was just before Norman's death, and now no one's even speaking to her."

"Okay, then. I'll talk to Chloe. Thank Nick for that. It's because I trust *him*, not you. I'll do my best, but I can't promise anything. I'll tell her what Nick and you've just told me, but I can't influence her decision. I want you to get that."

"Thanks, Benson!" he exclaims. "I mean, Vicky. Just talk to her. My money's on you."

He notices that Nick and I exchange glances and gets that it's time to leave us alone.

"Can we meet later?" I ask Nick. "I want to tell you about my weekend."

Well, I need to tell someone or I'll burst.

"Sure," he says as his face lights up. "Let's meet after school."

As soon as I see Chloe, I relay everything I've heard from Ted and Nick, "Ted's desperate for you to believe him. Why don't you talk to him and hear his side of the story?"

"Do you really think I should?" she asks, looking hopeful. "Maybe you're right."

"Yes, I really think you should," I respond, "and I'm sure I'm right."

*   *   *

"I'm back with Ted!" Chloe announces as soon as we sit down for lunch. "Thanks to Vicky and Nick."

She tells Liza, Alex, and Jackie how the big reconciliation happened.

"I also have news," I announce. "Two, actually. One I'll tell you now, the other after Liza's party." First I tell them about my almost-date with Nick on Friday. "I've decided to give him the chance," I state with a grin. "As a matter of fact, we're meeting after school."

"Well, it's about time!" Liza proclaims. "Thank god you've come to your senses!"

"Oh, Vicky, it's turned out great for both of us," Chloe claims. "I'm so happy!"

"Mazel tov!" Jackie exclaims and sighs.

"What did you say?" Chloe asks as Liza and I laugh.

"Chloe, haven't you ever heard that expression? Maybe in the movies?" I ask, surprised.

"But what does it mean?" Chloe persists.

"I don't know the exact meaning, but people say it all the time, at weddings, for example," I reply.

Liza nods in agreement, but we all look at Jackie, waiting for a translation.

"In Hebrew, *mazal tov* literally means *good luck* or *good fortune*," Jackie explains, "but it's been incorporated into Yiddish as *mazel tov* and is now used as *congratulations and best wishes*."

The girls look at each other and exclaim in unison, "Mazel tov!"

Everyone but Alex. She doesn't say a word. She just sits there, like she doesn't hear anything we say.

"Alex, are you so happy for me that you're speechless? That's a first," I say with sarcasm in my voice. "Don't you have anything to say? Any comments? Remarks? Quotes?"

"Yeah, Alex, isn't it great that Vicky and Nick will be together?" naïve Chloe asks.

I see Alex's face flush as she looks down and says, "If you're happy, Vicky, then I'm happy for you."

Happy, my ass! If I had any doubts before about her having the hots for Nick, I don't anymore. They've just dissolved. My suspicions are confirmed: one of my best friends is my rival, my competition for Nick's affection!

Not now. After the party. I don't want any confrontations right now, before Liza's party, but after that, I'm sure confrontation is inevitable. I can't pretend any longer that I'm a total moron and don't see or understand what's been happening with her. *I've had enough of this bullshit!*

"You're bringing Nick to the party, I hope." It sounds more like a statement than it does a question from Liza. "Especially since Chloe's bringing Ted. Guys, can you imagine? The entire house is ours! We'll have fun, I promise. But please, let's not drink like pigs, okay?"

This is something we can agree on since the last party, so we all nod in agreement.

Sure we'll have fun. I can see it now: Liza with Craig, Jackie with Jamie, Chloe with Ted, I'm with Nick, and last but not least, Alex with . . . Alex. I can imagine how she must feel.

"It's time to go to class," Alex announces.

As usual, she's in charge and has the last word.

*   *   *

I meet Nick after school. The weather is wonderful. It seems that nature has finally come to terms with Norman's death, and I'm slowly starting to do the same. It's sunny and quite warm for the end of March. It's such a splendid afternoon that instead of going to eat in a café or a diner, we decide to have a picnic on the grass. First, we go to the store and get some sandwiches, chips, and sodas, and then we drive to the park.

As soon as we spread out the huge towel Nick always keeps in his car (hmm, I wonder why), I tell him about my weekend with the Bensons between bites. He listens to me without interrupting.

"So what do you think?" I ask when I finally finish my story. "Was I right or what?"

"I can't tell you whether you said and did the right thing, but I can tell you this: you did the right thing by saying and doing what you *felt* and what you thought was right for *you*."

"You always make me feel better," I say. "Listen, Nick . . . umm . . . Liza's birthday is this Saturday. It's nothing big or anything. It's just the five of us, but we can bring dates. So I was wondering . . . Would you like to be my date and come to the party with me?"

"Well, well, well . . . Victoria Benson, does it mean what I think it means?" He smiles, giving me a piercing look. "Are you ready to go steady?"

"I believe it does, and I am," I respond, smiling back.

"How come?" I see he's glad, but truly surprised. "You were afraid of being judged and hurt. You didn't want any strings attached because you didn't trust me. You thought it was the wrong time for us. Now suddenly you want to be my girlfriend. What gives?"

"What can I say? You've kind of grown on me," I reply, shrugging and smiling.

"Or maybe you've just mellowed a little?" he asks. "In this case, I'll be happy and honored to be your date this Saturday, and your boyfriend for all Saturdays to come."

He smiles at me with that killer smile of his, revealing those perfectly straight and white teeth.

"Thanks," I say, relieved and pleased. "And about the strings . . . Let's take it one string at a time, deal?"

I give Nick a long stare and wait for his reaction.

"Deal," he agrees, and leaning closer to me, adds, "Now let's seal it with a kiss."

We kiss. Slowly, gently, tenderly . . .

*   *   *

"Daddy's secretary really knows how to please him," Liza states when she calls me on Saturday morning. "No wonder he sings her praises. You wouldn't believe how efficient this freaking woman is! She just had to wake me up at nine o'clock this morning via a delivery boy with flowers my father had supposedly sent. I've decided that this is the year I punish both of them. Since his idea of a birthday present is that I buy myself whatever I want, I'm going to want something that's impossible to find because it doesn't exist, and I'm going to make *her* search for it. What do you think of that?"

"I think you're mean! When she woke you up, you were in righteous indignation, but now you're pulling the same trick on me. You call me at nine-ten and wake me up as well. So tell me, how does it work?" I'm furious with her, and before she has a chance to open her mouth, I continue to give her a hard time. "The poor woman shouldn't have to suffer just because you want to stick it to your father. She's just doing her job. Her only fault is that she does it well!" I shout. "Get over yourself, Liza!"

"Bummer!" she exclaims. "I'm so sorry, Vicky, for waking you up. I was so angry that I had to call you and complain. I didn't realize that I was doing the same thing to you. And about the poor secretary, you're absolutely right: I can't make her pay for Daddy's sins."

"It's okay," I say a little softer. "Forget about it."

"No, it's not okay. I'm sorry. Go back to sleep."

"Ha! Easier said than done," I say, and then remember what today's about. "Oh, Happy Birthday, by the way. Be well and happy. I wish for you to take over your father's business before he's ready to leave it to you. That's how you'll stick it to him. That'll teach him!"

*   *   *

Since we couldn't think of anything to give the poor little rich party girl, we've decided to give her *the party*. Liza doesn't have to do a thing (as if she could!); we'll be taking care of everything. We'll supply the food and decorations to make the party more festive, and the guys will provide alcohol and flowers. Even a rich girl loves and needs flowers for her birthday. Every woman does.

At 3:00, Liza tells her housekeeper, who has fried tons of steaks, baked a huge fish, grilled lots of vegetables, and is about to bake a cake, to take the rest of the day off and go home. The woman tries to resist, but Liza practically throws the poor thing out. We do the same thing to Liza when we ditch *her* (send to the beauty salon, that is) and take over the kitchen.

I prepare several seafood dishes; Chloe makes some appetizers and beautifully arranges the cold cuts on platters (having a caterer for a mom *does* help); Alex cuts and shreds veggies, fruits, and walnuts for the salads and cakes; and Jackie bakes two scrumptious, mouth-watering tortes: one a crunchy vanilla-chocolate cake with walnuts, and another soft, kind of like a sponge cake, topped with fruits and whipped cream. She writes, *Happy Birthday, Liza!* on one, and *Best Wishes, Birthday Girl!* on the other. Now we're ready to set the table and put up the decorations.

By the time Liza gets home, exhibiting old-Hollywood glamour, everything's ready. Now we can go home. It's *our* turn to make ourselves beautiful.

*   *   *

Nick rings my doorbell at exactly seven o'clock. As soon as I open the door, he hands me a huge bouquet of assorted flowers and says, "Beautiful flowers for a beautiful lady."

After I thank him, he gives me a long, appraising look, and I can say that he's pleased with what he sees. (He's not so bad himself, I notice.)

"I'm awestruck!" he exclaims. "I'm totally captivated by you."

"That sounds like a pick-up line," I joke, flattered. "Do you always tell the truth?"

"I have nothing to lie about," he replies and shrugs playfully. "You mesmerize me."

I say, "Oh, really? How nice. You don't look too shabby yourself."

"Thanks. A magnificent diamond deserves a lovely frame. You're my diamond; I'm your frame. We complete each other, creating a perfect harmony."

He takes my hand and kisses it. Wow! How refreshing and totally unexpected. *He belongs to another generation!*

"Hmm . . . you probably say and do this to all the girls," I mumble, "but I can live with it."

"Let's go, but leave your flowers home. You can't outshine the birthday girl, can you?"

We pick up Chloe and Ted, both looking good and cheerful, and drive to Liza's house. As we approach the driveway, we see Jamie, Jackie, and Alex getting out of the car, carrying a huge basket of flowers and a bag with alcohol. Nick and Ted pay Jamie for their share. Ted approves Jamie's choice of alcohol, and we all admire the flowers.

We go inside and are greeted by Liza and Craig. They both look elite and . . . blond. Immediately, I think of Barbie and Ken revived, but intelligent and articulate.

"Thank you, guys, for these gorgeous flowers and for the party," Liza says. "Guess what Craig's present is?" Happy and excited, she doesn't wait for us to guess and announces, "It's a week-long stay at a Mexican resort on our spring break. Isn't it great?"

"It's great, Liza!" I exclaim.

Oh-oh! That's when the big event will happen: she'll become a woman. As I think that, I look at Nick. *Why did I look at him*, I wonder.

The party goes well. The food is delicious and the guys compliment us all night long. We drink in moderate dosages, since we all remember the last after-party hangover. Dancing, of course, is the highlight of the party. Nick and I can dance as close and as intimate as we want—we're now officially a couple—and we kiss a lot, which I enjoy enormously. I love being in Nick's strong arms and having my head on his chest, or dancing cheek to cheek and feeling his breath in my ear—either way, my body begins to tremble.

All four guys take turns dancing with Alex. And no matter how well she tries to hide it, I can see her face burning when she dances with Nick.

Since it's a huge house and it's all ours, the couples try to sneak away to different rooms. When Nick and I are alone at last, we kiss more passionately than before. He kisses my face, my neck. There's a lot of heavy breathing going on, but every time Nick tries to put his hand on my breast, I try to take it away. His hands are so beautiful and warm . . . I'm losing control . . .

Wait! Should we go check on Chloe? What if Ted hurts her? Alex is there all alone! Shouldn't we go back? I suddenly stop and ask Nick those questions.

"Aw, jeez!" he exclaims, breathing heavily. "Perfect timing for questions, as usual."

"I'm sorry," I defend myself. "I can't help it!"

"Listen, Chloe's totally sober," he says, a little agitated. "If she goes all the way tonight, it's because she wants to, not because Ted is forcing her, and Alex is a big girl. I'm sure she understands those things."

He takes me in his arms and starts kissing me again, but I stop him.

"Pretty please," I beg.

He's disappointed, but does as I ask, and we go back to the living room, where Alex, of course, has been left alone. Jackie and Jamie return at the same time. They must've had the same idea.

"Well," Alex says. "It's time for me to go."

I see sadness in her eyes, though she smiles.

"Nick," I whisper in his ear. "Can you take her home and come back?"

"Do you think it's a good idea?" he asks and looks me straight in the eye.

He knows!

"It's okay. I'll call a cab," Alex says. "I don't want to ruin it for you guys."

"Actually, we're about to go," says Jackie. "It's almost one o'clock, and Jamie's leaving in the morning. We brought you here, Alex, and we'll take you home."

After they leave, Nick and I call everybody in. We put the dishes into the dishwasher, then wash and dry the glasses so the housekeeper doesn't know we had alcohol. In about twenty minutes, the four of us say goodnight to Liza and Craig and leave.

After we drop off Chloe and Ted, Nick takes me home.

We kiss a few more times and, as hard as it is, I finally say, "Goodnight. I had a wonderful time with you" and go inside.

*   *   *

On Sunday we all talk on the phone and discuss the party. I notice that it's not the same as usual. It seems that we don't share the *details* anymore. *Maybe we're growing up.*

Amelia calls me on my cell phone, explaining that she was afraid that if she called our home number, Mom could pick up.

"How's Mr. Benson?" I ask politely.

"He's slipping away," she responds, and I can hear her swallowing. "How are you, Tori? I still think about our time together. I enjoyed it so much. Oh, by the way, has your mother finished that decorating job? The reason I'm asking is that one of my neighbors wants to remodel, and our friends are moving to a new house and need to decorate. Do you think your mother will be up to doing those two jobs?"

She sounds really involved and excited.

"I don't know," I reply. "I'll have to talk to her, but thanks anyway."

Wow! Two potential clients! Maybe it is possible for Mom to start a new career, after all.

"Now listen. I'll give you their numbers. Please mention it to your mother and see what she says. Also tell her that she needs to create a portfolio. When she finishes the job she's doing right now, she has to take pictures of the house, and your house, from every angle of every room, and put them in the portfolio. If she takes these two referrals I'm giving her and does the jobs, her portfolio will be quite impressive."

An online portfolio hadn't even occurred to her! *Mom could create a website and display those pictures there.*

"Thank you, Amelia. It's very thoughtful of you. I'll tell Mom."

I'm really very touched.

"You're very welcome. I hope you come and visit again soon, before . . . well, you know."

"I'll try," I promise and hang up.

∗   ∗ · ∗

On Monday morning when we get to school, I see Nick by my locker, waiting. The girls look at each other, say hi to Nick, and leave us alone. We hold hands and steal a few kisses.

During lunchtime, however, I sit with the girls and he sits with his friends. That's fair. I feel a little coldness from my friends, but don't say anything. Chloe starts first.

"You promised to tell us something important," she says. "Well?"

"Listen, guys," I say, "it's too long of a story to tell over lunch."

"Is it ever a good time for you anymore?" Alex asks.

I see my friends exchange glances.

"What's that supposed to mean?" I inquire, clueless.

"Are you interested at all in what's happening in *our* lives?" Liza wants to know.

"Is something happening? I thought I knew," I say, confused, but they all just stare at me. "Okay, be that way. We'll talk later, and I want an explanation." I get up. "No, wait. I'm meeting Nick after school. Let's talk tomorrow."

"Nick, of course," Alex says, kind of sarcastically.

"Okay, forget Nick. Let's go to the Indulgence after school," I say, and everyone agrees.

After I explain to Nick, to his disappointment, that I need to spend some time with my friends, we all go to the café. Chloe's very anxious—she can't wait to hear my story. After ordering my usual, a tall latté and an éclair, I tell my friends the entire story of my visit with my non-grandparents. As I suspected, their reactions and opinions differ.

"I'd never go there and I definitely wouldn't forgive them," Liza claims, as she did before.

"Umm . . ." Chloe starts, but I don't pay attention to her.

"Well, you can't even forgive your dad's secretary for waking you up early," I say to Liza.

"I think you did the right thing," Alex states. "I've said this before, and I'll say it again: you should let go of the past. But if you forgave them, why didn't you accept the gifts?"

"Yeah," Chloe says, but I ignore her.

"Because I don't want them to buy my affection," I respond. "Isn't it obvious?"

"They're not trying to buy your affection," Alex speculates. "They're trying to make it up to you. Why don't you give them a chance?"

"Vicky should do what *she* feels like, what she thinks is right for *her*," says Jackie.

"Yeah, that's right," Chloe states, but who cares what Chloe says, since it's her third opinion.

"You know, Jackie, Nick said the same thing you did," I say and see Alex's face change.

"How long has Nick known about this?" Alex asks as Liza raises one eyebrow.

"Well," I start, "actually, I told him before I went there."

"So you thought he could handle that information, but we couldn't?" asks Jackie, and I hear irony in her voice. "Why do you feel you can talk to Nick and Tina, but not us?"

"Yeah," Chloe finally gets the chance to put in her two cents. "Ever since Norman's death you only want to be with Tina and Nick. What about us? We're your best friends!"

She sticks her bottom lip out, making a perfect offended-and-abused-child face.

"Oh, so that's what it's all about," I say. "Hmm, funny how no one feels the need to share the details of their big evenings with me anymore, but I'm expected to share the info of my private life. How does that work?" I ask, narrowing my eyes. "And FYI: I only talk to Tina about Norman. We need each other . . . you wouldn't understand."

"Has it ever occurred to you that *we* might need you?" Jackie asks.

"Yeah, maybe we wanted to share the details with you, but you didn't seem interested," Liza adds, looking sad.

"There was your birthday party, Liza," I continue, "so I decided to tell you afterward." I look at my friends, but they remain silent. "I was wondering why the cold treatment. You were exchanging glances, but didn't say a word to me. I didn't think that Nick—"

"It's Nick, Nick, Nick!" Alex exclaims angrily. "Is there anyone else anymore?"

Whaaat? My jaw drops! This is the third time today. She's never spoken a word when anybody mentioned Nick, and suddenly *it's Nick, Nick, Nick?* What's up with that?

"What is that supposed to mean?" I ask.

"It means that since you've found out that Nick is into you, you forgot that we're your friends. You don't spend any time with us anymore. You're always with Nick."

"I can't be with my boyfriend?" I ask her, furious. "You're insane! Do you know that?"

"You *can* be with him," Alex says, "but you spent months pining over your feelings for Nick and we were there for you. I'm so sick and tired of listening to your complaining *I-want-him-I-want-him-not*. Well, now you've got him, but we lost you. So *do* him already, for god's sake! Get it over with and be our friend again."

"I will, if I want to. Not that it's any of your damn business! By the way, for months you've never said a word when we mentioned Nick's name. Why's that? You've always interrupted when his name was mentioned."

I finally have to tell her what I think.

"Where are you going with this?" she asks, all flushed.

"I've bitten my tongue and kept my mouth shut for too long." I wave my hands and shake my head in indignation. "I've been wondering for months why you're so much against Liza pushing Nick and me together. Then I started to suspect that you like him too! You're my competition for Nick's affection. My best friend is my rival! Am I wrong, Alex? Am I?" I shout.

A few people look our way as I confront her and she doesn't deny it.

"Why all these questions? Are you afraid I'll make a play for Nick myself?" she asks.

"Will you, Alex? You *do* want him, don't you?"

I strike just the right chord.

"And what if I do? Not that it's any of *your* damn business! Anyway, he doesn't want me, he wants you. So what difference does it make?"

Alex starts crying. *Oh, no! Shit!*

"So it's more like, if you can't have him, I shouldn't either, right?" I ask, a little softer.

"Stop it, Vicky, for crying out loud!" Liza yells. "How could you? There are some things you just don't do. You don't put a tea kettle on a cheese board; you don't commit a lucid person to a mental institution; you don't bury someone alive; you don't kick people when they're down; and you don't *ever* hurt your friends."

"I didn't start this, she did," I say, pointing at Alex.

I can't believe it! Like it's my fault!

"In this world, perception and response are everything," I go on. "It's simple: if you're nice to me, I'll reciprocate; if you're mean to me, I'll retaliate. Relax, Liza. Why are *you* so intense?"

"It's a very intense conversation," Liza responds.

"And long overdue," Alex, who has stopped crying, adds.

"Is this a conversation I want to keep on having?" I ask, making a face.

"Too much has gone down with us in the past several months to ignore it," Alex insists.

"What is this? Intervention or something?" I ask sarcastically.

"You can call it that, if you want, but I was thinking of it more like a confrontation," Alex replies. "Let's recap, shall we?"

"Let's!" I retort.

Should I take it seriously?

"Okay," she begins, "for the past year you've been behaving like Jekyll and Hyde. It's like you have a split personality. One minute you're kind and considerate, and the next minute you're arrogant and rude. The bottom line is: we don't want to put up with it anymore."

"Look who's talking! Ever since Brianna's party, nobody behaves more like two different people than you. It's like good-cop-slash-bad-cop all in one. One minute you talk us into going to the party, you encourage us to drink and to, and I quote, *live a little,* and the next minute you give us a lecture on how to behave. One minute you talk about how wonderful love is, and the next you say that all men want is sex. So what is it? A double standard? Do as I say, not as I do? You're the biggest hypocrite of all, Alex!" I shout.

"Please, guys! I don't want anybody to boil over it," Chloe begs.

"I think you've gone too far with this," Jackie says to me. "Stop before it's too late."

"Don't worry. There won't be any bloodshed," I assure them. "Come on, cut me some slack! I know I get stressed out over every little thing, but these past seven months have been long and difficult for me, and Norman's death hit me pretty hard. I still can't get over it."

"Don't use Norman's death as an excuse for your actions. We all lost Norman, even though you and Tina felt closer to him than the rest of us," Liza says, looking annoyed."

"Listen," Alex starts again. "You've got a little setback in your family. First, your mother loses her job, and then you think she's got cancer. Thank god she's okay. You should be happy, but you're not. Why? Because you can't maintain the lifestyle you're used to. Well, that's a real reason to be unhappy and make people around you miserable. Now grandparents who made a mistake years ago want to make up for it. A real tragedy, isn't it? The most gorgeous guy in school wants you. Someone should be so lucky! But you don't think so. You still complain.

"You always complain that life sucks. It doesn't always suck, but it's not always fair, either. You've been dealt a bad hand, but it's not the worst hand, so deal with it. Imagine this: you're a queen, and everybody worships you, but one day they stop worshipping. What then? Are you ready for the other side? If you get my point, stop whining already. Don't play the victim. If you want us to help, we'll help, but otherwise you're on your own. Seriously, get over yourself and grow up! There's a very good quote about it, if you'd care to hear it."

"I won't have peace of mind unless I do, so shoot, put me out of my misery."

"Well, then. I don't remember who said it, but it's perfect for this conversation. 'You can either complain that rose bushes have thorns or rejoice that thorn bushes have roses.' "

"You're losing your touch, Alex," I say sarcastically. "You're forgetting the names of the people you quote. How can you live with yourself?"

I know it's a bad attempt at a joke.

"And you're losing touch with everything that's real in your life," she retorts.

"I don't consider myself a queen!" I exclaim, furious. "Why did you say that?"

"Because you're always so self-involved," Alex replies. "Ha! And I thought you had started to change. You don't stop to think of other people. You're not the center of the universe, so why is your attitude all over the place? And what about that ego of yours!"

My ego? Ha!

"You love to quote, Alex, so how about this? Donald Trump said it, by the way. 'Show me someone without an ego, and I'll show you a loser.' But seriously, I'm so humble. Don't you know that?" I try to joke again. "I always criticize myself."

"There's a saying," Alex says. "Humble people don't think *less* of themselves—they think about *themselves* less."

That's it! That does it!

"In other words, you hate me, right now, you hate me!" I paraphrase Sally Field, trying to turn everything into a play.

I really don't feel like fighting, but Alex has a different idea.

"Oh, puh-leeze! Don't be your grandmother-in-training."

Is it true? Is it even possible? Omigod! I'm a teenage drama queen! I need a comeback! I really do. Fast!

"Okay, maybe I'm melodramatic sometimes," I begin, "but let's talk about you, shall we?"

"Let's stop this stupid verbal ping-pong! Stop bickering and start acting civil," says Jackie, but I ignore her.

I can't let Alex tear me apart and not do the same to her.

"You're such a control freak!" I declare. "You looove being in charge. It's your mission in life to control people, to lecture them, to tell them what to do and how to do it, and to boss them around. Well, guess what? If you think you're going to push *me* around, you'd better think again. I'm no pushover, and don't you ever forget it, because if you do, I'm going to push back, and push back, and push back until you remember for good."

Inhale . . . Exhale . . .

"You say *I* have attitude!" I continue. "And what about *your* know-it-all-slash-mother-knows-best attitude? You remind me of a headmistress in an all-girl boarding school, where all the girls hate you for being so annoying and obnoxious."

Alex doesn't say a word. She just looks at me, astounded, hurt and anger on her face.

"Vicky!" Liza exclaims. "Stop being such a jerk! What's gotten into you? Alex is right about you being two different people. You were such a caring friend to me about Craig, but sometimes I just don't recognize you. Alex was just tough, but she only told you the truth. And what did you do? You've hurt her."

Why is she on Alex's side? What about me? It's not fair!

"Are you having a brain freeze or something? Or is it just another *blonde* moment?" I ask Liza. "How come you heard that I hurt Alex, but didn't hear that she hurt me? Or were you thinking about your next shopping spree at the moment, Senorita Fashionista?" I know I keep saying the wrong things, but I just can't stop—I'm on a roll! "What else do you do? Oh, yeah, blame everybody for your father's sins."

"I'm going to ignore that because you're upset," she says. "Don't make me wish I hadn't."

"Aw, jeez. You're totally blowing it out of proportion!"

I need to stop this.

"But, Vicky, you've just hurt Liza, too," Chloe says.

Even she's not supporting me.

"And you, little troublemaker, you. What do you want?" I ask Chloe. "Miss Clueless! Do you think I care what you think? You don't even have an opinion. You have four!" I smile, but I really feel like crying. "Leave me alone!"

That's enough, Vicky," says Jackie. "You've gone too far already. Please don't get to the point of no return."

Jackie! You always understand me. Please try to under- stand me now.

"And you're against me, too, Miss Goody-two-shoes."

Oh-Oh . . . Strike that! Too late. Now I want to cry badly. *What am I doing? I'm burning all my bridges!*

Jackie doesn't respond to my comment. She just shrugs and shakes her head.

"Well, thanks for the thorough analysis of our charac- ters," Alex speaks again. "I think you need to reconsider your career choice and become a psychoanalyst instead of a journalist."

"And do you know what you need?" I ask, ready to retaliate again. "You need a set of drums so that you can join the band marching down the street to screw themselves! But then again, a control freak that you are, you'd probably want to *lead* that band."

"If you think it's funny, do you know *where* you can shove it?" Alex asks.

"Is this a biology question or geography?" I counter, but Alex ignores it.

"Someone really needs a major attitude adjustment," Liza announces.

"Is that someone me or Alex?" I ask, knowing very well who she means.

Liza doesn't answer. She just gives me a long stare.

"My attitude's just fine, thank you very much," I say, "and if you don't like it, it's your problem, not mine."

"This state you're in. Do you know what it's called?" the relentless Alex asks. "It's a namesake for that river in Egypt called *De Nile*. And by the way, you also need to take some anger management classes."

"You're so smug!" I exclaim. "Spare me the righteous indignation. Please don't give me ammunition to hate you."

I really mean it. I'm so sick and tired of her lectures. *God, she's pissing me off!*

"You know, Vicky, you've never been an angel," Liza suddenly says, "but now you're terribly rough around the edges. Is it because you're laying all your anger meant for Amelia on us? It's like you've become this bitchy persona that I don't like at all. I want the spirited, vivacious Vicky back, and I want this angry, bitter, and unbearable bitch to go away."

"Shut up, Liza!" I yell. "I'm not a bitch. Screw *you*!"

We both start crying, and Chloe, of course, joins us—it's a given.

"Seriously, Vicky," Alex starts again. "You need to do something about your attitude. Otherwise, this bitchy persona might become persona non grata and end up walking down a very lonely path."

"I don't want to change!" I spit. "I like myself the way I am."

"Even if it means losing your best friends?" Liza asks.

"Even if it may cost you people you love and who love you?" Alex inquires.

I open my mouth, ready to respond, but Chloe cries, "Vicky, please don't say it."

"Please, Vicky, stop," Jackie implores, and then, with a sad irony in her voice, adds, "It might feel exhilarating to you, but is it worth it?"

I want to scream, *No!* I want to apologize, but I won't give them the satisfaction.

"Suit yourselves," I say instead and wait for the other shoe to drop.

Liza gets up first, throws the money on the table and declares, "I'm done with you!"

Alex does the same and adds, "Well, it's been emotional. Nice knowing you."

They both say goodbye to Jackie and Chloe and storm out of the café. Nobody speaks. I want to kill myself.

What has just happened here? Have I just lost my two best friends? Or maybe four? Have I really burned all my bridges?

"You're still here," I finally say. "It's a good sign. Does it mean I haven't lost you two?"

"You're never going to lose us, but it doesn't mean we think you were right," Jackie replies. "We love you unconditionally, but you were totally wrong. If not for the fact that you were very upset, I wouldn't be here either. You said some terrible, mean things to us."

"I'm sooo sorry," I mutter and start crying again. "Please forgive me. Both of you."

"Oh, Vicky, I'm not even angry with you for calling me clueless. I love you anyway," Chloe claims.

Sweet little Chloe. How could I have been so mean and cruel to her?

"Well, it's not us," Jackie says. "It's Liza and Alex you were really mean to."

"What about them being mean to *me*?" I demand, infuriated. "Are they so innocent?"

"Vicky, they told you what they thought about your attitude," answers Jackie. "Maybe they did it the wrong way and used the wrong definitions, but they didn't really hurt you. You, on the other hand, hit them where it hurts the most— Alex with Nick and Liza with her father. You didn't have to be that graphic. What were you thinking, anyway?"

"What now?" I ask.

I still think that even if I was rude and mean, so were they. Totally.

Chloe shrugs. I can't believe her! Now, when I actually need her opinion, she doesn't have one.

"Give them some time to calm down," says Jackie, "and then apologize."

No way!

"I apologized to you and Chloe because you didn't say anything mean to me. You were just trying to help. You didn't leave, and that means a lot, but they're a totally different story, especially Alex. They were pretty mean to me, too. Let them apologize to me first."

*   *   *

When I come in, Mom knows right away that something's wrong. I don't feel like talking, but she insists. I tell her what happened. Well, the cut and edited version, of course.

"So you had a huge fight with your best friends, huh?" Mom asks.

"It wasn't a fight. It was a falling out," I lie.

"But you shared some fighting words, right?" she persists.

"Rather *exchanged* some fighting words," I clarify the information.

"You *had* a huge fight, all right," Mom proclaims and sighs. "Give Liza and Alex the chance to calm down and then talk it out—and I think you need to apologize."

In my room, I think about the fight over and over again. I try to do my homework, but I can't concentrate. I take my journal and write about the huge fight, as Mom called it, and everything that was said. I analyze the situation.

Was it really my fault? Was I really rude and inconsiderate? Is my attitude really that bad and does it have to be changed? Even my mother assumes by default that I'm the one who owes an apology. Am I that obvious? They say I should give it some time and apologize. Why should I? What about them? What do I do now? Why does it hurt so much?

Later, as I lie in bed, trying to fall asleep, I still think about it, and I still have tons of questions, but no answers.

Do I tell Nick about the fight? What if he changes his opinion of me? What if he shares this with his friends? Would he do that to me? What if from now on I'll be known as the bitchy person who deals with her issues by bad-mouthing and hurting her best friends? What if . . . shit! I forgot to tell Mom that Amelia gave me those two referrals for her.

Now I think about Amelia and Richard Senior. Then . . . about everything. Rumors and speculations . . . trials and tribulations . . . bits and pieces of my life . . .

*   *   *

Over the next few weeks, something strange and uncomfortable goes on. On the mornings Mom can't drive me to school, Jackie has to go in the opposite direction to do Liza's chore and pick me up. I could ask Nick to do it, but then I'd have to explain why, and I don't want him to know that Liza and I aren't talking. He brings me home, though, and is only too happy to do it. We feel like the most star-crossed lovers who got a break.

At lunchtime, we all sit together, though. Where else would we sit? I could sit with Tina, of course, but I don't want the *Jewelry Collection* to speculate about it, and I do want to spend time with Jackie and Chloe. Poor Jackie and Chloe—they're so stuck in the middle.

Spring recess starts. Liza goes away with Craig to a Mexican resort. I feel bad that I can't say goodbye, but I'd have to say *I'm sorry* first, and there's no way I'm doing that. *I'm sooo not doing that!* Jackie's parents leave for a business trip to New York, and she trails along for the opportunity to spend some time with Jamie. Chloe visits me and Alex a few times during the break. She says Alex misses me (I'm sure she tells Alex the same thing about me) and it's time to apologize. *I'm sooo not doing that!*

I'm restless! I catch myself missing both Liza and Alex terribly. I'd give anything to hear Liza's voice, even if she complains about her daddy neglecting her or tells me what she bought lately. I'd give anything to hear one of Alex's lectures—*anything* but an apology. I'm not going to apologize first. *I'm sooo not doing that!*

I feel miserable. My chest's tight, but at the same time I have this emptiness inside me because something big is missing. I tell Mom about it, and she expresses her opinion.

"Victoria, you need to understand something," she starts. "The earth won't stop turning just because you were mean to your friends. Their life will go on. You just won't be a part of it unless you do something about it, and I think you know what it is."

"Well, it wasn't supposed to be a permanent arrangement, you know," I say. "I wasn't going to throw in the *friendship* towel, but now I'm afraid that they might."

"Then maybe you should try to do your best to stay *in* their life instead of doing everything possible to stay *out* of it."

*   *   *

We're back in school. Jackie looks happy. She had a wonderful time with Jamie in New York. Liza's got a great suntan. It looks perfect with her blonde hair. She still doesn't talk to me, and neither does Alex, just as I don't talk to them. But now, at least, we occasionally glance at each other. And that's pretty much the way it goes for the next couple of weeks.

Jackie's birthday is on May eighth. It's Tuesday. Jackie doesn't want anything big, so we take her to a restaurant after school.

There, happy and excited, she announces, "My father has to go back to New York Saturday morning. I'm going, too. We'll stay at a friend's place and I can meet Jamie. He's taking me out to dinner and to see a Broadway play."

"You're glowing, Jackie," I tell her. "I'm so happy for you and Jamie. Have fun."

"My brother's having a barbeque at his house on Saturday," Chloe proclaims. "I can bring Ted and friends, meaning you. Are you up to it, guys?"

"Thanks, Chloe, but I already have plans with Nick," I lie.

I could take Nick with me, but I just don't feel like going. Liza says that she doesn't feel like going either (she looks kind of tired lately and not herself). Alex is the only one who accepts Chloe's invitation.

*   *   *

My cell phone rings around noon on Saturday. It's Liza! My heart starts beating faster.

"Vicky, can you come over right away?" she cries. "I need you."

I'm speechless!

"Hello! Vicky, are you there?"

"Yeah, I'm here," I answer softly. "It's just . . . you've caught me off guard. What's wrong? Your voice is kind of shaky. Are you crying, Liza?"

Now I'm concerned for her.

"Please come fast, Vicky. I think I'm having a miscarriage."

Whoa! Somebody kill me!

"Are you sure?" I yell.

Why am asking stupid questions? Liza's in trouble, and she needs me.

"Never mind. Do you want me to call an ambulance?"

"No!" she shouts. "I want you with me. Please come and take me to the hospital."

"Okay. Don't move! I'll be there soon."

Easier said than done. Mom took the car. I know that Jackie, Alex, and Chloe aren't home. I could call a cab, but it's going to take too long, and it's very impersonal. I could call Nick, but I'm not sure Liza would be comfortable with Nick knowing. (Oh, I have to call Nick and cancel our date.) *Think, Vicky. Think fast.*

Suddenly, it hits me. There is someone who lives close to both me and Liza. I dial Tina's number. *Please be home. Please be home.* She is.

"Hi, Tina," I say when she picks up, my voice shaking. "I need a huge favor. Do you know where I live? Can you be here, like yesterday? Thanks. I'll be waiting."

I run upstairs, throw some clothes on, grab my purse, and run outside just as I see Tina approaching our house.

"Hi," I say. "Thanks for doing this. Don't ask any questions. We need to pick up Liza and take her to the hospital."

She doesn't say a word, just nods and starts driving. When we stop by Liza's house, I ask Tina to wait for us, run to the door, and ring the doorbell. Liza opens right away and hugs me. She looks very pale and her eyes and nose are red from crying. I expected to see a lot of blood, but it's not like that at all.

"How are you holding up?" I ask. "Is your housekeeper here? Do I need to clean before we go so she and your father don't see anything?"

"I'm not that bad," she replies. "No, you don't have to clean. Luckily, it happened when I was in the bathroom. I was late, and suddenly I felt cramps and I saw blood. I thought I got my period, so I used pads, but then the cramps got so bad that I knew."

"Can you walk?" I ask.

She nods. Then she grabs her wallet and her cell phone and throws them in my bag. I help her outside. She's surprised to see Tina and looks at me inquisitively, but she's so weak that she doesn't care about my explanation.

When we approach the hospital, I ask Liza whether she wants to go to the ER or the maternity ward.

"Let's go to the maternity," she says. "We'll page my doctor and he'll know what to do."

"Thank you so much," I say to Tina. "You didn't see Liza today. Forget about it, okay?"

Tina opens her eyes wide and looking innocent and confused, asks, "Forget what?"

"Smart girl," I say and smile. "I really appreciate what you've already forgotten."

"Call me if you need me for anything at all," she says and leaves.

*   *   *

The doctor confirms a miscarriage. He can't explain the reason. He just says that it happens often in the early stages of pregnancy. Liza will have to stay under his watch for seventy-two hours. He hopes that her body naturally completes the spontaneous abortion. If not, she'll be given a drug to induce contractions and to empty the uterus completely. Fortunately, Liza didn't lose a lot of blood. And if everything's okay, and there's no infection, a surgical procedure won't be necessary.

Finally, Liza is transferred to a room. I ask her how she feels. She's exhausted. When she's able to listen and talk, I tell her how sorry I am about our fight and how I wasn't there when she needed me.

"I missed you so much," I say. "Why didn't you tell me you were pregnant?"

"I wasn't sure. Well, I suspected because I was late, but I wasn't sure."

"So you've finally had sex, huh?" I say.

"It happened on my birthday, after you left," she responds, looking away.

"And? How was it?" I'm curious.

At least one of us did it. That's huge!

"Well, sex is overrated," she states. "I think that the sense of anticipation is greater than the process itself. Though, I have to say, the more you do it, the better it gets. When we were in Mexico, we did it all the time, and it started to feel good. Craig was very gentle and very considerate the first time, but I must've gotten pregnant then."

"Has either one of you ever heard of a device called a condom?" I ask with indignation.

"We're using them now. But the first time . . . how could I tell the difference? I think I saw Crag putting it on, but you know they're not a hundred percent effective."

"Speaking of equipment improvement!" I exclaim. "Does he know?"

"No, I didn't tell him," she says sadly. "I didn't want him to think I'm tricking him."

"You should tell him now, and you should tell your father," I try to convince her.

"No!" Liza shouts and begins to cry.

In a few minutes, she's sobbing relentlessly, tears rolling down her cheeks, her body trembling.

"Liza, what's the matter?" I ask, concerned. "I'm here. I'm not going anywhere. We'll get through this together." I lie down on the bed next to her and pat her head. "Why are you crying so hard? Everything's okay. It happened naturally, just as your doctor hoped."

"I feeel sooo emptyyy!" she weeps. "It's like I lost a part of me," she squeezes out through chattering and grinding teeth.

What? Did she want to have this baby or something?

"Liza, I understand that you feel bad," I say, "but you're sobbing like all your dreams have been shattered. Would it have been better if you had the kid? Even if Craig married you, what about college? What about your career? Listen, the doctor said that nothing's been damaged, so you can have as many children as you want—and you'll have them in time, but not now." I see she's sobbing less intensely and continue, "Calm down. Everything's going to be all right."

I reach into my purse, take out several tissues, and hand them to Liza. She blows her nose a few times, sniffles, and continues to shake. She doesn't say a word for a long time. Then she blows her nose again and finally speaks.

"How can I tell Craig? I'm scared."

"I don't understand why you're always scared to talk to Craig. He seems like a nice guy, and there's not always fire where there's smoke." I speak the familiar phrase. "Besides, it's all over now. If he makes you scared and nervous all the time, maybe you don't need him. You don't need this emotional roller coaster. Choose. You can say to yourself, *Fasten your seatbelt and get ready for a bumpy ride* or you can say, *I need peace and serenity.*"

"No!" Liza exclaims. "He's not like that. You're right: he *is* nice. I'm not scared of *him*. I'm scared of what he might think. If it happened once, it can happen again. He doesn't need a commitment now. What if he leaves me? I can't live without him."

"I once heard this saying," I start. "It goes like this: *If you love something, set it free. If it doesn't come back to you, it was never yours to begin with, but if it does come back to you, you get to keep it forever.* Talk to Craig, Liza, and see what happens. Call him." I get her cell phone and hand it to her. "And let's call your dad. He needs to know, and you need him."

"Okay, but let's do it tomorrow," she begs. "Let's sleep on it."

"Logical," I say. "When did you become this wise? What kind of a blonde are you?"

"The smart kind," she chuckles, but wrinkles her face right away because of the pain. "Vicky, can you spend the night here, with me?"

"I can, but I don't think they'll let me," I say as I shake my head.

"Leave it to me," Liza says. "Hand me my wallet, please."

I do what she asks, and the next time the nurse comes in to check on her, Liza tells her how much she needs me here, and slips a fifty-dollar bill into the nurse's pocket.

I call Mom and tell her I'm spending the night with Liza, but don't tell her where. I see that Liza's falling asleep, so I decide to walk to the nurses' station and find out how early Craig and Jeffery Tollan can come to see her.

As I walk toward the station, I see . . . Brianna Gold! She smiles and walks toward me. *Shit! What is she doing here? What do I say to her? I need to make something up, but what?*

"Hi, Vicky," Brianna says. "How's Liza doing? Is everything all right?"

Oops!

"What? What do you mean?" I ask.

How much does she know?

"I saw you guys when you came in. You don't have to tell me anything. I just want to know if she's okay."

She sounds and looks sincere.

"She's fine," I respond. "What are *you* doing here?"

"Oh, I've been here since morning. My whole family is here. My sister just had a baby girl. I'm so happy and excited, I can't tell you. I have a niece! I'm an aunt!" she exclaims.

"Congratulations," I say. "Listen, Brianna. You didn't see Liza and me here, okay?"

"Were you and Liza here? I didn't know," she says seriously.

Another smart girl.

"Well, in case you remember seeing us in the hospital and tell someone, I'll kill you," I proclaim. "I've never committed a murder before, but I wouldn't rule it out. I'm wide open to every opportunity and look forward to a new experience. Of course, I'd have to make it look like an accident."

We both laugh, but she knows I'm dead serious.

"By the way," Brianna says. "Do you know about Ruby's upcoming bash? It's kind of a debutante, coming-of-age, and end-of-year celebration, all in one. I know she intends to invite all five of you. Will you go?"

"I would neither dare nor dream of missing it," I say, making a serious face. "I just hope she doesn't cancel it. As a debutante myself, I'd feel so robbed and deprived being just thrown into society without celebrating my coming-of-age."

"You're baaad," Brianna giggles. "Are you kidding me? She's not going to cancel it. Not in a million years! She lives and breathes it. All she thinks about is how she's going to look at the party. By the way, Jackie's her icon. Ruby dreams she could look like Jackie."

"*My* Jackie?" I ask with dark thoughts on my mind. "Does Ruby have a boyfriend?"

"Yeah. A friend of the family. I saw him a few times. Wow!"

So much for my sexual confusion theory!

"Okay. Have to go. Say hi to Liza for me, will you? Take care of her," Brianna says.

"I will. And you take care of your sister and little niece."

By the time I get back to Liza's room, there are two dinners on the table. *Money talks.*

* * *

In the morning, Liza feels much better. She looks relaxed and rested. Her cheeks are rosy, and despite of everything, she's glowing. *Yeah, when you got it, you got it.* She calls Craig, and he comes right away, very worried. When he finds out what happened, he's upset with Liza for not telling him. I leave them alone.

Later, when I sneak a peek through the door, I see Craig lying next to Liza, his arms wrapped around her, his lips touching her temple. I don't have any more questions.

"You looked so beautiful together," I tell Liza after Craig leaves.

"I hope I didn't drool or snore," she says, worried.

"Even if you did drool, I'm sure you did it like a cover girl," I reassure her, "and your snoring was music to his ears."

"He's angry that I didn't tell him. He says he'd support any decision I make because he loves me," Liza says, pleased. "This is the first time he's ever said he loved me."

"He does love you. I'm sure of it now," I say. "He's a keeper, that one, so grab him, hold on to him, and never let him go. And now . . . are you going to call your dad or should I do the honors?"

Liza's reluctant at first and says, "I'm so afraid he won't understand, that he'll judge and lecture me for having sex. What if he says he's ashamed of me?"

"Stop it, Liza!" I exclaim. "He's your father and he loves you. Just give him a chance to prove it to you. Call!"

She wants me to do it. I call Mr. Tollan and ask him if he could come to the hospital as soon as possible. At first, he thinks Liza's been in an accident, but when I tell him exactly *where* she is, he gets it. He thanks me for calling and promises to be there soon. He walks in twenty minutes later. I leave them alone so that they can talk.

When I come back and walk in the room, I see them hugging and crying. *Wow! Some talk they must've had.*

Jeffery thanks me for taking such good care of Liza.

Then he bends over, kisses his daughter on the forehead and says, "Forgive me, baby. I promise that from now on everything's going to be different. I'm going to get my priorities straight. I'll be back later with Craig."

He leaves, and Liza tells me what a wonderful conversation they had.

"He called himself a jerk," she begins. "He said I should've talked to him a long time ago because he's so stupid. He thought that I, as a young girl, needed my mother, not him. Can you believe it? You were right, Vicky. *Communication* is the key to a good relationship."

Later, Liza asks me to call the girls (they're supposed to be back by now).

"Are you sure you want them to know?" I ask. "It can be our little secret."

"I'm positive," Liza nods. "We've never kept anything from each other."

I call Jackie and ask her to get Alex and Chloe and come to the hospital. They do.

"Why did you call Tina?" Jackie asks after I brief the girls on the current events and report on Liza's medical condition.

"Well, excuuuse me for acting on impulse," I reply. "There wasn't enough time to stop and analyze the situation. It happened too fast, and Liza needed my help pronto. So it was between Tina, Nick, and a stranger-cab-driver."

I gesture to Alex with my head to go outside the room. There, with just the two of us, I apologize for everything and ask, "Is my attitude really that bad? Have I really become such a bitch?"

"Umm . . . yeah and yeah," Alex replies, and we both laugh.

"Okay, I admit I need to change my attitude," I say. "Not much, though, just a little. I'll work on it, I promise, but is it possible to forgive and cleanse a tainted soul?"

"I think so," Alex answers. "I wasn't much better myself. Instead of lecturing and controlling *you*, I should've tried to control my temper and maintain my coolness. Otherwise, what kind of a surgeon would I make? Do I really remind you of an annoying and obnoxious headmistress in a boarding school?"

"The first answer is: a great one; the second answer is: sometimes," I respond and ask, "What's gotten into us that we were so mean to each other and then suffered for it?"

"It takes less time to do a thing right than it does to explain why you did it wrong," Alex replies. "I forgot who said that, but somehow people always do the wrong things."

"Henry Wadsworth Longfellow said that," I say. "I just happen to know."

She looks at me, surprised, sighs, and says, "Yeah. We're quite a pair, you and I."

"But we're always there for each other when it counts, right?" I tell Alex lovingly.

"It's because 'the language of friendship is not words, but meaning,' as Henry David Thoreau said."

I see and hear *my* Alex, and I feel something warm inside me. I swallow.

"Oh, Alex, I missed you so much!" I exclaim, giving her a hug and a kiss on the cheek.

We laugh, and then go back inside, with our arms wrapped around each other. The girls are happy to see that we've made up, especially Chloe.

"We're all together again!" she declares. "BFF!"

"Because a real friendship is the one that never goes away," I state with tears in my eyes. "You can slap it in the face, you can kick it in the butt, you can push it away as hard as you can, but it still doesn't go away—and even if for some reason it does, it's like a boomerang—it always comes back to stay with you." I stop and look at the girls. "I love you guys so much!"

Suddenly I have an idea. I take the pitcher on Liza's bed table and pour some water in five little plastic cups. Then I distribute four among the girls and take one myself.

"I have a toast. Let all the pain we cost each other go away and all the tears dry. Let all bad stuff be forgiven and forgotten. Let's remember just the good and funny stuff—the smiles and the laughter, the joy and the happiness."

Poor Little Rich Girl: A Little Girl With Big Dreams

"If rich people could hire other people to die for them, the poor could make a wonderful living."

—Yiddish Proverb

For the next week or so, the laughter and the good stuff continue. No fights, no tears. I enjoy spending time with Nick, but now I'm more considerate of Alex's feelings. I try not to be lovey-dovey with him if there's even a slight chance that she could see us. He's not happy about it, but doesn't argue. I'm sure he knows why I behave like this.

Liza and Craig are better than ever, and Liza's relationship with her father has improved tremendously. He spends more time at home with her, and they really talk. He keeps his word. Brianna and Tina also keep theirs. The incident hasn't been mentioned at all.

Ted asked Chloe to be his prom date, and Jackie asked Jamie to be hers. Both couples are happier and closer than ever. Both Nick and Ted got accepted by a prestigious private school in New York, based on their sports (and academic, in Nick's case) achievements.

Jackie, Alex and I have already received acceptance letters from all the colleges we applied to, including NYU. Liza and Chloe are still waiting to hear from NYU.

Mom has started a remodeling job for Amelia's neighbors, and is about to start decorating a new house for her friends. At first, I was afraid to mention that Amelia was the one who gave me those referrals, but Mom said, *A job is a job,* and following Amelia's advice, started building up her portfolio.

Today, when I come home from school, I see her on the couch, her legs crossed, looking at some new pictures on the coffee table. She's so into it, she doesn't even react to me walking through the doorway. I look at the coffee table and . . . *omigod! Can it possibly be dust?* I wander around, touching other pieces of the furniture, and corroborate my horror: it's definitely dust!

"Mom!" I exclaim. "You have to see something."

I'm sure I look disturbed and distressed because that's how I feel. *I can't believe I live in a dusty house!*

"Do I even want to know what it is?" she asks, without lifting her head up.

"I'm sure you don't," I reply, irritated, "but I'm afraid you absolutely have to."

"What?" She finally tears herself away from the pictures and looks at the spot I'm pointing to. "So what's your point?"

Is she really clueless or just pretending?

"What's my point?" I shout. "We have dust all over the house. Look at the furniture, and the floors are even worse. Didn't you have time to clean the house?"

"Sorry, I didn't. Maybe *you* should start cleaning," she says matter-of-factly.

"Whaaat? Me?! I *never* clean!" *Is she for real?* "And how about *you*? Are you too *busy* to clean? You're not even working."

Is she serious? Who am I? The cleaning lady?

"I know, it was better when we had a cleaning lady, but we can't afford her anymore, unfortunately," Mom says, stretching her legs out, "and you're right. You *never* clean. So maybe it's about time you started. Oh, and in case you didn't notice, I *am* working."

"You know what I mean."

It pisses me off when she plays innocent.

"I'm afraid I do," she says. "I thought you supported me since you gave me that book."

"I do, but Mom, you're apparently not making enough money for a maid and—"

I stop in mid-sentence. *I'm trying to change. Let's not go back to the way we were.* The old Vicky in me wants to scream, *No way! You clean!*

But the new Vicky just huffs and spits, "Fine."

I get the dusting brush and start dusting. Soon, Mom joins me.

"Is that how it's going to be from now on?" I ask, still angry. "Me cleaning?"

"It doesn't have to be," she answers. "We can alternate or we can make it a team effort so it goes faster, but I'm not going to do it alone."

By the look she gives me, I know she means business. *Stop being selfish. She's not asking too much. What's fair is fair.*

I start mopping the floor, but I'm so angry, and my movements are so aggressive that I slip and fall. I'm furious! I want to shout, *It's all your fault,* but I just sit there with my butt and legs wet, as Mom looks on.

"It's going well, I can see," she says, barely able to hold in her laughter. "Since you don't need me anymore, I'll go back to work. Do you need help to get up?"

That does it! I pull her toward me and in a second she's on the floor next to me, as wet as I am. *I'm dead!*

There are three kinds of laughter: a *throat* laugh, a *chest* laugh, and a *belly* laugh. Let's say someone tells you a joke, but you don't find it funny; so you make this sound with your throat, kind of like, *hah-hah-hah,* just to be polite. Or you hear a joke, and it really *is* funny; so you laugh loudly, *mhu-mhu-mhu-mhu,* with your heart and soul, which makes your entire chest tremble and shake (boobs not excluded). The same happens with your stomach when you hear something totally hilarious, and that's a *belly* laugh. But there's this rare case of your whole body exploding, laughing hysterically, which occurs with the combination of all three types of laughter. That's exactly what happens with Mom and me, sitting on the floor, wet.

We end up cleaning together, laughing, singing, and surprisingly having fun with it. Suddenly, I feel content: doing something around the house once in a while isn't that bad, and it's kind of a bonding thing for me and Mom. And then, it happens: I get the news.

Amelia calls as Mom and I are having dinner in the kitchen. She informs me that Richard Senior has just passed away. I don't feel a thing. She wants me to come. I wish I could say, *How awful; I'm devastated,* but instead, I say, *I'm so sorry* and promise to come as soon as I can.

"You don't have to go if you don't want to," Mom says when I fill her in.

"I'd rather be taken to a hospital to have my appendix removed without any anesthesia, but I think I *do* have to go. She needs me. Mom, please understand." I look at her, hoping for support, and I get it.

"Can I have the car?" I ask, then remember, "Oh, never mind. I forgot that you need it for work all the time." I realize that this is the first time I call whatever Mom's doing *work*.

"Come on, I'll drive you." Mom gets up. "And I'll pick you up whenever you need me to. Let's go. I'll call one of your friends and tell them you won't be in school for a couple of days. Go pack a bag."

"Thanks, Mom, and please tell Grandma and Grandpa."

I run upstairs and start packing.

*   *   *

The very thin grey-haired man from my dream (but with a face) looks yellow and grey at the same time lying in a coffin. Amelia, however, is holding up well. She's a strong woman, I must say. Not a single tear on her face! She keeps me by her side and introduces me to all her friends and neighbors. They try to console me. *Like I'm totally crushed!*

The memorial service is beautiful. Many people speak. In a few hours, I learn so many things about my non-grandfather that it feels like I've actually known him for years.

When they put the coffin into the grave, I think of Norman, and tears start to fill my eyes. Amelia sees it and, though misinterpreting it, appreciatively squeezes my hand.

I spend three days with Amelia and when she offers to drive me home, I accept.

*   *   *

When I come back, I tell everybody about my first experience with losing a family member, though it feels more like learning of a stranger's death and attending his funeral. Everyone says I shouldn't feel bad about it because my non-grandfather practically *was* a stranger to me since I only saw him once in my life.

"It's not your fault he was a stranger," Nick says while we wait for coffee in a diner. "Let's not talk about him. I've missed you so much. Listen, I know I don't even have to ask because it's a given, but I'm going to make it official and ask anyway." He takes my hand and says, "Vicky Benson, would you do me the honor and be my date for the prom?"

Ouch! I haven't even thought about it yet. *What did you expect?* My heart and the old Vicky in me want to scream, *Yes! I'd love to be your date for the prom.*

But my head and the new and improved Vicky think of Alex, and I state, "I'm sorry, I can't."

When I see his jaw drop in astonishment and shock and his eyes inquisitively searching for a reason, I feel that I need to clarify. I owe him that much.

"Don't get me wrong—" I start.

"Don't bother," he interrupts angrily. "I hope it was a joke and you're about to tell me what color dress you're going to wear so I know what corsage to get you."

"Yes, of course I'll go with you, but as a friend. I mean we'll be together, but we can't kiss and . . . you know," I mumble. It's not going well at all. "Let me explain—"

"You don't have to, " Nick says. "If you're doing this just so Alex can have a good time, you're crazy, and I'll never understand that!"

"Alex?" I exclaim. *Double-ouch!* "You mean—"

"Yes, Vicky, I know she likes me. I'd have to be blind not to notice, but I can't help her with that. *You're* my girlfriend and I want to be with *you* at the prom. Let her find her own date."

Is he kidding me? He'd have to be blind not to notice? How about Amber, then?

"You're totally right, but please think out of the box for a moment. We can do it. We'll dance, but we have to watch it."

I sound desperate, and I am. Nick looks at me as if I'm a lunatic and should be committed to a psychiatric facility.

"Are you coming with me as my girlfriend or not?" he asks. "It's your only option. Speak now or forever hold your peace."

"But Nick, please understand. I've loved Alex since we were born. She's my best friend. I can't hurt her. I can't lose her!"

I say it all with such passion that it pisses Nick off even more.

"But it's okay to hurt *me*? It's okay to lose *me*?"

He puts the money on the table and gets up.

"Well, Amber will be thrilled to be my date. I hope Alex appreciates your sacrifice and I hope you'll both be very happy together."

He walks away, and I sit there alone, crushed, and think, *So it went from the Nick factor to the Alex factor. What do I do? Who do I choose and who do I lose? Why should I have to choose or lose anyone? Why does it have to be so damn hard? It was much easier when I was thinking of myself first. Being selfish and self-centered does have its advantages.*

I need to talk to someone. I need someone to reassure me that I'm doing the right thing. My opportunity comes the next day. Alex has an appointment to get her eyes checked for new glasses. She has to skip the last class, so it gives me a chance to talk to the girls without her being present. I tell them what happened with Nick.

"Have you lost you mind?" Liza yells.

It's what I'm getting for being selfless!

"You told me that I can't kick a person when she's down, especially my friend," I try to justify my actions. "I don't want to hurt Alex and I know how much it hurts her when she sees me with Nick—and please don't yell at me."

I feel like a child that did something bad.

"We told you to be more considerate, not more stupid!" she shouts again. "We told you to get rid of your ego, not to have your brains removed."

"Vicky," Jackie gets involved. "You can't lose Nick just because Alex likes him."

"Yeah, Vicky—" Chloe starts, but I interrupt.

"Come on, everybody! This *non-selfish* thing is new to me. I'm really trying, you know, so give me a break, will you?"

I'm ready to cry.

"What exactly did you say to him?" Liza asks.

"Oh, no!" I exclaim. "I'm sooo not doing the self-incrimination thing."

Of course, I relay my entire conversation with Nick to my friends, and we all agree on two things: we have to find a prom date for Alex, and we need to use some major damage control with Nick. Considering how cold he is toward me today, it'd better work.

The next morning, Chloe casually asks Alex if she has someone in mind for the prom.

"Well," Alex responds, laughing. "I've been trying to get that lover-boy from cyberspace who used to send me those X-rated messages to take me to the prom, but I can't get through because all circuits have been overloaded."

Bravo! She deserves an Oscar.

*   *   *

Several days later, I get a call from Ira Cohen, the Bensons' attorney, who informs me that my presence is required at the reading of the will at his White Plains office. I call Amelia and ask her about it, but she confirms that my presence is a must, nothing else. She gives me directions to the office, says, *See you there,* and hangs up. *What is it about?* I call Alex.

"Alex, what do you think it's all about?" I ask. "I've already turned down their money."

"Go and find out," she says. "I smell a surprising bequest. It's so intriguing."

Mom also thinks I should go. I've got nothing to lose. It's not far, and I don't think it's going to be that long, so I take Mom's car and go. We don't mention it to Grandma yet.

*   *   *

I listen to Ira Cohen read the last will and testament of Richard Benson, Senior, and all I can think is, *What's all of this got to do with me?* I was a stranger to that man. He didn't even meet me until just before his death. I don't get the whole legal rubbish, but then I start hearing numbers, and *that* I get. I understand that Amelia rightfully gets the house and everything in it. She also gets a trust fund, like a pension she can live on. But what I hear next, really blows me away! First, I get his Mercedes as a sentimental token, a keepsake, a memento. *Like I have tons of memories of him!* Then, I get a hundred thousand dollars right away for living expenses, and a hundred and fifty thousand as a college fund. I also have a trust fund set up that I'll get access to when I turn twenty-five, in the amount of . . . two hundred and fifty thousand dollars! That totals a mind-blowing half a mil! I've never even dared to imagine such numbers, and it's all mine! *Wow! Poor little me gets all of it!* I wish I could say it doesn't get a major resonance, but I can't, because it absolutely does. With a bang!

Does my jaw drop? Does my stomach flip over? Does my heart stop for a moment and then start pounding? All of the above. And then some. I realize that my lifelong dream of being rich has finally come true.

Suddenly, this surprising bequest from my dearly-newly-departed non-grandfather makes me feel guilty for not caring for the man, for calling him "my non-grandfather," "the old man," "a stranger."

If he can hear my inner voice from up there (or down there—wherever he is), he's probably rolling over in his grave.

There's a struggle going on inside of me: the old Vicky versus the new Vicky. The old one says, *It's your money. Take it. You can have everything you've ever wanted,* but the new Vicky replies, *How can I take it from people that don't mean anything to me, that didn't want me? How can I betray Mom? How can I hurt my real grandparents' feelings?*

Mr. Cohen sees my almost-catatonic state, and gives me "some time alone with my grandmother so that we can discuss it as a family." *Some family we are!*

"Are you all right, Tori?" Amelia asks as she strokes my back. "What's wrong?"

"I don't know," I reply. "It's just that this whole *legacy* subject is too overwhelming, I guess. I'm not sure I'm entitled to it, and I don't know how my family will feel about it."

"It's understandable. Your life will change completely. This money won't make you very rich, but it will make you secure and comfortable, and that's a good thing. You should be happy about it. I'm sure your mother and your grandparents want you to be secure, too." She looks into my eyes and goes on, "Your grandfather wanted you to inherit everything he saved for you. Part of it would go to your father, if he was here, but eventually he'd leave it to you, as well. After my death, you'll also get the house."

If he didn't want me, why did he save money for me? He had to start saving when I was born to save so much. Am I starting to have doubts?

"I'm not ready for this inheritance thing," I mumble.

"Nobody's ready for a 'thing' until they acquire it," Amelia says with a smile.

"I've always dreamed about being rich. All poor people want to be rich."

Be honest, Vicky. You haven't been anything close to poor in your life. Ever!

"Yes. And all rich people wish to be happy. You've always been happy because you have a great mother and two wonderful grandparents, while Richard and I—"

"I'll take the car," I interrupt. "So I can always think of him."

"Thank you. It would mean the world to him."

She squeezes my hand.

"Amelia, what will happen with everything if I don't accept it?" I ask.

"It will remain where it is, but after my death it will all go to charity," she responds with concern on her face. "I hope you're not thinking of turning it down."

"Well, I have to think about it more, and I need to talk to my family and my friends."

"Take your time. I'm sure you'll make a wise decision."

* * *

"The money belongs to you," Mom says, to my surprise. "Your father would get it and leave it you, so it's rightfully yours. You're their granddaughter, for god's sake!"

Grandpa agrees with Mom, but Grandma keeps saying we don't need anything from the Bensons.

"We?" Mom exclaims. "Nothing's coming to *us*, Mother. It's coming to Victoria. Don't you want her to be financially secure, to get a good education, and to lead a comfortable life?"

I tell the girls about my visit to Ira Cohen's office and about my inheritance.

"Congratulations!" Liza exclaims, and the others join in. "At least you know that you didn't forgive them for nothing. Now I can also call you *a poor little rich girl,* just as you call me. You're one of us now, Vicky." She turns to Jackie and says, "No offense."

Jackie shakes her head and waves her hand, meaning, *none taken.*

"I'm not rich yet," I say. "I'm just a girl with a Mercedes and big dreams, a girl in pursuit of happiness." I look at each girl and say, "I'm not sure I should accept it."

"Whaaat?" Liza exclaims. "Have you totally lost your mind?"

"Vicky, are you insane?" Chloe asks, her eyes open wide.

"Did the reading of the will affect your brain in a bad way?" Jackie wants to know.

"You're a nut case," Alex declares. "Do you know that?"

"No. Believe it or not, I'm absolutely, completely, and totally lucid," I reply.

"What's wrong with you, then?" Liza asks. "You love money so much, so why not take your inheritance? Earth to Viii-ckyyy! Did you have a personality transplant or something?"

"Stop it, Liza," I say. "I just can't think of a reason why I should feel entitled to it."

"Oh . . . I can think of five hundred thousand reasons," Liza states. "If that number doesn't convince you, I don't know what will."

"But if I take it, won't it be a sell-out?" I ask. "How can I take something from a man I don't feel anything for? Forgiving them is one thing, but taking their money would mean like going into a totally new dimension."

"Yeah, right," says Jackie. "A dimension of real *life*, financial *liberty*, and a successful *pursuit of happiness*," she paraphrases Thomas Jefferson. "Listen, Vicky. Take it from someone who knows. Your ambition and drive can take you as far as you're willing to go, if you just *grab the torch and run the distance*, but believe me, and you know this yourself, it's much easier to run that distance and to carry that torch when you're rich."

Nice argument.

"Anais Nin said," Alex starts, "There are only two kinds of freedom in the world: the freedom of the rich and powerful, and the freedom of the artist and the monk who renounces possessions." She looks at me and says, "You're certainly no monk, and you're not an artist, unless you consider being a struggling writer the same as being a struggling artist. Well, do you want to be a struggling writer, Vicky? Struggling, but free!"

Good point.

"Okay, okay, guys. You've made a very strong case, Counselor Millerman," I claim. "And your statement, Doctor Malone, was very convincing and it will definitely influence my judgment, but I don't have to make it right now, do I?"

I stop and then remember about the car.

"Listen, guys, who wants to volunteer to drive me to Amelia's the day after tomorrow to get the car? I'll drive it from there myself, but I need to get there somehow."

"I do, I will," Alex jumps at it.

I wonder why. The girls look at each other and smile. They probably think that Alex hopes to talk me into taking the money on the way. *Does she?*

Later, I see Nick and ask him if we can talk. He seems cold, but agrees.

"If you don't want to be my girlfriend, it doesn't mean we can't be friends," he says.

"But I want to be your girlfriend!" I yell.

"Well, you have a funny way of showing it. Okay, go ahead, tell me what happened."

I tell him the entire story and wait for a feedback. *He's smart and reasonable.*

"I'll always be your friend. You can always count on me," he says after I tell him about the inheritance. "Whatever you decide, I'll always be on your side."

"Are you offering me friendly, non-romantic comfort and support?" I ask sarcastically.

"Yes, you can say that," he answers. "Call it whatever you want. If you want my opinion, I think your mother and your friends are right. You *are* entitled to the money, but remember: you shouldn't have to accept it if you don't feel like it and really don't want to."

"At least now I know you're not in it for the inheritance," I laugh. "It's nice to know that you don't want me for my money."

If he still wants me, that is.

*   *   *

"Why did you volunteer so fast to drive me?" I ask Alex on the way to Amelia's.

"I wanted some time alone with you," she replies. "We need to have a little talk."

"I knew it!" I exclaim. "You want to talk me into accepting the inheritance."

"No. Nick asked me to talk to you. Why don't you want to be his date for the prom? A *real* date."

"What did he say to you?" I ask in astonishment.

Did he tell her he knows about her feeling for him?

"He just said that for some reason you turned him down, and he thought that I could talk you into changing your mind. He pretended like he didn't know the reason, and I pretended I didn't know that he knew." She looks me straight in the eye and asks, "You did it because of me, didn't you,

Vicky? You thought it would hurt me to see you two together, right?"

"Yes, I didn't want to hurt you," I admit. "I'm trying not to be selfish anymore."

"And you don't think I'd be selfish if I accepted your sacrifice?" Alex asks. "Or maybe the three of us could dance together? Three's an odd number. No matter how you do the math, there's always someone left over. Three's a crowd, and a love triangle is not for me, especially since there *is* no love triangle. There's Nick, and there's you. I'm not part of the equation. I don't fit in the picture. If you don't go as his girlfriend, it will hurt me more because I'll know I'm the reason for your misery. I don't want to build my happiness on your unhappiness."

I want to jump up and down and scream, *Wooh-hooo! Yes!*

Instead, I ask, just to make sure, "Are you sure, Alex? Will you and I be okay if I'm with Nick?"

"I'm positive," she says. "If I can put a smile on your face, if I can make your heart sing, we're more than okay. I just have to start looking for my own date, don't I?"

*   *   *

I introduce Alex to Amelia. They hit it off right away. We have lunch together and tittle-tattle for a little while. Then Alex makes an excuse and leaves us alone.

"Listen, Tori," Amelia starts when she sees me still doubting the whole legal affair. "Is your mother against it? I can imagine that since you've been here, there's probably a rift between the two of you, and I certainly don't want that rift to widen. I didn't mean to wreak havoc in your home and family when I called you first. I honestly don't want to cause troubles for you and your mother, but she loves you, and she has to see that it's good for you."

"Amelia, Mom's all for it. She's on your side," I reassure her.

"Really?" she asks. "Well, then. I'll give you a reason why you should accept your inheritance. If you don't want to do it for you, do it for your mother."

"What do you mean?" I ask.

"Your mother is very talented, but she needs an office and resources. You can provide them."

"But she'll never take the money from me," I say, "especially if she considers the source."

"Don't give her the money," Amelia says. "Invest it in her business. This way you can help her and show that you believe in her and support her."

How can I fight that?

"You make a lot of sense," I say, "and I'd love to do something good for Mom."

"Very well. It's settled, then," Amelia proclaims.

*   *   *

Alex loves my Mercedes. Before we get into our cars, I tell her that I've decided to be smart and become rich.

"How could Amelia change your mind so fast?" Alex asks. "I thought it would take longer than that to convince you. She must be a real master manipulator. Were you under duress?"

"Let's say she made me an offer I couldn't refuse," I reply with a low, husky voice and Italian accent.

"What did she do?" Alex asks. "Stick a horse's head in your bed?"

"It wasn't that drastic," I laugh.

I tell her the reason, and she says, "Omigod! You're taking such a risk by investing in your mom's business. Aren't you scared? We told you to change your personality a little, not get a new one. I don't recognize you anymore."

"I believe in Mom, and I support her," I defend my position. "Please don't give me a hard time about it, Alex. It's my first attempt at being rich and powerful. I've never been an heiress before, so be gentle. Go easy on me."

"I just wanted to say I'm very proud of you."

We smile at each other and drive away, each of us in her own car.

*   *   *

As I drive home, I fantasize about the prom, and Nick and me as King and Queen. *King and Queen? Gosh, it's sooo not me. When did I get a personality transplant?*

I can't wait to tell him the good news! *What if I'm too late? What if he doesn't want me anymore?*

Then, I imagine presenting Mom with my investment on her birthday. I'm so happy!

I think of everything that's happened this past year—good and bad—and how it's affected my life. I've changed so much and I've experienced so many new things.

I realize I haven't made any entries in my journal in the past few weeks. And suddenly, I feel like I want to share everything I've learned about life with the world.

School is almost over. I have one final editorial to write. My last school article ever! I know what it will be about, and I know what I'll call it.

The Twenty Commandments for Living

by Victoria Benson

*"Life moves pretty fast. If you don't stop and
look around once in a while, you could miss it."*

—Ferris Bueller

Life should come with a user's manual, instructing us step
by step on how to live it. Then we'd always know what
to expect and what to watch out for. We'd embrace the good
things that come our way and prevent the bad things from
happening. We'd never make any mistakes, and even if we
made some, we'd know how to correct them. We'd always
succeed and never fail.

If we at least had a handbook with a set of rules and some
tips on how not to break them, we'd know what we can and
can't do, should and shouldn't say. There'd be no hurt, no
pain, no problems in the world, and life would be perfect.

Unfortunately, life doesn't come with a user's manual or a
handbook. There are no instructions, no tips. That's why we
screw up, break the rules, make mistakes, get hurt, and have
lots and lots of problems. That's why we do things we wish we
hadn't and say things we regret later.

Regrettably, there's no user-friendly machine that can
erase everything we're sorry for or ashamed of, and we can't
press the rewind button so we can go back and start all over
again. We can never go back to the way we were.

If we could know where and when we might fall, we'd
throw a pillow under our knees right before it happened. If

we could know when we were going to die, we'd never keep our calendars clear for that day. Instead, we'd look into other options and make other plans that would keep us far away when death came.

We can never know what's ahead. Life is unpredictable. It's like a deck of cards. You never know what cards you're going to pick or what hand will be dealt. Life deals us cards, and we have to deal back.

We search for things, we look for people. Sometimes they're useless things and the wrong people, so we start our quest over and try again. We have lots of questions we need answers to. Sometimes we get them, sometimes we don't. We learn many new things, but there's always more to learn.

Life is full of surprises—good and bad.

Some of us succeed and then fail, others struggle and then get lucky. Sometimes we can build a life, and sometimes we have no control over it. Some live the way they choose to because they can, others live the only way they can because they don't have a choice.

Life can be easy or tough, sweet or bitter; life can be full or empty, interesting or boring; life can be fun or duty, joy or obligation; life can be happy or miserable, a blessing or a curse. One thing is sure: Life as we live it is not black and white—it's mostly grey, and it's up to us to make it more colorful.

We can't just wait for what we want; we have to go for it and get it. We don't know how much time we have on this earth. Let's just make the most of it. Let's try the best we can to make this time and this experience we call LIFE more meaningful.

I've decided to invent my own list of tips and directions to a successful and happy life, based on my own experience and on what I've learned from the people around me.

Useful Tips:

If you don't like the hand you've been dealt, deal with it anyway.

If you want the horseshoe to bring you luck, work as hard as a horse.

If you want your relationship to last, compromise.

If you see your life as a piano keyboard (black and white), improvise.

The Twenty Commandments for Living:

1. *Accept and embrace life as it comes, but do your best to make it better.*
2. *Accept and like yourself the way you are, but remember: there's always room for improvement.*
3. *Be good to yourself and life will be good to you.*
4. *Always be yourself and never change just to please somebody. An original of yourself is better than a copy of someone else.*
5. *Reevaluate your attitude and try to adjust it according to different life situations.*
6. *Don't underestimate the power of education; gather information, always be prepared, study hard, and learn as much as you can, because the more you know, the less you don't know. Apply your knowledge to all aspects of life. Remember: intelligence is the key to success.*
7. *Accept challenges, trust in your abilities, and never give up. It's not being the best that's important—it's trying your best.*
8. *Realize your dream and hold on to it tight—never let it go. It's not that hard to get to the top, but it's hard to stay there.*

9. *Never judge a book by its cover—its contents might surprise you. Don't judge, and you won't be judged.*

10. *Never put off for tomorrow what you can do today because today's already here, but there's no guarantee that tomorrow will come.*

11. *Think hard before you do something you might regret later and can't undo.*

12. *Never agree with someone if you really don't agree. Defend your point of view or your position; always stand by your principles and fight for what you believe in.*

13. *Don't settle for the one you're with; wait for the one you can't be without.*

14. *Help someone today and someone will help you tomorrow. Pay it forward.*

15. *Always treat people the way you want to be treated. Remember: what goes around comes around, so be nice to everyone.*

16. *Learn how to forgive and forget. Everyone deserves a second chance, so give it before it's too late.*

17. *Always have your priorities straight. Otherwise, you might miss out on something important for something that doesn't mean a thing.*

18. *Remember the past, think of the present, and dream about the future.*

19. *Always appreciate and treasure your loved ones and never be afraid to show your true feelings and affection. It's worth the effort.*

20. *Appreciate and enjoy every second you have on earth because life is too short.*

Every moment we have on this earth is a miracle. Life is a moment in time between birth and death, and this moment is the greatest miracle of all. Let's cherish this moment in time. Let's celebrate this miracle called LIFE.

Celebrate the Moments of Your Life

*"If we take care of the moments, the
years will take care of themselves."*

—Maria Edgeworth

"Living in the moment brings you a sense of reverence for all of life's blessings," Alex proclaims as we sit in my room, gabbing. "Oprah Winfrey said that, and I totally agree with her. Vicky's last commandment states just that." She looks at me and adds, "Your article shows how much you've learned and how much you've changed. You even think differently."

Jackie, Liza, and Chloe also sing me praises for the article and I feel proud of myself.

"Thanks, guys. It means a lot, coming from you." I say. "I'm so happy! And it's not just because I have money now. Even if I didn't, I'd feel the same way because now I have my priorities straight. I have you guys and I have my family, and you all love me, and I love all of you. There's no pain anymore. That's what I call happiness."

"I believe you," Alex says. "Do you know why you feel this way? Because you have a more positive attitude. Do you know what Martha Washington said about it?"

"I don't, but I'm dying to find out," I reply. "Go ahead, I'd really love to know."

"I am still determined to be cheerful and happy, in whatever situation I may be; for I have also learned from experience that the greater part of our happiness or misery depends upon our dispositions, and not upon our circumstances." She looks at me and asks, "Great, huh?"

I suddenly realize that Alex's quotes don't annoy me the way they used to.

I nod and say, "That's exactly how I'm going to think from now on. And now, let's talk about school."

"What's there to talk about?" Chloe asks. "We're almost done with exams and in a few weeks we'll have our prom, and then, bye-bye school."

She looks giddy and excited.

"I meant college," I elaborate. "Have you heard from NYU yet? Have you, Liza?"

Chloe glances over at Liza, and Liza answers for both of them, "No, we haven't. I don't think our SAT scores were good enough for NYU. Actually, we don't care if we don't. We wanted to tell you," she sees our astonished faces and goes on, "I've decided to go to FIT, Fashion Institute of Technology."

We're speechless!

"I've been accepted there," she continues. "You see, fashion and merchandising is more my thing, and Chloe . . . Well, you tell them, Chloe."

"Well," Chloe mumbles. "I've been accepted by several art schools, and I just have to choose which one I want to be in."

"But what about our plans?" I ask, upset and confused. "Jackie belongs in an Ivy League school, but she chose to go to NYU just to be with us. We wanted to be together."

"And we will be," Jackie says. "NYU's schools are at different locations anyway. It's not like we'd be in the same building and live in a dorm. We'll rent an apartment together, just as we planned, somewhere in the middle, so we can all get to our schools by bus or subway. We *have to* use public transportation to be real New Yorkers, don't we?"

"Jackie," Alex says, looking at her strangely. "What aren't you telling us?"

"Well," Jackie starts, "actually, I was about to tell you that I've already been accepted to Columbia on a scholarship."

"And you didn't tell us?" I exclaim.

"I wasn't sure what would happen," she responds. "Jamie took my papers and brought them to the admissions office. When they saw my GPA and my SAT scores, well—"

"Jamie, of course. You'll go to the same school and see each other every day," Alex says.

"But I'll live with *you* guys and see *you* at home every day," Jackie defends herself.

"It's just the way it should be," I say, suddenly realizing that everything is exactly right. "Jackie belongs in Columbia, Liza belongs in FIT, and Chloe deserves the best art school."

"So, it's just you and me, kid," Alex says. "We started together, and we'll continue it together. Okay, then. Let's find a big apartment and live happily ever after."

"Not very expensive, though," Jackie says. "Not all of us are rich, you know."

"Don't worry" I say. "I want a nice apartment. You'll pay what you can, and we'll cover the rest. We're family, remember? All for one, and one for all."

"No way!" Jackie exclaims. "We pay equal shares or no deal."

"Can we *not* discuss this right now?" I ask. "Let's talk about something interesting."

"Are we going to Ruby's party next Saturday?" Chloe cuts in. "I want to."

"I can't wait to see her boyfriend," I claim and immediately see the inquisitive looks.

I suddenly realize that I didn't tell the girls about my conversation with Brianna, regarding the Ruby-Jackie thing, and how my sexual confusion theory was blown to smithereens. So I do.

"That's what happens when you speculate and overanalyze," Alex says.

"I'm changing, aren't I?" I chuckle.

"See, Vicky, your intuition let you down this time," says Liza. "Now let's talk about the prom. Oh, and we have to plan Chloe's birthday party. It's right after the prom."

"By the way," I say. "It's Mom's birthday tomorrow. She'll get the surprise of her life."

We chat a little more and then Jackie and Chloe leave. Liza gets up next.

"Do you have to go already, Liza?" I ask. "And you, Alex?"

"Nah!" Alex answers. "I can stay a little longer."

Mom knocks on the door as soon as Liza leaves. She informs me that she invited Nora Brickman and her son, Ben, to spend the weekend at our house. *Wow! Great! Fireworks!*

"Am I supposed to be happy and cheer about it?" I ask sarcastically.

"Just be civil," Mom answers. "Alex, please stay for dinner. You'll keep Vicky in line."

"It's a great idea!" I exclaim. "Please, Alex, don't leave me with that brat, Ben."

"I don't want to intrude," Alex starts. "And—"

"You won't be," Mom interrupts. "I insist."

Alex looks at me, sees my begging eyes, and says, "Well, okay, then. I'll stay. Thanks."

Soon we hear a car pull into our driveway. Mom runs outside to greet the guests.

"Vicky, you remember Nora," she says as she walks through the doorway with a plain-looking woman, slender, medium-height, with dark hair and glasses framing her big brown eyes.

Before I have the chance to answer, a tall young man walks in, carrying two bags.

Omigod! Ben! Well, he's grown up quite nicely—handsome, with beautifully-cut dark hair. Just like his mother, he's wearing glasses, which make him look serious and intelligent.

"Ben, you remember Vicky, don't you?" Nora asks.

It's not me Ben looks at. It's Alex!

"Sure," he replies with a deep, low voice. "How could I forget?" He makes a face. "Do you still behave like a diva with a capital 'D?' "

"Excuse me?" I exclaim. "You should talk! You acted like a spoiled brat with a double 'B.' You didn't want anything to do with me."

He still doesn't, considering the way he looks at Alex. *I bet he wants to do a lot with her.*

"Oh, Vicky," says Nora. "It was a long time ago. He was what, eleven then? He's nineteen now. He goes to NYU, by the way. Pre-med."

Another match made in heaven!

"This is my best friend, Alex," I say, believing that it's time to introduce her.

"Nice to meet you," Nora and Ben say in unison.

Ben takes Alex's hand and holds it a little too long, looking straight into her eyes. *Another love connection!*

"Let's go upstairs, Nora, and get you settled," Mom says. "You'll stay with me in my room and Ben will stay downstairs in the guest room. Vicky, please show Ben to his room. Then you and Alex can start setting the table while I check on dinner."

*   *   *

All through dinner Ben and Alex throw little glances at each other. I think Mom and Nora also catch what's been happening between those two—since they look at each other and smile.

When we're almost done with dessert, my cell phone rings. It's Nick. He wants to go for a walk in the park and go down to the pond. (Translation: he wants to make out under the stars.)

Suddenly I get an idea. Why not take Alex and Ben with us? I mention it to Nick. At first, he's not happy about it, but when I tell him that there might be a love connection developing, he's glad for Alex, and even more for me, because I don't have to worry about Alex's feelings being hurt. Alex and Ben jump at my offer to come along.

God, I'm good! I should make a second career in match-making and make tons of money.

We go in Nick's car. Nick and Ben, who hit it off from the start, talk all the way to the park, which is about ten minutes from my house. Once there, we find a nice bench, and all four of us talk together for a little while. Then we go down to the pond.

"Let's take a walk," Nick whispers in my ear. "I want to be alone with you."

I nod and say, "Guys, we'll meet you by the car in about an hour or so. Okay?"

We walk hand in hand away from Ben and Alex. It's such a beautiful and romantic evening. It's warm, but breezy. The sky's clear, the moon's bright, and there are lots of shiny stars looking down at us. We can see their reflection in the water.

I remember how glad Nick was when I apologized and told him about the green light I got from Alex for us to be together at the prom as a real couple.

"I'm so happy I'm here with you," I say to Nick. "I'm glad you still want me after—"

"How could I refuse an heiress?" Nick jokes. "Especially after such a wise editorial."

He stops and takes me in his arms. We stand there under the stars, looking into each other's eyes. Nick starts kissing my neck, my face, my lips. There are a few people passing by, looking at us—young, smiling; old, in indignation.

"What are you doing?" I ask playfully. "People are watching!"

"I'm kissing my girlfriend. Is that a crime?"

He pulls me closer.

"I guess not," I mutter, my head spinning, my heart pounding, my pulse racing. "But if it *is* a crime, feel free to commit it again . . . and again . . . and again."

*   *   *

It's Saturday morning and it's Mom's birthday. I get up early. Mom, Nora, and Ben are still asleep. I drive to the flower shop to get Mom's favorite spring flowers: tulips, peonies, and lilacs. Who do I run into there? Brianna! It's her sister's birthday, too. She tells me about her baby niece and how much she enjoys her. Then she asks how my friends are, but I know she really means Liza. I tell her we're all going to New York to study.

"Me, too," she says. "You know I take dancing lessons, right? Well, I'm going to study dance with the best of the masters in New York. Our friends are going to Europe for a few years. They want to sublet their apartment. It's gigantic and very expensive. If I could find a few roommates to share it with, it would be great. It's in midtown Manhattan, and it's huge enough for ten people, but it can fit six easily. Do you think you and your friends would be interested?"

"I'd love it," I say. "Let me talk to the girls. Find out what the rent would be."

I say goodbye to Brianna, pick the flowers, and leave.

On the way home, I think of Brianna's offer. The apartment must cost a fortune. She said it's big enough for ten people. *It would be cheaper if we split it by seven instead of six.* I dial Tina's number, and she answers right away. A little small talk, and then I pop the question.

"What school are you going to go to?" I ask.

"Art school in New York," she replies. "I don't know yet which one."

How great is this?

"You should talk to Chloe about it. Listen, Tina, we're meeting at Indulgence tomorrow afternoon. Can you be there?"

She says yes, so I call Brianna to ask her if she'd mind if Tina lived with us. She says she wouldn't. *Yay!* I ask her to be at Indulgence, as well.

*   *   *

Mom's in the middle of making breakfast. She's touched by the flowers. We kiss and she tells me she has reservations made in a nice restaurant this evening for six people—me, my grandparents, Nora, Ben, and herself.

"Can we change it to eight?" I ask. "I want Alex and Nick to join us. Alex will be Ben's date and I think it's time for my family to meet my boyfriend. I'm paying. It's my first present."

"You've got more than one?" Mom asks.

"Yes, wait." I get a flat box from my room and hand it to Mom.

Inside the box is a sign, a letterhead, and a business card that I created on my computer. All of them say: *Fine Interior Designs*. Mom looks at me, confused.

"It doesn't have an address yet, but I think it's time to find a space," I say. "Seriously, Mom, you can't run a business from home anymore. Don't you agree?"

"I don't understand," she murmurs.

"It means I'm investing in your business," I declare. "I'll be your silent partner, but you can use me to write slogans and promotional stuff for you. And you'd better start bringing in some profit, because I expect a nice fat return on my investment by the end of the year."

"I don't know what to say," Mom says and starts crying. "Are you sure about it?"

"I'm more than sure. That's how much I believe in you. Have faith in yourself."

"I can't believe it's you, Victoria. You've changed enormously," Mom says tearfully, with a shaky, vibrating voice. "You've grown so much as a person over the past year."

"I've evolved!" I joke. "Though I have to say, the evolution process has blown into a major time-consumer."

"I wouldn't call it an evolution process," Mom plays along. "I'd call it a major personality revamping."

"I know," I laugh. "I'm new and improved!" Then I say seriously, "Mom, forgive me for every bad thing I've ever said to you. I'm grateful for everything you've done for me, and you've given me so much. You've been instrumental in all aspects of my life. You had the most profound impact on me. Only *I* know how I was affected by you and to what extent."

"Wow!" Mom exclaims. "That was unexpected. I didn't know you felt this way. All I've ever wanted, and still want, is to be there for you and to guide you through life the best I know how. I'm in it for the long haul."

"*We're* in it for the long haul," I say and join Mom in the crying game.

"You're the best daughter a mother could ever have."

She smiles, her chin quivering.

"You're my mother. You're biased." We both laugh and hug. "Now we need three GH's: good health, good health, and good health. Everything else we can buy."

Mom shakes her head in disbelief and says, "Thank you for being my lifeline."

* * *

The dinner goes well. Everyone loves Nick. He charms everybody, especially Grandma. Grandpa just winks at me, approving my choice.

After dinner, the four of us go to the park again, where Alex, as I later find out, ends up asking Ben to be her prom date, and he gladly accepts.

"Can you take me someplace tomorrow morning?" I whisper into Nick's ear.

He nods.

The next morning, he picks me up early and takes me to the cemetery. When we find the grave, he leaves me alone with my grandfather. I put flowers on the base of the monument and start talking.

"Hi, it's me, Vicky, your granddaughter. People call me sharp-tongued, acid-tongued, a real mouthpiece. I prefer very outspoken. So here goes . . ."

I let him have it. I talk passionately, putting all my anger and bitterness that I couldn't lay on a dying man into my conversation with a dead one.

"Well, I feel much better now. I forgive you, and I want to thank you for making up and for changing my life. Rest in peace."

I wave for Nick to come back.

"It's ironic, isn't it?" I ask him. "A man who never wanted me in his life when he was alive has changed my life so tremendously after his death."

"But he *did* want you," Nick says. "He planned ahead for your future, didn't he?"

I nod.

Later, I get a call from Amelia. She just came back from the cemetery.

"Thank you for visiting him," she says.

"How do you know I was there?"

"I saw the flowers. They're not mine. Friends and neighbors wouldn't go without me."

"I felt I had to thank him in person. Well, kind of."

"Thanks. It means the world to both of us. I'm sure he knows."

* * *

In the afternoon, I meet the girls at the Indulgence Café early to warn them.

"I hope you don't mind," I say, "but I invited Tina and Brianna to join us."

"I see that the camaraderie is developing between you and those two," says Liza.

"I don't mind. I like both of them," Chloe claims.

"They're decent," Jackie declares.

"In the words of my grandmother," I say, "*the girls are courteous.*"

"I don't know," Alex says. "The jury is still out on this one."

"Come on, Alex! Don't be such a grouch," I tell her. "Aren't you forgetting how you were bugging me to be polite to Brianna?"

I tell them about Brianna's offer.

"I told you to be decent to her, not to play house with her," Alex says.

The others, however, like what they hear.

Brianna and Tina show up almost at the same time.

"What about your own friends?" Alex asks Brianna. "Why can't *they* live with you?"

"Their grades are only good enough for a local community college, unless their daddies buy them spots in some little private schools. So what do you say, guys?"

We all decide to give it a try and start making plans right away.

"What's happening with Heather?" Chloe suddenly asks.

"I have no idea," Brianna replies. "I don't think anybody talks to her since . . . since she's become the town pariah."

"So Heather's all alone," I say. "Good. Her happiness would bring me grief. Her every success would be my personal tragedy. I'm glad she lost all her friends. That's what I call a real *revenge of the nerds*."

"Don't overdo it, Vicky," Jackie says. "You're a changed woman, remember?"

"I know," I respond. "That's why I'm letting her live."

We all giggle.

"Let's drink to Norman," Tina says, and we all take our sodas and toast Norman Fixx.

"Maybe some day Heather will change and become a decent person. Maybe she'll even become somebody, and then her ex-friends will respect and love her again," says Jackie.

"A real friendship is when you love your friends for what they *were* and for what they *are*, not for what they might become," I say. "Just like our friendship."

"You're right," Jackie says and then adds, "Okay, New York, here we come!"

"Watch out for us!" Chloe warns all New Yorkers.

"Let's go conquer the new depths and heights!" Alex, the leader, exclaims.

"Let's kick some ass!" Liza dares us, and she's not kidding.

"The moment of triumph," I elaborate to Tina and Brianna, and they laugh with me.

They seem to fit well with us. I'm not saying we'll become one big happy family overnight, but I won't be surprised if one day the *Fabulous Five* become the *Magnificent Seven*.

*   *   *

And so it all ends . . . and begins again. Out with the old life, in with the new. The new Vicky says goodbye to the old Vicky. Don't get me wrong. I'm still me, only better. I still stand by my principles and fight for my beliefs, but I've learned how to compromise. I can't say that my attitude has changed completely, but let me put it this way: it's been significantly adjusted. I think more positively now and money isn't the most important thing in my life.

It's not *everything* to me anymore. Love and friendship are. Totally! From now on, love and friendship mean to me what fashion and shopping mean to Liza, what supporting everybody and agreeing with everyone mean to Chloe, what scores and grades mean to Jackie, and what lecturing and being in charge mean to Alex . . . well, you get my drift.

ABOUT THE AUTHOR

 In her debut novel, a first-place winner in the Arizona Authors Association Annual Literary Awards contest, Ludmila "Mila" Bernadkin draws on her experience as a teacher, mother and advanced graduate of the Institute of Children's Literature to identify with the tremulous world of confusing emotions and mixed messages of "maturity" today's teens live in as they feel their way through the process of becoming young adults

Born and raised in Odessa, Ukraine, a beautiful resort city on the Black Sea, Bernadkin emigrated from the former Soviet Union and came to the United States in 1977. She graduated from the Brest Music College with a BA-equivalent degree in theory of music and music literature, and accepted a teaching position at a children's music school. After moving to the States, she became a Senior Programmer-Analyst, working at several of the largest financial institutions in New York City. However, medical reasons forced her early retirement, which turned out to be a blessing as she realized her life-long dream of becoming an award-winning published writer.

Bernadkin, who loves to travel, listen to music and read, now lives in Brooklyn, New York, with her daughter, a graduate student working on her masters.

REVIEWS

"In *The Attitude Girl* we meet Vicky, 17 years old and with a self-proclaimed attitude problem. As Vicky changes through the story, teen readers will find her to be a very strong and appealing character, and while she may not lose the attitude by the end of the book, we're cheering for her as she discovers that maybe there's a lot more to her than she realized. Vicky's voice is authentic, the whole plot and conflict seem very real and timely, and the story moves along at a good pace because there's so much great interaction and dialogue between the characters. The style of writing is casual and will definitely appeal to teens."

Marcia Lusted
Assistant Editor, Cobblestone Publishing, and author of over 20 books for young readers

*   *   *

"Sometimes outrageous, nearly always outspoken teenage Victoria brings both smiles and sad reflection to this impressive coming-of-age story. I am most impressed with how Ms. Bernadkin reveals her main character through her expressions. And more. Bernadkin's novel could well serve as a lively guide for a girl's survival of the wicked teens."

Greta Manville
Author and Steinbeck Fellow

"With use of authentic dialogue, Ms. Bernadkin has done an incredible job of capturing the heart and mind of a 17-year-old girl. Her story of Vicky Benson and her relationship with her family and four closest friends will perhaps make you look differently at the 'Attitude Girl' in your own life. Or it may just make you remember those days when you too had a touch of that attitude."

Patty Nagle
Mother of Five and IT Professional

* * *

"I loved *The Attitude Girl*. This realistic story is deeply emotional and at the same time deliciously humorous. It made me cry and it made me laugh. It was absolutely impossible to put the book down. I couldn't wait to find out how it ends and I wasn't disappointed. But then, I didn't want it to end. This novel isn't just for girls; it's for their mothers and grandmothers as well."

Alla Leibman
IT Specialist and Mother

* * *

"Victoria is an outspoken 17 year-old with whom most American teens would easily identify. She starts out as a self-involved young woman, struggling to proclaim and nurture her outspokenness despite all. As the story develops, however, she is faced with sobering obstacles, which guide her into the realization that being outspoken may not be all she needs and desires out of life."

Anna Dunevsky, M.D., PhD.
Director, Comprehensive
Rehabilitation Medicine Corporation

"In *The Attitude Girl*, every parent with teenage girls can find themselves in familiar terrain, reassured they're not there alone. The expressions and dialogs of the main characters are so real, you start feeling your presence in the plot. A very easy and enjoyable read."

Yuriy Pavlov

IT Professional and Father of 2 girls